LEARNING CURVES

MOLLY O'HARE

This book is dedicated to anyone who has felt they weren't good enough. Anyone who has been looked upon like they are less.

YOU AREN'T.

You are a fucking unicorn. I mean it. The world is a hell of a lot better because you are here. Be you. Be Proud. And, most of all, rock your shit, 'cause damn, you are a fucking Rockstar!

P.S. Can I have your autograph?

PREFACE

It's no secret that I, Molly O'Hare, have learning disabilities and I'm dyslexic. I've made them public and I've talked about them openly in my reader group along with other author friends.

So, why in the world am I telling you this?

Here's why.

When I was in school many many years ago, I needed to see a psychologist to be evaluated once again. This wasn't new to me since it's something you have to go through a lot. I've had reading, writing, spelling and math issues, my whole life. Every few years, you had to be re-evaluated. No big deal.

However, this particular psychologist took one look at me saw that I was overweight, I was a woman, and that I've had these disabilities my whole life and decided right off the bat, I was a waste of his time. After he'd completed my evaluation, he returned with an attitude. I won't even mention the snide comments he made under his breath when I had trouble with a word or my math was off during the test. He then proceeded to tell me I would never amount to anything. I would never be able to read, write, and spell like a *"normal"* person. I would never make it in the world, and I might as well give up now.

As I said before, this wasn't my first evaluation. I was older here. Not only was I older, but I'd already overcome so much. Nonetheless his words still gutted me. I'd be lying if I said his words didn't ultimately shape me for a *long* time. They put me into some really dark places and even to this day, his comments and the eighty-page document with his spewed garbage (that I promised myself once I publish this book I will burn), still creeps into my head every once in a while.

I can remember days I would have trouble comprehending something I read or I'd get bad marks on a paper for spelling and grammar mistakes. His words would always echo the loudest at those times. I foolishly thought I would never amount to anything because of this person. The same person who was in charge of helping people just like me, who had multiple doctorate degrees told me I was nothing. So, it had to be true and why bother, right?

No.

That couldn't be the answer. I wasn't willing to give up. Instead I used his cruel words spoken with disgust as my driving force. Not only to prove him wrong about me, but to prove no one should be thrown into a box of not good enough. Those words made me fight harder. They made me push myself. They made me stronger in the end. And for that, I thank him.

My reading disabilities, my dyslexia, my spelling disabilities, and hell even my math disabilities, did not and would not define me. Before I realized it I was moved up to regular and even honors classes. I tutored kids that were just like me. I was able to show them tips and tricks I'd figured out along the way.

Because of *him*, I made a difference. Not only in myself, but with people that were struggling exactly how I was.

Just because someone learns something a little bit differently than others, does not mean they are stupid or they are less. They do not get thrown into a not good enough box because they need help.

I come to you with my story now because after his words, if I had read something like this or knew there were others out there like me, I might not have fallen so hard as I did.

This book goes out to anyone and everyone that has ever been looked down upon. Who's ever been told they weren't good enough, not pretty enough, not thin enough, whoever has a learning disability or something different about them. Something that sometimes they try to hide.

That's bullshit.

Those things do not define you. They make you who you are as a whole. And, that's pretty fucking awesome if you ask me.

As for me, I can look back and smile. I was told I'd never be able to read or write and I'm publishing this book. My *sixth* book.

You can accomplish anything you want in this world if you believe in yourself.

I hope these words can touch anyone that was or is feeling the way that I did. Even just a little bit.

The moral of the story: you are who you are. You can do anything in this world. I believe in you. And if I can do it, so can you.

As I say in every book I publish, you are a mother-fucking unicorn. Own that shit. Be true to who you are and live the best goddamn life that you can live.

Oh yeah, and before I forget. I say wholeheartedly, fuck that dude. Fuck him in his fuckity face and I mentally punch him in the fucking throat, because look at me now, bitch! And I can't wait to burn that fucking document.

CHAPTER ONE

"I DON'T WANT to go to school!"

Spencer Hurley sighed as he looked down at his nine-year-old daughter, Annabelle.

"Come on, Dad. Please, don't make me." She pouted. Which any other time would have gotten her anything she wanted, but not today. "Can't you be one of those cool dads that lets their kids—"

He gasped. "I am one of those cool dads!" Spencer narrowed his eyes at her, daring her to deny it.

When Belle responded with an eye roll, Spencer's jaw dropped.

"Sure, sure, the coolest, Dad," she placated him. "But you know what would make you ten times cooler?"

"I'm on the edge of my seat." He crossed his arms over his chest. Belle was too good at this. But then again, she was *his* daughter.

"Daaaad, would you please listen? Don't you want to know how to get into the Cool Dad Hall of Fame?"

Spencer artfully cocked his brow. "How about not negotiating with my nine-year-old."

"No, it's letting your most amazing, coolest *daughter* stay home with you." She smiled sweetly at him, trying her best to win her argument. "I don't know if you can even handle being alone here. How would you survive without me?"

He held his hand over his heart in mock hurt. "Who are you? Grandpa?" His father probably put her up to this... actually, he could bet money on it.

Belle ignored him as she continued, "There's more unpacking I can do. I'll even make sure everything goes in the *correct* place. Maybe I can even help you pick out some graphics for your clients? You don't need school to pick out graphics. How hard could it be?"

"So, my master's degree is what? A fire starter?" Both Spencer's brows shot to the ceiling, as he stared down at her.

As soon as Belle realized what she'd said, her eyes widened.

"Exactly."

"What? No. Come on, you know I didn't mean it like that, Dad."

"Sure, you didn't." Spencer rolled his eyes before he smirked at her. *His* signature smirk, the same smirk Belle sent right back to him.

He had to hold in his pride. She was the spitting image of him in every way. And with each day that passed, she acquired more and more of his mannerisms.

Case in point, the killer smirk.

He'd be lying if he said it wasn't a little frightening, though. Especially when she played him like a master. His little prodigy. Spencer's chest swelled.

Thank fuck Belle got nothing from her mother. He shuddered at the thought. They both dodged a bullet there.

As their smirk stand-off continued, Spencer studied her. One of them was bound to break first and with having a daughter exactly like him, he'd never live it down if he was the one.

He was *not* going to break first.

Hell no.

That's how you let the terrorists win. Okay fine, she had him wrapped so tightly around her finger, that if she'd said jump, he'd say how high. He knew that, and she knew that, but he'd be damned if he lost in a smirk standoff.

Over his dead body.

He did have pride after all.

Just as he thought he was about to win though, something flashed in Belle's eyes. Then to his shock, she looked away, quickly darting her eyes to the front door and then back to him.

Spencer jolted back as a haunted look appeared on her face; it was a straight sucker punch to his gut.

Fuck.

Spencer knew what that look was. It was one of the reasons why he'd waited longer than he needed to get her re-enrolled in school.

Mustering all he could Spencer did his best to give Belle an encouraging smile. "I know, Belle, but you have to go. You can't avoid it forever."

She spoke her next words in such a quiet whisper he had to strain to hear them. "Please, Dad. I don't want to go through that again. What if they all make fun of me like before?"

Her words were like a knife to his soul. As a father, you do everything you can to protect your children. And when you fail, there wasn't a worse feeling.

The education system failed her.

Her mother had failed her.

And, he'd failed her.

It's why a month ago he packed up all their belongings and moved giving them a fresh start. He vowed to do whatever it took to make her see how truly special she was. And, he refused to ever have his daughter feel any less than she was again.

Annabelle looked up at her dad with large worried eyes making his heart break the impossible inch more.

This had absolutely nothing to do with a child not wanting to go to school.

No, this was much more.

Spencer crouched at his knees so he could look Annabelle in the eyes and prayed she would believe him. "No one is going to make fun of you, Belle," he promised. "This isn't going to be a repeat of your old school. That won't happen again."

"How do you know?" she asked.

"We moved here because I know for a fact this school can help you. They have teachers that specialize in what you need. I did my research." The corner of his mouth turned up. "Besides, if anyone does, let me know. I'll punch them." He said it with such conviction, Belle's face broke into a toothy grin as she laughed.

"You can't punch kids, Dad."

Spencer's eyebrows knitted together. "I can think it. No rules against that."

"And you say *I'm* a drama queen?" She threw herself into his arms almost toppling him over. "Love you, Dad."

"Love you too, kiddo." He squeezed her tight for a few seconds before letting her go. "Let's get you off to school. Nothing worse than showing up late on your first day. It'll set a bad example."

Belle cocked her brow looking over his right shoulder. "You do know we're already late, right?" A small giggle escaped her lips causing Spencer to snap his head around to look at the clock. "Shi— I mean shoot."

"It's okay, Dad. I'm sure being late on your first day in a new school won't follow me for the rest of my life." She shrugged, giving him an evil grin. "And if it does, I'll make sure the blame is on you."

"Wow." He placed his hand over his heart. "That's real thoughtful of you."

The little she-devil winked. "Just doing my part."

Is this the shit my father had to deal with raising me? The man needs a fucking medal... "Thanks for that."

As she smiled happily at him, Spencer shook his head. "How did you get so smart?"

"Not from you," she shot back.

"Oh, you little shit. I'm gonna get you." Spencer pounced going into an all-out tickle war between them.

Within seconds Belle was screaming "Uncle" as she tried to kick him off as she laughed. After a few more seconds, Spencer let up playfully narrowing his eyes at her. "That's what you get, missy. I'll remember this the next time you ask me for a dog."

"I take it back! I take it all back. I get all my smarts from you. And my looks, and my personality. It's the *best* person- ality there is. Yep, one hundred percent. I've got all my good parts from you. None from Grandpa. Just you—"

"Nope. Too late, Belle. You can't soften the blow now." He pointed to his head. "It's locked away. I've got at *least* ten good uses for it."

"Daaaaad," she groaned.

"Don't dad me. You might be smart, but —"

"Not that smart." It was as if all the air was sucked out

of the room.

Without hesitation, Spencer dropped back to his knees, pulling his daughter into his arms. "No. None of that. You hear me. You *are* smart, Annabelle. You're a hell of a lot smarter than I was at your age."

"That's not what *she* said."

It took everything inside of Spencer not to scream in frustration at Belle's words. This was another reason why they moved.

Fuck that woman!

Hell, it had been years since they'd seen her mother, but that bitch's parting words of Annabelle's struggles had left a permanent mark on his baby.

Fuck, Spencer wanted to murder his ex. Bring her back to life, and then murder her again.

Fuck her.

The *only* good thing that came from her was Annabelle, everything else was a disaster.

He scolded himself just as he'd done countless times before. It was a one-night stand that ended in her getting pregnant and his life changing forever.

His father's words came rushing back to him. *This is why you always wrap it, son. 'Cause that one night could end up being one hell of a mess.*

Spencer hated himself for getting so drunk that night he forgot to do just that.

Not because he got Annabelle out of it, no. Her coming into his life was the best thing that could've ever happened to him.

It was everything else that went along with it. Some people were pure evil and only cared about themselves. He learned that the hard way, multiple times when it came to Belle's mother.

He tried, Lord knows he did.

As soon as she found him a few weeks later and informed him she was pregnant he tried to make them work. The whole time they were together, if you could even call it that, was a disaster. If she wasn't cheating on him, she stole from him. Money, car, you name it. And if she wasn't stealing it from him, she was demanding it. And every time he called her out on it, she'd threaten him with taking his daughter away, or worse. He wasn't willing to take that chance.

So, he put up with it. He had to.

Spencer was going to be a father.

After giving birth to Belle, she disappeared for the first year. Just up and left him and Belle alone. It was so bad, he had to move them in with his dad.

Thank the Universe he had his dad.

And when Belle's mother did come back, she demanded more money. Money that he didn't have. And if he didn't give it to her, she threatened to have Belle taken away from him.

Then, once Annabelle was diagnosed in the first grade with her learning disabilities it got worse.

Way worse.

Children never forget their first scar. Especially, when that scar came from someone that was supposed to love them unconditionally.

"She's stupid, Spencer. She's pretty much wasted space if you ask me..." As her parting words hung throughout the house, Spencer looked behind him only to see Annabelle staring blankly at the spot her *mother* just vacated. Those words spoken with such disdain and directed toward a tiny Annabelle hiding behind him, changed his girl forever.

He hated her mother with every ounce inside of him.

She was never allowed to step foot in his home again, nor was she allowed near his daughter.

The next day he asked his dad to help him figure out the legal process to gain sole custody of Belle. It took some time but it happened. Along with a restraining order, and actually following through with it a couple of times, Belle's mother finally got the picture.

Spencer just wished he could erase the words she spoke to Belle along with it.

"She is *not* your mom," he remarked. "She might have given birth to you, but not once has she ever done or said something that would constitute her as motherly. Your Grandpa is more of a mom to you than she ever was. Her words were garbage —" He stopped himself before he went too far. He could hate her mother with a fiery passion but he wouldn't push that hatred on his daughter.

He looked at Belle's broken face. "Come here, sweetie." He pulled her into his arms as he let out a heavy sigh.

This was supposed to be a new beginning for them.

A fresh start.

One where Annabelle was free to be a kid, learn, grow, and discover who she was.

Way to go, dumbass. Add this to the enormous list of screw-ups you've made.

After a few moments of silence, Belle pulled back from his arms and smiled sweetly at him. "So, about that dog?"

His jaw hit the floor. *That little...* A deep laugh erupted from his gut. "You're an evil genius. You know that, right?"

"Duhh." She smirked. "Of course, I am. You raised me that way, didn't you?"

"I'm trying to decide if I regret that or not." His finger tapped his chin.

"You don't." Belle looked at the door and then back at him. "Uhh, Dad?"

"Yeah, kiddo?"

"Will you help me with my reading after school? I'm sure I'll have a lot to catch up on." She pulled away from him and grabbed her bag.

Spencer's head slightly cocked to the side as his brow rose. "Don't I always?"

"Yeah," she answered before turning back to him. "But this time I want to try and read it myself first. Like when we read books together at night."

His heart tightened.

Since her diagnosis, it'd been a struggle for both of them. Every day, especially in the beginning, it was a new learning curve. Him giving her what she needed and Annabelle figuring out what would help her wasn't always easy.

Absolutely nothing was cut and dry, but as time went on, they figured it out the best they could.

Even through all her struggles she never ceased to amaze him, though.

Annabelle was smarter than any kid he knew. Just because she learned things a different way didn't make her less than others.

To him, it made her smarter.

Innovative.

A force to be fucking reckoned with.

Belle Hurley was going to kick all the ass and take every name. And until his dying breath, he would stop at nothing to prove that to her.

"Sure, sweetheart. Now, let's get you to your new school."

CHAPTER TWO

ELLIE RYAN WAS LATE.

She'd like to say that was a rare occurrence, but then she'd be lying. And lying this early in the morning would be bad juju for the day.

Besides, her morning was already going downhill and fast, she didn't need to add to it.

Ellie's black and white Border Collie, Roxy, had decided she'd forgotten what their own backyard smelled like and she was determined to sniff every last inch of it.

Every freaking last inch!

Now, don't get her wrong. She loved Roxy more than anything. They were a pair, hell if Ellie could take her to work with her, she would. But this dog, who made it clear, she only did things to amuse herself, and mainly at Ellie's expense was going to drive her to drink.

Seriously, Ellie found out as soon as she got Roxy home from the shelter that her favorite pastime was to annoy her.

The exact same way her students strived to do each day.

Oh, and she couldn't forget that Roxy's other favorite

thing was food. The girl *loved* to eat, and she made everyone aware of it.

To add insult to injury, this morning as Ellie watched Roxy walk around sniffing, that dog had the audacity to look at her with pure amusement as she hobbled on one foot, flailing about as she tried to put on her shoes.

Then that bitch went back to sniffing.

Zero respect.

It was as if Ellie was only there for her entertainment, and to be her food servant. That was it.

Then of course, once Roxy had determined she'd sniffed every blade of grass, she demanded breakfast.

Like Ellie said, the dog loved to eat.

Then, just like it happened every morning since getting her, that devil-dog demanded a second breakfast. And because Ellie had no backbone when it came to Roxy, she always gave in, which led to her demanding a third breakfast...

Normally, it wouldn't have been an issue to deal with Roxy and her antics, but since the little mishap with her alarm clock a week ago, her internal clock hadn't calibrated correctly.

Or ever.

She glanced down at the clock in her car...

Shit.

Why the hell had she flung her alarm clock across the room last week, breaking it into a million pieces?

Could she not have any self-control?

Whatever.

Fuck alarm clocks.

Those dirty bastards. No one should be jolted awake from their sleep.

Don't doctors say you need to get eight to ten hours of

sleep each night? At least that's what her mom had always spouted. How the hell is someone supposed to get eight hours a night when you're laying all nice and warm in your comfy bed, then a foghorn goes off in your ears making you almost pee yourself?

Huh? How?

Exactly.

Naturally, that meant every one of Ellie's alarm clocks over the years had ended up across the room, shattered to smithereens. It's the reason she had to go old school and not use her phone.

Trust her, after smashing three screens in a row, you go the less expensive route.

Why was adulting so freaking hard?

Ellie's car rolled to the stop sign causing her to let out a dramatic sigh.

This wasn't any old stop sign, though. No, this was *the* stop sign. The one she had a fight with every day she had to drive into work.

Ellie looked both ways. "Take the chance? Or not take the chance?" She thought about her karma for the day.

What's Bob really going to do if he catches me sneaking into my classroom late again? He wouldn't really fire his best friend's daughter, the same girl he considered his own, would he?

She tapped her finger against her chin. He'd been threatening to fire her since day one and it hadn't happened yet. Chances were....

Ellie looked both ways once again.

Go left, end up at the school.

Go right, end up at the coffee shop.

Might she add, it's the best coffee shop in town? That

kind of pull was hard to look past. They were the ones that made the greatest croissants in the *world*.

And Ellie would proudly fight anyone who disagreed with her. They were flaky, buttery, melt in your mouth deliciousness.

How could anyone say no to those?

You couldn't, and the only people that could, were monsters.

See if I don't go right, it's like I'm a monster. I can't be a monster this early in the morning.

She groaned at her own dramatics.

Ellie glanced at the clock in her car again.

She was late.

As in really freaking late. The on the verge of it being an issue and her not being there when her students arrived late after morning announcements.

"Oh, fuck me!" Ellie looked to the roof of her car. "Make note I'm doing the right thing here, Universe. I want to cash in these brownie points later. You know, become the ruler of the Universe, have a high rank in the apocalypse. I'm not too picky, but I want it noted I'm doing the right thing."

With one last longing look toward the direction of her favorite coffee shop, she turned left toward the school.

"I swear to everything, if Mr. Douglass left the coffee pot empty again, I'll make some and march right into his class and pour it on him." She clenched the steering wheel tighter. "That bastard."

After another ten minutes, and what Ellie would consider an Oscar-worthy driving performance and stealth-like ninja skills to get into her classroom *completely* undetected, she placed her purse in her desk drawer and headed to the teacher's lounge. Her students would still be in home-room for another ten minutes.

Ellie: One.

Talley: Zero.

With an extra pep in her step, she hurried down the hall in search of her liquid gold. Once she got to the lounge, she yanked open the door. "Come to, momma!" She took two steps into the room before she froze. "That bastard!"

Ellie stomped over to the pot, cursing. "I should've known better. I was already late, what would have been another ten minutes *and* I would have gotten a lovely flaky delicious treat out of it. But no, I had to be a freaking adult and come to work. Stupid coffee. Stupid Douglass. Stupid alarm clocks."

"You still haven't gotten a new one?"

Ellie spun around to see Sally, the school's art teacher and Ellie's best friend, sitting at the table. "No, for your information. I still haven't gotten one," she mocked. "And if you were in here when that asshole left with the pot empty, why didn't you make any of this garbage mud?"

"And miss your meltdown? I think not." Sally held up her cup. "Besides, I only drink tea. Coffee's disgusting. Why would I make it?"

"I am *not* having a meltdown," Ellie protested. The coffee might be horrible but at least the new machine brews it fast. "I'm having a cool-up."

"What the hell is a cool-up?"

Ellie stared at her best friend like she had five heads. "The opposite of a meltdown, duh."

"How are we friends?"

Ellie proudly straightened her shoulders as she grabbed the coffee and poured herself a cup. "You cover for me when I'm late, so I keep you around."

"Sally can't cover for you when you're late, because I already *know* when you're late."

Not turning around Ellie swallowed. "Sally, he's right there, isn't he?"

"Yep." Sally popped the 'p' making Ellie want to strangle her. "This is going to be good. Glad I already got my tea."

I'll kill her.

Turning on her heels, Ellie faced her boss. The same boss that she'd known her whole life. "Who said I was late?"

Bob Talley stared at her unmoving. Kind of like a lion about to pounce.

Okay, Ellie girl, never back down from a stare-off. You learned this years ago with your students. Do not show any sign of weakness. Stay strong.

He raised his left brow at her.

Oh, freak. Shit. The pressure. I'm losing and he knows it!

Ellie snapped. "Okay, fine, whatever, you dictator. I was late. Sue me. Or fire me. But I want it duly noted I'm an adult. I made good adulting decisions this morning."

Sally sat back in her seat, joy radiating off her. "Told you this was going to be good."

Ellie snapped her eyes toward her soon to be ex-best friend before moving them back to her boss.

In rushed out words she continued, "I didn't take the right and go to the coffee shop. Instead, I did the *responsible* thing and came here to drink this lousy mud water!"

"Mud water?" Both his brows shot to the ceiling.

"And there are no croissants here. So, in reality I pulled up my big girl panties and did the adult thing. I am in the positive."

"Doubling down." Sally took another sip of her tea watching the scene over the rim. "Nice."

Ignoring her, Ellie propped her arm on her hip aggressively. "I'm here, aren't I?"

After a few awkward moments, Bob sighed heavily. "Late, but you are here, yes."

"That should count for something."

Bob's right hand went to his head as he rubbed one of his temples. "If you weren't the best special education teacher out there, you would've been gone a long time ago. Do you understand that?"

Ellie's mouth fell open as her hand went to her chest in shock. "I'm telling dad you threatened me." Ellie lifted her chin at him in defiance causing Bob to roll his eyes.

"Yes, it also seems to help your lack of unemployment seeing as your father is one of my best friends. I'm sure Dean will be outraged." Bob gave her the stare down once again giving Ellie the heebee-jeebees.

Okay, so playing the dad card wasn't her smartest move. And with the way Bob was giving her the eye right now, yeah, she knew it wasn't her finest moment.

Screw it.

Whatever, she was blaming it on the lack of caffeine.

Holding her mug up, she made a show as she took a large swallow fighting the urge to upchuck since she hadn't put sugar in it yet. "Did I say mud water? I meant *love* water. Yum, yum." She held back her gag as the unsweetened beverage hit her tongue.

"Are you done?" he finally asked.

Ellie bent over the nearby sink spitting the coffee out. "Blah!! Gross and hot. Too hot." She waved her hand over her tongue for a moment before she turned back to Bob. "Yes, now I'm done."

"Sigh. These are the mornings I live for." Sally took another sip of her tea.

With a quick shake of his head, Talley did like he'd done every other time Ellie spazzed. He acted like it didn't happen and continued on. Although Ellie knew she'd be getting a call from her dad before the day was over. "You'll have a new student for your morning classes."

Ellie nodded as she turned to add a gallon of sugar to her drink. "Did they just test in or are they a new student?"

"Brand new."

"Okay."

"Her father and she moved here a few weeks ago—"

"A few weeks ago? Why is she only starting school now? Do you know how far behind she could be? Especially if she needs the extra help?"

"Simmer down." Bob held up his hands. "Her father assured me this morning he'd been working with her as they settled in. You were supposed to meet with them with me this morning..."

All the color left her face. *Was that meeting today? Oops...*

"I've set up a meeting with both of you tomorrow after school," he announced. "I sent you an email." He gave her a stern warning look. The one that said she had no choice, and if she missed it again, she'd be sorry.

It's not like she was out there dealing drugs to her kids, she was very unorganized... Plus, mornings were a bitch.

Oh crap, Sunday dinner with her parents was going to suck balls. She rolled her eyes at herself. *This is your own fault, Ellie.*

Her eyes caught Sally.

The same Sally that was supposed to have her back, but instead was turning red trying to hold in her laugh.

She sent her an evil glare. *I'm gonna deal with you later, just as soon as I get my shit together.*

Ignoring her, Ellie calculated in her head how she could help her new student, then Bob's words registered...*Wait a second. They'd been there for a few weeks now?* Something inside of her snapped. A few weeks. Like in more than two? What the hell was her father thinking? Someone that was already possibly behind....

Ellie let out a hard growl as she mumbled into her coffee. "Sounds like a real winner. He could have enrolled her two weeks ago. Two weeks!" she yelled. "That's fourteen days. I'm not good with quick math but that's a hell of a lot of hours she could be behind now."

"Three hundred and thirty-six," Sally jumped in.

"Did you hear that?" Ellie shot her eyes to Talley. "That's almost five hundred. Which is close to a thousand!"

Bob's eyes darted to Sally for a second before moving back to Ellie.

"Don't give me that look, *Robert*. When a child already has difficulties sometimes having to play catch up will make it ten times worse." *Then again,* Ellie thought. There was a possibility she could be overreacting. It could just as well go the other way and her new student was ahead of where her class was now.

And, if that was the case, she'd just made a fool of herself...

"Ellie..." he warned.

"You know how I get when it comes to my students. I will always be their advocate even if I've never met them yet."

"I know." He sent her a pleading look. "Like I said, you're the best. No matter how many times I want to fire your ass, I can't. It'd be doing an injustice to the kids that need you."

Ellie puffed out her chest at Bob's compliment. She

then looked him square in the eyes with a smirk on her face. "I'm telling dad you said ass."

With another shake of his head, Bob ignored her. "After speaking with her father, he'd like to have her start fresh and be re-evaluated. Maybe one day get her moved to regular education classes."

Ellie's nostrils flared. "Why? There is nothing wrong with my classes." She hadn't met the guy and she already hated him.

"It has nothing to do with that. Apparently, there was some bullying at her old school."

Everything inside of Ellie switched on a dime as she saw red. "I will gut them like a pig."

"Nice," Sally remarked from over her cup as she took another sip as she hid her grin. "Threatening violence against children."

"Can it. No student of *mine* will be bullied because they learn a little differently than others. If my fat ass can push through my learning disabilities, graduate at the top of my class, become a special education teacher and be successful at it, then anyone can do anything. You hear me, and let me tell you one more thing, if it wasn't for the extra help who knows where I'd be. I will do everything in my power to make sure she gets the education she deserves the way she *needs*. Even if that's not the same as everyone else." Ellie huffed as her past came rushing back to her.

"I know," Bob replied. "That's why you're the best there is. If anyone can help her and get her on the path to success, it's you. Don't forget, Ellie, I was there too. I watched you grow. I know what struggles you went through. I know what you overcame. I was there firsthand. If I remember correctly, I believe *I* was the one to help you with math. That's why I continue to say you are by far the best special education teacher there is. Not only do you help *all* kids succeed. You went through it yourself."

Ellie nodded curtly. "Damn straight."

"Do what you do best." Before she could say anything else, Bob turned on his heel and left the lounge.

"What the hell, Ellie?" Sally stared at her.

"What?"

"I'm not sure if it's the lack of coffee or what but, damn."

"There is no but damn, Sally. I get heated about this. There is nothing wrong with kids just because they need to learn a different way."

A warm smile appeared on Sally's face. "And you make sure every one of your students knows that."

"Always."

"But I don't think it's as serious as you made it seem." She quickly held up her hands in surrender. "All I'm saying is take a chill pill every once in a while."

Ellie glared at her, but she knew Sally was right. She couldn't help it though.

Sally stood from her seat before walking toward the door. "I wonder if one day he'll actually succeed in firing you?"

Ellie shrugged as a wicked smile spread across her face. "Maybe, maybe not."

With that, Sally let out a huff before walking the other way. "See you at lunch. You're buying."

"Bitch." Ellie rolled her eyes as she made her way toward her classroom.

CHAPTER THREE

SPENCER WALKED BACK into his house after dropping Belle off at school. It was probably one of the hardest things he'd ever done. And that was after dealing with his ex.

Seeing the emotions in Belle's eyes as he'd left the office would haunt him forever.

But he'd done his research. He knew Belle was now at a school with one of the top-rated special education teachers.

Although, he did wish he was able to meet her new teacher. A one Ms. Ellie Ryan.

Spencer had to admit he was a little more than pissed she didn't show for their meeting. Yeah, they were able to reschedule it, but he couldn't help the concern if this was going to be just like her old school.

If the one person that was supposed to help his daughter couldn't show for a meeting, that didn't sit right with him. He'd give her the benefit of the doubt though. Principal Talley had assured him Ms. Ellie Ryan was the best.

Spencer walked into his office and sat at his desk. He was in the middle of redesigning two of his client's websites, along with redoing two digital media packets. He was glad he freelanced his web consultation and graphic design business. It was the only reason he was able to pick up and move him and Belle so effortlessly.

He could work from anywhere.

Ten full minutes went by with Spencer staring at a blank screen before he gave up. There was no work getting done today.

Is this how parents were supposed to feel? How was it that he was more a nervous wreck than Annabelle was?

He looked at the clock. Five hours and forty-five minutes. A lot could happen in that time.

What if she had a horrible first day?

What if kids picked on her?

What if her new teacher was just as bad as her old ones?

Is this what being an overprotective parent felt like? Damn... What was he going to do when she started talking about boys?

Nope. Not going to happen. Spencer shook his head. Belle was forbidden from dating until she was forty-five.

Yep. That's how that was going to go.

Pushing aside the horrible thought of Belle dating, he wondered how her day was going for the millionth time since he got home. He tapped his fingers on his desk. He knew his daughter. She was probably having the time of her life right now. Making new friends, laughing. All of it.

She might have resisted this morning, but she was resilient.

Spencer pushed back from his desk, his work forgotten. He walked to their kitchen to put away some of the random stuff lying around. Maybe if he kept busy, he could fool himself into believing he wasn't a mess on the verge of driving to the school and bringing her back home.

She was his kid and parents just want the best for their children. It was in the handbook. A handbook he still didn't have, but his father would refer to it often.

As he took his first step into the kitchen his phone rang. "Hello?"

"How's my little girl?"

Spencer rolled his eyes at his father's voice on the other end. "Why, yes, I'm doing fine, Dad. Thanks for asking. How are you?"

"I'm not calling to shoot the shit, numb-nuts. How's my grandbaby?"

A wide smile spread across Spencer's face. "She's still asking for a dog."

"That's my girl."

"Have you been pushing that?" he asked with a growl. "You know we need to wait until we're settled."

"You've been there a couple weeks and if my grandbaby wants a dog, you damn well better take her to the shelter and get her one. Do not make me fly over there and do it myself."

"I'm not saying it's a no, Dad. We need to get settled more first. It's just us here. We're both starting from scratch."

"Fine," his father growled. *"But, make it snappy. If it were up to me you would've never moved."*

"We had to, Dad. You know that."

"I still don't have to like it."

Neither did he at times. He hated being away from his dad. He was their only lifeline. "She's at school now."

"First day?"

"Yeah. I was going to enroll her last week, but I couldn't." The unspoken words of wanting to keep her safe hung in the air. "I couldn't push it off anymore."

"She'll be fine," he was quick to reassure. "My Bella will rule that school in no time."

The corner of Spencer's lip turned up.

"Just like she rules your house."

"For fuck's sake, old man. You pretend she doesn't also have you wrapped around her little finger."

"I don't deny it. I think she hung the moon and I make sure she knows it."

That was true. For what Annabelle's mother lacked, his father made up for. "I know, Dad."

"I'm coming to visit soon."

"Dad..." He better not bring a fucking dog.

His father huffed into the phone. "Don't you dare dad me. You took my little girl from me, so I'm coming. End of story."

"You want to check up on us."

"That's part of it. The other part is seeing my girl."

Spencer let out a small chuckle as he leaned against the counter. "When are you thinking of coming?"

"I want it to be a surprise," he answered. "But if I get a wild hair across my ass, make sure my room is ready sooner rather than later."

"Already beat you to it. After her room, Belle insisted we got your room together. You know just in case you surprise visit us."

"She's a smart one, your daughter."

"As smart as they come."

The phone went silent for a few moments before his dad spoke. "Son?"

"Yeah?"

"What did the school say?"

Spencer sighed. "I did my research before we moved, remember? It's the best. They are going to test her again, to get her accurate reading, writing, and math levels. I don't think they trust her last school evaluations. At least not after what I told the principal."

"Did you meet her?"

"Who?"

"Bella's new teacher. You gotta make sure she's not like—"

"No," he cut him off. "She missed the meeting this morning. I'll be meeting with her tomorrow after Belle has her evaluation."

"Good. You're going to give it to her straight, right? Ask the hard questions. Her education style? What she has planned to help Annabelle? The whole nine yards."

"Of course, Dad, this isn't my first rodeo. I've got it covered." He pushed himself off the counter as he went to the box sitting on the table.

"And you'll call me as soon as you meet her?"

"Am I five again?" Spencer chuckled as he removed a chipped cup from the box.

"Spencer," he warned.

"You can't Spencer me anymore, Dad. I have my own kid now."

"I'll Spencer you until I'm ten feet underground, you hear me? Just 'cause you have your own offspring, doesn't mean I'm not still your father."

"Fine. And yeah, I'll call you after I meet with her."

"That's more like it." Spencer fought the urge to roll his eyes as his dad continued. *"Once Annabelle's home, have her call me right away. I want to know how it went."*

"Sure thing, pops."

"Pops? Don't make me fly over there and kick your ass."

"Would you rather I call you Randal?"

"Boy, I know I raised you with more respect than that."

Spencer couldn't help his laugh. Calling his dad by his first name always got under his skin. Something about being proud he was a father and he'd earned that title. But he'd be lying if he said his father wasn't starting to give him a headache. "We'll call you later."

"You better." With those parting words, he hung up.

Spencer looked at the clock again. Five hours and fifteen minutes. Damn, today was going to take forever.

CHAPTER FOUR

The moment Ellie placed her coffee cup on her desk, the morning bell rang.

Showtime.

Quickly, Ellie tossed her hair in a messy bun on top of her head. Any chance of looking halfway decent ended twenty minutes ago while she was still arguing with Talley.

Ehh, her students were used to it by now.

Messy hair, usually accompanied by a stain on some article of clothing. Might she also add she *never* knew how the stain got there.

Ellie yawned as she tucked a stray piece of hair into her bun. There was no use in trying to hide who she truly was.

A freaking mess.

At this point, she took pride in it. Even with how chaotic her life was, she always did right by her students. They have been and always will be her top priority.

Ellie could spill a gallon of coffee down her shirt, accidentally cut off half of her hair, and trip over someone's backpack causing her to bust a lip and break a tooth, but as long as her kids still got what they needed she considered her life a job well done.

Besides, messy hair wasn't *that* bad. It's not like she walked in from the bathroom with her skirt tucked into the top of her bright green underwear giving everyone a show.

A blush crept up her cheeks as she tried pushing away the memory.

No matter how hard Ellie tried, she *still* hadn't been able to live down that nightmare and that was *two* freaking years ago. But when you show your underwear to a group of elementary school kids, they never forget. It didn't help that Ellie was a specialized teacher, so most of her kids stayed with her during their whole grade school experience.

Psshh, and they say elephants never forget. Try a group of seven-year-olds.

She wouldn't even talk about the time she came in with her shirt on backwards giving everyone a perfect view of her *dinosaurs eating cupcakes* bra.

Why was there a new fashion trend in shirts with a hole in the back anyway? That was just asking for a disaster.

Whatever, none of it mattered. Today was a new day, and she was positive somewhere along the line something else would happen to be the talk of the school.

As the minutes dragged on, her students slowly made their way into her classroom.

Since Ellie's days were broken up according to age and grade, her room was a revolving door. For the first few hours, she had third and fourth graders, the hour after lunch she taught her fifth graders, and the last part of the day she had her young-ins. One of the perks of being a special education teacher was working with all ages as they developed. She was privileged to watch each one of them grow throughout the years. She loved that about her job.

Now, she would take it to her grave, but she liked her morning students the best. There was something about eight to nine-year-olds that always had her laughing. Maybe it was their unfiltered wit, or their ability to talk your ear off about some random thing they found fascinating? Nevertheless, she enjoyed them the best.

Okay, that was maybe a lie. There was one of her morning kids that drove her up the wall.

Travis Cummings.

Nine out of ten times she wanted to strangle him. And, he knew it, which made for an interesting day. Don't get her wrong, she loved the kid like he was her own. But Travis made a game of, how much can you annoy the teacher and get away with it?

Which was always, since she found it amusing most of the time.

Ehh, what could she complain about though? There was always bound to be one in the group that tried to push all her buttons. It just so happened to be Travis for the last three years… and counting.

There were echoes of 'good morning, and mornin' Ms. Ryan' as her students found their seats.

Music to her ears.

Ellie joined in on the good mornings as she gave them all a welcoming smile. "Take your seats, my little prodigies, let's get today kicking."

Then, right on cue, Travis walked in. "Hi, can we watch a movie today?"

Ellie rolled her eyes. He hadn't made it to his seat before he asked this time. "What do you think my answer is gonna be?"

"Yes. 'Cause you want to be the coolest teacher in the school and to be that, you gotta let us watch movies."

Ellie's hand slapped over her heart. "That hurts, kid. I'm already the coolest teacher in the school."

"Isn't that Mr. Douglass?"

Ellie fell back in her seat. "How could you?"

He shrugged. "Then there is art. I've always liked Ms. Sally."

"You're pitting my best friend against me now?" Her mouth fell open. "I thought we were friends, Travis?"

An evil grin appeared on his face. "So, about that movie?"

You little twerp.

Ellie had to hide her smile. She couldn't blame him for trying, the kid had gumption. "What do I tell you every day when you ask?"

"Yes."

"No. I don't."

Giving up, he plopped into his seat. "Fine, but one of these days you'll say yes."

"And one of these days you'll actually do your homework." Ellie crossed her arms over her chest as she stared down at him.

Travis completely unbothered, shrugged. "Maybe one of these days, but today's not the day."

The whole room laughed as they watched the daily negotiation between the two.

"Why am I'm not the least bit surprised?"

It was Ellie's own fault really. She never penalized her kids for not completing their homework. You never know what someone's home life was like. Ellie knew all too well the defense mechanisms of pretending to "forget" to do your homework rather than try it and fail.

That's why the moment they entered her class each day,

she did her absolute best to be there for them any way she could. That's the way her parents were for her.

"You try my patience, kid." Ellie stood from her desk before walking to the workbooks on the shelf. *Remember Ellie, you are helping shape these kid's futures. Murder is not an option.*

Once she grabbed their workbooks, she turned to do a quick scan of the room. No new faces.

There was Tommy in the corner picking his nose, which was normal for him.

Then there was Kimberly, who was hurrying to do her homework hoping Ellie wouldn't see. Again normal.

And of course, Travis had started making paper airplanes.

Ellie glanced at the clock. Huh, a new record for him. At least he was always good for a laugh, and even though he tried her last nerve, Travis was a good kid.

For the most part.

A knock on the door alerted her attention to Bob standing with a little girl by his side. Ellie took a quick scan of her.

She was cute, in the little girl, first day kind of way. She had on blue jeans, an adorable top with a dog in a tutu on it. *I wonder if Roxy would let me put her in a tutu? Probably not, but it would be worth a try.* She also had brown hair that went to her shoulders and deep blue eyes.

"Ms. Ryan, I've come to deliver someone to you." Principal Talley's voice interrupted Ellie's musings.

"I'm not a package," the girl said as she looked up at Talley with a huff.

Ellie liked her already.

"I'm a human. You can't deliver me unless you're a doctor."

31

Oh, hell yes! *Thank you, Universe! You've just given me the best gift. Wait a minute, are these my brownie points being cashed in?*

Ignoring her grievance with the Universe she saw the little line between Bob's eyebrows appear. *Oh shit, that's the look he got when he held his tongue.* Lord knew he'd done it enough with Ellie.

Ignoring it, she focused her attention back on the girl. Ellie liked her. A lot. Anyone that could manage to get under Bob's skin that fast was a-okay with her.

A pinched expression appeared on his face. "Correct Annabelle, you are indeed a human and doctors do the delivering for those."

"That's not true," Kimberly yelled. "Right, Ms. Ryan? Didn't you say you were brought into this world on the backseat of a car? That's not at a doctor's office or the hospital."

Bob's eyes almost popped out of his head as he snapped his face toward Ellie. "Excuse me?"

"That's not what I said." She held her hands up in defense. "Don't believe them."

"Yeah, it was," Travis interjected. "You talked about how the backseat of the car hadn't seen luckier days until you were born. Something about the best thing since sliced bread."

"Oh, really?" Bob studied her for a second before he reached into his pocket and pulled out his phone.

Oh shit! She wanted to scream at him to stop, but it was too late. Ellie knew by the end of the day she'd have a text from her dad. *Son of a biscuit.*

Bob pocketed his phone, focusing his attention back to the child next to him. "Annabelle, this is your morning teacher Ms. Ryan. She's different." Bob raised his eyes to

Ellie causing her to shudder. She knew that look meant this was far from over.

Annabelle cocked her left brow at Bob. "You're weird."

Holy shit! Ellie couldn't stop herself from laughing. Yep, she really liked this one. See this is why she loved her morning students the best. And it seemed as though Miss Annabelle was going to fit in just fine.

As Bob's left eye began to visibly twitch, Ellie knew it was time to step in. She took a step closer to the door. "I'll take it from here." She held her hand out. "Hi. I'm Ms. Ryan, and from what Principal Talley said, I assume your name is Annabelle."

"My grandpa said assuming is bad since it makes an ass out of you and me."

The whole room erupted into laughter.

At first, Ellie was taken aback, but then she was right there with her students laughing. "Oh, man, kid. I can tell you right now, you and I are going to get along just fine."

Ellie ignored the annoyed groan that came from Bob.

"Annabelle is right," the spitfire said, holding out her hand to Ellie. "Annabelle Hurley, most people call me Belle though, except my grandpa. He calls me Bella."

"It's nice to meet you." The corner of Ellie's mouth turned up. "Which would you like me to call you?"

"Belle is fine."

"Belle it is, then. Come on in, and pick your seat." Ellie bent so she could whisper in Belle's ear. "I'd avoid the kid in the striped shirt. Unless you like to watch him pick his nose all day."

"Eww!" Belle giggled.

"Ms. Ryan, I heard that!" Tommy shouted with a smile as he stuck his finger in his nose again.

"Was it a lie?"

"No." Tommy sent a toothy smile her way.

Never a dull day...

"I can sit anywhere?" Belle asked.

"Sure, as long as it doesn't become a problem."

"My old school we had to sit in alphabetical order. I was always at the front."

"Then sit in the back for a change."

The girl's eyes widened like she'd just been given candy. "Okay!"

"I see you've got it handled," Bob remarked with a nod toward her. "Ms. Ryan, before the day is over, please see me in my office."

The room broke out into laughs, along with Oos and 'you're getting in trouble'.

See always something new to talk about. She wanted to fist bump the air. *My panties were not coming up today.*

Once Bob left, Ellie turned back to her class and sighed. "Really guys, you had to bring up the backseat thing?" She gave Kimberly a strained look which resulted in that little shit winking at her before smiling from ear-to-ear.

Dear Universe, why do my students walk all over me? Better yet, why do I let them? Ellie shook her head with a smile. She knew exactly why she let them. As long as no one was getting hurt, why not have a little fun?

"What's the fun in that, Ms. Ryan?" Travis asked.

"At least, you guys always keep me on my toes." Ellie made a sweeping statement with her hand as she glared at them. "If I get in trouble, you're all getting an extra three paragraphs added to your book reports." She wanted to pat herself on the back for holding in her smile at her idle threat.

"That's not fair."

"Life ain't fair kid and you might as well find it out now."

"We already know," Travis spoke up. "That's why we're in this class."

Ellie sobered.

It was one thing to have an issue working through your schoolwork; it was another to realize you were different. Outside this classroom, the world could be cruel. Lord knew she'd been there.

With a heavy heart, Ellie pushed back her own feelings of inadequacy. "You are in this class because you need a tad more help than some of the other kids. That doesn't mean anything negative. Just because you might learn a different way, does not make you any less than them. You got me?"

"We know," Tommy answered. "It's why you're my favorite teacher."

"Mine too," Kimberly echoed.

"Good." With a quick nod, Ellie took a calming breath before her eyes glanced at Belle.

Poor girl, she had no idea what she just walked into.

New plan. Instead of passing out the workbooks, Ellie walked to the front of the room.

"Did you cave? Are we gonna watch a movie?" Travis eagerly asked.

"No." He was going to give her a migraine. "I figured we could play a game first."

"TAG!"

Oh, for fuck's sake!

"No." She huffed. *Give me strength, Universe.* "Let's go around the room introducing ourselves."

"What kind of game is that?" Kimberly scoffed.

"Why? We already know each other," Travis added.

"Belle is new, maybe it would be nice if we took the time for her to feel welcomed. Maybe make some new friends."

Travis turned to Belle. "Hi, I'm Travis, we're friends now." He turned back to Ellie. "See, done. Friends. Can we watch a movie?"

Is it normal to want to squash your students like a bug? Is that frowned upon? Rubbing her temples, Ellie pointed at Travis before she hitched her thumb behind her. "Get your butt up here. You go first."

"Do I have to? Didn't I just introduce myself?"

"Now."

"Fine." He clunked to the front of the room. Ellie glanced back at Belle to see her smiling face.

Good.

One by one they all introduced themselves to Belle each telling her something interesting. Once the last student finished Ellie stood. "As you know, I'm Ms. Ryan. I like to read and watch movies in my spare time."

"That's 'cause she doesn't have a boyfriend!!" Travis screeched with a devilish grin on his face.

"And how do you know that?"

An evil glint appeared in his eyes. "You were talking to Ms. Sally at lunch the other day about how it's been too long since you—"

"And that's enough from you today. Another word and it's detention."

"You always say that."

"I mean it this time." *Universe if you're listening, a fire drill would be perfect right now.* Ellie turned back to Belle. "Anyway, I like reading and music. I also love coffee."

"Coffee's gross," Belle replied.

She gasped. "Just when I thought you were gonna be my favorite."

That's when Belle's whole face brightened in amusement.

"Hey, I thought I was your favorite," Travis grumbled.

"Only on Fridays."

"What about me?"

Ellie smiled as she looked at her students now fighting over who was her favorite. See, this is why she loved them. "You're all my favorites. Now pipe down." Ellie moved her attention back to Belle. "Would you like to go?"

Hesitantly, Belle looked around the room. "Uh, sure."

She slowly made her way to the front. "Umm. Okay, most people call me Belle. My dad and I just moved here."

"What do you like to do for fun?" Ellie asked, encouraging her.

"I don't know. Draw sometimes, watch tv. Mainly I like to annoy my dad."

Travis sat up. "Told you we were friends. See, Ms. Ryan, Belle can help me annoy you now."

"Trust me, you need no help."

Belle laughed as she continued, "I'm trying to convince him to get me a dog."

"Aren't girls supposed to like cats?" Tommy asked.

"Aren't humans not supposed to pick their nose all day?" Belle countered, making Tommy shrug unbothered.

"I've always wanted a dog. I hope once we're here a little while he'll let us get one."

"My friend has a dog that's a human," Travis replied.

"Dogs can't be humans," she stated matter-of-factly, which caused Ellie to chuckle.

"You haven't met Lord Waffles yet."

"What?" Belle looked at Travis like he was insane.

"I'll introduce you at lunch or recess," Travis replied. "His name's Jimmy."

"I thought you said his name was Lord Waffles?"

Ellie held up her hand stopping Belle. "It's best to leave it alone. Trust me."

The little spitfire's face scrunched for a moment as she looked at Ellie. "I think you're all weird." She walked to her chosen seat in the back. When she sat there was a ginormous smile on her face. "But I like it."

This was the life.

Looking at the clock, Ellie knew they needed to get started. If she waited any longer Talley would have another thing to talk about her with. "All right class, it's workbook time."

A groan came from Travis' direction. *Do not engage. If you plan on getting any work done this morning. I repeat. Do. Not. Engage.* "We're starting on page forty-two." She looked at Belle. "You can start on page one. I'll be over to help you in a moment, have no fear. We'll get you up to speed with everyone else before you know it."

"Do we have to read out loud here?" Belle asked, genuinely fearful.

"Not if you don't want to." Ellie's heart sank as Belle relaxed into her seat.

"Okay, good."

Ellie watched Belle for a moment as she saw her younger self there. When she was in school, there were countless times a teacher would spring reading out loud in front of the whole class on her. It used to paralyze her. She never wanted her kids to feel like that. Reading out loud, although it could be beneficial wasn't a requirement, nor would it ever be for her. But even if they wanted to, she needed her to know it was safe here. "Belle, if you ever want to read out loud, you don't need to be worried, okay? We're all here to help. We're a team."

"Team Green!" Travis yelled to the room causing Belle to look at him strangely.

Before Ellie could stop him, Travis all too willingly explained himself. "One day we came into class and Ms. Ryan had her skirt tucked into the back of her underwear. They were bright green."

Seriously...

Belle looked back at her, before bursting into a deep belly laugh.

Oh well, no harm done, and at least they didn't remark about the size of her actual ass, just the color.

"Team Green!" Belle shouted.

Oh, for fuck's sake.

Belle turned out to be farther along than Ellie thought. And not surprisingly, when Belle came across something she didn't know, she would work through it. Only asking for help if she absolutely had to.

Just like Ellie did when she was younger. She now knew what drew her to Belle. She reminded her of herself.

"When's lunch?" Travis yelled from across the room.

"Same time it always is," Ellie replied, not looking up from her desk. "Do you have to ask every day?"

"How else would I annoy you?"

Ellie bit her tongue to stop from saying just by being alive. Instead, she forced a smile on her face. She did love the kid, but sometimes... "Ten minutes."

"I'm hungry now!"

"Aren't we all?"

"Plus, I wanna go to recess."

She rolled her eyes. After their morning work Ellie took everyone to lunch. After, they would disperse to gym, art, or back to their mainstream class to work on social studies.

"You know, what? Get your stuff together. I'll bring you down now. Maybe Ms. Sally is already there. It's her lunch duty week."

"Yay!"

"I'll introduce you to Jimmy," Travis announced, looking at Belle.

"Line up by the door, and make sure to have all your things. None of this coming back here. I'm looking at *you*, Travis."

Ellie turned to Belle. "Do you have any questions?"

"I don't think so."

"Is there anyone to help you at home? If not, all you have to do is let me know and I'll make sure you have time here with me."

"My dad can help. He did at my old school."

"That's great, Belle. Whenever you need any help, just let me know. It doesn't matter what subject. History, even art, if I can't help you, I'll have Ms. Sally do it."

"Math?"

"Yep, math. Well, kinda." Ellie's eyebrows knitted together. "Wanna hear a secret? I still don't get half of the math stuff."

Belle's mouth fell open. "Really?"

"Yes, really. But math's important, so when I don't understand how to do something, I figure it out. Or, I ask for help."

"You have times you don't know things?" she asked, wonderment in her eyes.

"All the time."

"Come on. I'm starving over here!" Travis hollered, standing first in line. *Travis. Oh, Travis, how I would love to stick a sock in your mouth.* "All right, gremlins. Let's go."

CHAPTER FIVE

"Dad!" Belle screamed as she ran to Spencer's car at full speed. The sight of her infectious smile caused his face to break out into its own ear-to-ear grin.

"Hey, pretty girl, how was your first day? Tell me all about it." *And put my mind at ease.*

Belle jumped into the backseat of his SUV and buckled her seat belt. "It was really good. I like Ms. Ryan. She's funny. She's the teacher that helps me with reading, spelling, and math. But she said she wasn't that good with math." She looked at him with a cocked brow. "She even said she has trouble sometimes and instead of getting frustrated or upset, she figures out the perfect way to learn it. Just like me!"

Spencer glanced at his daughter in the rearview mirror, as he continued down the road. He made a mental note to ask her why she'd tell a student she wasn't good with math. He wasn't quite sure if he liked that idea. "That's great, kiddo."

"She's really really funny, Daddy, and pretty. She's got blue eyes just like me and brown hair, too. But I don't think she brushes it." She giggled. "It was in a huge mess on the top of her head."

Spencer chuckled. "That so?"

"There was also this boy named Travis."

A boy? His lips thinned.

"He told me her name is Ellie. That's such a pretty name, don't you think so? But Travis said we have to call her Ms. Ryan. She gets annoyed if you call her Ellie. He's always fighting with her. They go back and forth all the time."

Spencer had to agree. That *was* a pretty name. *Wait a minute...*

"What do you mean fighting?"

"Not like for real fighting. More like what I do when I want to annoy you."

"So, you're telling me you'll be friends with him in no time." His brows pulled together. "Not sure how I feel about you making friends with boys. Boys are supposed to have cooties at your age." *Forty-five, kid. Forty freaking five.*

"Does that mean you have cooties since you're a boy?"

"I'm a man. There's a difference. When men hit a certain age, we no longer have cooties. It's in the rule book."

"What rule book?"

"The one your grandpa keeps from me."

At the mention of his father, Belle let out a scream. "When's Grandpa coming? Did you talk to him today? Does he miss me?"

"Holy shi-shoot, kid. Blow out my eardrum why don't you?"

"If you're hearing doesn't work, then you can't answer me when I ask if we can get a dog. No answer means, yes."

Spencer's eyebrows shot to the roof of the SUV as he looked at his evil prodigy in the back. Who just so happened to be sporting the Hurley smirk on her face. "I spoke to him while you were at school. Yes, he misses you. He's demanding you call him as soon as you get in the house."

"Yay!"

"Settle down there. First, finish telling me about your day."

"There isn't really much to say, Dad. Ms. Ryan gave me a workbook I have to go through to get caught up with the other kids in the class. She also said if you couldn't do it, she would stay after school to help me. Can you believe it? My old school never wanted to help unless it's what they were teaching. Ms. Ryan said she'd help me with art if I needed it. Or get Ms. Sally to help me." She relaxed back into her seat. "I really like her. She wasn't like my old teacher."

"You know I'll help you."

"I told her that, Dad. But she said if I ever needed extra help, she'd make time for me. It was nice."

A smile appeared on Spencer's face. Sure this Ms. Ryan was late, but if she was willing to help his little girl this much, she couldn't be all that bad right?

"None of the teachers in my old school would do that; they'd rather laugh. I don't think anyone's ever said they'd help me."

"Hey, what am I chopped liver?"

"No, Dad, gosh. I know you and Grandpa used to help me all the time, but it's nice to know I have a teacher that wants to do it too." She looked out the window. "When I'm in her class I feel like everything's okay. You know? I can't wait to go back to school tomorrow. At least for the morning."

For the first time since she'd gotten into the car, her

voice sounded small. Which made Spencer's ears pick up. It was probably nothing though.

"After art, I had to go back to my regular teacher."

"Yeah?"

"Her name's Mrs. Grady."

"How did you like her?"

She shrugged. "Okay, I guess."

"What about Mrs. Grady?"

Belle shrugged again. "I don't know. I like Ms. Ryan's class better. I wish I had her all day." She turned to her dad. "I really really like her."

"That's great, sweetie." Spencer pulled into their driveway, and before he got a chance to ask Belle to elaborate, she was out of the car and running toward the front door. "Where are you going?"

She turned back to him appalled. "To call Grandpa, duhh."

"My bad. I thought you would want to hang out with me for a little while before you throw me away for him." Spencer's bottom lip jutted out.

Belle ran back to her father jumping into his arms giving him a kiss on the cheek. "I'd never throw you away for Grandpa."

He held her tight as he used his hip to shut the car door. "It's nice if every once and a while you remind me."

"Unless Grandpa gets me a dog. Then you're tossed out the window."

His mouth hit the floor. "Right through the heart, kid, damn."

She smirked his way before letting out a laugh.

Damn.

Spencer placed her on the ground before tapping her back. "Come on, let's call Grandpa. You can tell him how

I've been demoted once again in your book. I'm sure he'll want to hear all about your day. You can tell him about Ms. Ryan."

"Only a little bit demoted." She held up her pinched fingers.

He shook his head. "You kill me, kid."

Ignoring him, Belle took off toward the front door. "Hurry up, Dad!"

"Geez, kiddo, I'm old. I don't work like I used to, give me at least two seconds to get to the front door. Plus, I'm over here trying to mend a broken heart my little girl just gave me."

"You're talking too much."

"Right in the heart, baby. Right in the heart. I'm adding this to the bank when you ask for a dog."

Belle's eyes popped out of her head. "Can we get a dog?!"

"Did everything I say just go over your head?"

"Well, I am smaller than you, so maybe."

"And a smarta—butt."

Belle started bouncing on her toes with excitement. "There's this kid at my school that has a dog named Lord Waffles."

"That's an interesting name." Spencer opened the door.

"Yeah, everyone said he is more human than dog."

That caused Spencer to cock his brow.

"I know it's weird, right?"

"Yeah."

"Waffles is a weird name for a dog," Belle remarked, kicking off her shoes. "Don't worry when we get one, I won't name it something like that. "

"Generous of you."

"I know."

Spencer shook his head as he chuckled. "Go call Grandpa. Once you're done, we'll get to work on your homework."

He didn't have to tell her twice. She took off through the house to get the phone. "Okay!"

Relief swept through him. It seemed as though Belle had a good day. See, he had nothing to worry about.

Besides, he couldn't wait to meet the teacher that had his little girl, the same little girl that hated everything about school, completely smitten.

Tomorrow couldn't come soon enough.

CHAPTER SIX

ELLIE RUBBED her temples with her fingers trying to ward away the tension headache she was getting.

Some days were hard, some were easy.

Some days she wanted to strangle Travis.

Today was one of those days.

After lunch, the devil incarnated ended up back in her classroom five more times, you know as he so eloquently put it, "to shoot the shit."

Nothing surprised her anymore.

Remarkably enough, Travis wasn't the cause of her impending headache, though.

Nope, this was all on her.

Try as she might, sometimes Ellie's organizational skills got the better of her. Before she knew it, today had completely slipped by.

She glanced at the clock on her desk.

In less than five minutes she had a meeting with Belle's father, Spencer Hurley.

She rubbed her temples again, letting her fingers trail into her hair. She only stopped once she hit a knot.

Figures.

Doing her best, she tried patting down her hair. Lord knows it was probably a mess.

Real professional. Add that to your list of good qualities for the day.

Pushing away her own insecurities, Ellie looked down at Belle's assessment once again as she worked through the findings.

Belle had only finished twenty minutes before, and promptly, with a worried look went to Sally's art room to wait.

Ellie closed her eyes again. Administering these tests always sucked.

Seeing her kids struggle and not being able to help was honestly the hardest thing she would ever witness.

Even though it killed her, it was for the best. It had to be done to get an accurate reading of where the child was. Helping them when they were struggling would only hurt them in the long run.

She'd be lying if she said it wasn't murder on her soul, though. The test was designed to get harder and harder. They all struggled, no matter what.

Ellie sat back in her chair with her eyes still closed. Her mind drifted back to the countless times she had to take this very same test as a child.

She hated it.

And each time they got worse. Every time she'd put her pencil down, she knew what came next.

More people would put her underneath a microscope and place her into the box of not good enough. Ellie's fists clenched at her sides as she tried to fight off the memories.

Hell, thinking about it now brought up a part of her that she hated. A part she sometimes tried to hide.

There was one test in particular where the administrator, a — thought way too highly of himself, therapist — ate Ellie up and spit her out. No matter how hard she'd tried to forget his words over the years, they were always in the back of her head. *"You're pretty much dumb as a box of rocks, Ellie Ryan. Once your mother comes to get you, I'll talk with her about getting you moved somewhere better suited for your issues."*

Those words, even how untrue they were, had left permanent damage on Ellie's soul, psyche, and self-esteem. It took her years, and with the support of her family and teachers to realize that jerk was on a power trip.

As Ellie's eyes tightened, she did her best to push the thoughts away.

Those stories were for later. A time where she could get a bottle of wine and rehash them out with Sally who'd always been there for her. Just as she did every time she was thrown back into the hurtful memories.

Right now, though, *he* wasn't worth her time.

Besides, in the long run, because of him, Ellie worked her ass off. She graduated with honors in Special Education teaching, along with dual degrees in psychology and education. Just for the sole purpose, she'd be able to administer these tests.

She would *never* let what happened to her, happen to someone else.

Ellie's anger rose. How dare the education system leave the future of a child in some therapist's hands that had no idea what these children went through? Or better yet, someone who obviously gave zero shits about children all together.

Words hurt.

And, words can shape people's lives.

Thank the Universe for her, they made her push harder than ever before. She was a lucky one. She took his words and used them as drive.

Sadly though, not all kids got that, and Ellie couldn't help but wonder how many lives that therapist had potentially ruined by his misguided and asinine words... Because of that, she vowed to take back her power. She'd administer these assessments with nothing but love and kindness. She'd fight to her dying breath to make sure every child knew they were special. They were—

"Sleeping on the job?"

A deep agitated voice broke through her thoughts causing her eyes to snap open as she almost fell out of her chair.

Holy shit!

Once Ellie realized the building wasn't on fire or zombies hadn't invaded the school, her eyes adjusted. *Holy crap on ten million crackers.*

Her jaw hit the floor.

There, standing in front of her, was by far the most handsome man she'd ever laid eyes on. He wore dark jeans and a fitted dark navy shirt. One that showed off his toned arms.

Are you drooling, Ellie? You better not be drooling.

As she continued her perusal of him, her tongue popped out subconsciously wetting the bottom of her lip. His face had that chiseled look of a Greek god, and he had that messy brown hair of a hipster.

Usually, she wouldn't have been into that, but on him, it looked good.

Damn good.

And his eyes, oh man, his eyes.

They were like portals to the ocean. Such a deep-sea

blue-green they almost took her breath away. It didn't matter they were glaring death toward her. This man was someone straight out of a wet dream.

One she would gladly revisit later on in her fantasies.

Too bad he looked like he was ready to murder.

Okay, Ellie, game face. Most parents come in here with a chip on their shoulders 'cause they want what's best for their children. You're used to this. Smile, joke, and win them over. Which was never hard to do. Her students loved her, so did their parents. *Before you know it, all will be right with the world again, and you can help give Annabelle the proper education she needs.*

With a bubbly smile placed on her face, Ellie jumped from her seat and hurried toward the man with an extended hand. "Hi, it's nice to meet you. It's been a long day." She let out a laugh. "Wednesdays normally are, right? Hummmppp dayyy!" *Why did I say that? He's now looking at me like I'm insane.*

In for a penny, in for a pound. She had to keep going. At least that's what her deranged brain said. "It's all about getting over that hump. Once you do, the rest of the week is smooth sailing." *Who was this crazy person talking? Just because someone's attractive does not mean you get to blather on like an idiot. Why do you always do this?* She couldn't stop herself. "But, hey, hump day can also be fun if you have someone to hump. Maybe that's why they call it hump day?" Her hand shot over her mouth. *Kill me now.*

The room froze as Ellie stood there wishing the ground would open up and swallow her.

The attractive man's eyes almost popped out of his head. And could she blame him? Hell no. She was positive her eyes were doing the same.

Holy shit. This was not your first time talking to someone attractive, what the hell?

Ellie's eyes darted to her coffee. Did Mr. Douglass lace her drink because of her strongly-worded Post-it note that may or may not have threatened his family jewels?

The man cleared his throat, grabbing Ellie's attention.

Why in the hell is he glaring at me?

"First, you didn't show up at the meeting yesterday. I'm pretty sure I caught you sleeping. And, you're talking about humping people? What kind of place is this?" His brows darted to the ceiling as his arms crossed angrily over his chest making his muscles more pronounced.

Which of course Ellie's eyes snapped directly toward them. *Yummy.*

"I *thought* the Principal had assured me you were the best. I don't care what Annabelle said about you." He looked her up and down sending shivers through her body. "Doesn't look that way to me. I wouldn't be surprised if you're the worst teacher here."

Ellie's mouth dropped to the floor. *Oh, fuck no!* "Excuse me?"

It was like the air had been sucked from the room as she tried to compute his words. Who the ever-loving hell did this guy think he was?

His face hardened as he stared down at her.

She'd seen this look before. It was the same look she'd gotten countless times as a child. Scratch that, she'd gotten them as an adult, too.

It was the look to make her feel small.

Make her feel like she wasn't good enough.

Make her feel less.

Fucking less.

Anger shot through her. Ellie would've let that look

53

slide when she was a kid, when she wasn't strong enough to fight for herself, but not anymore.

Fuck that.

Never again.

Fuck him, and his handsome fucking face.

The superiority radiated off this asshole in waves. And Ellie gave zero shits if this guy was the hottest guy she'd ever seen. He was about to get schooled. "If I were you, Mr. Hurley, I'd take a chill pill," she snapped.

He jerked back. It seemed he wasn't prepared for her harshness.

Good.

Ellie shook in anger. "I'd appreciate it if you didn't look at me as if I were no better than gum on the bottom on your shoe." Her eyes were hard as she stayed strong. No one, especially a man, would ever make her feel less again. Squaring her shoulders, she held her stance. "I'm assuming you must be Belle's father."

"*Annabelle.* Yes." His eyes pierced into her.

Did he think that he was going to intimidate her?

Newsflash, bucko. No one intimidated her.

Stop. She scolded herself. Even though it would take everything inside of her, Ellie knew she had to stop this and now. Sure, she would more than happily slap this asshole across the face, but that wouldn't do any good.

Annabelle. Remember Annabelle.

How did sweet, sarcastic Annabelle belong to this prick?

That's why everyone was here. And even though it might kill her, she was going to swallow her anger and put Annabelle first. Ellie took a deep breath. "Mr. Hurley, I think it would be best if we start—"

"What do you mean looking at you like something on

the bottom of my shoe?" His brows pulled together as his face held genuine confusion.

Don't snap. Don't snap. Get through with this meeting, El. Then punch your pillow later pretending it's him. "Exactly that Mr. Hurley. I think it's best, however, that we move on and talk about what's important here. Your daughter."

She wanted to pat herself on the back. *This* was adulting.

See, Universe I'm taking the high road again. I'm expecting more brownie points in my bank by the end of this meeting. Especially, if I make it out of here without strangling him.

She pointed to the seat by her desk before she turned away. Ellie couldn't remember the last time someone looked at her like that. Her jaw tightened.

In a vicious motion, she grabbed her chair, tossing it back hitting the wall with a slam.

No one looked at her like that anymore and lived to see the next day.

Annabelle. Remember why you're here. Take another breath.

Ellie needed to calm down. Annabelle. She was all that mattered.

As the asshole, as she now deemed him, took a step toward her, she couldn't stop her mouth from speaking the next words. At least they were in a whisper. "Oh yeah, and before I forget. Fuck off."

CHAPTER SEVEN

*W*HAT THE ABSOLUTE *hell just happened?*

Spencer cocked his brow at the woman who stomped to the front of the room. And did she just... No, he *had* to have heard her wrong. There was no way in hell he'd heard her correctly.

His head was spinning.

It was safe to say this meeting wasn't going well. At all. Sure, he was partially to blame for that.

Okay, he was a lot to blame, but he couldn't help it. All the shit from Belle's old school came rushing back to him the moment he saw her eyes closed.

He couldn't stop himself from jumping back to his daughter's old teacher. The one that would degrade her students when they asked for help. The same one that would join in on the bullying.

He acted before he thought.

You couldn't blame him for going to bat for his daughter, though. It's parental instinct. You know, father bear and all that stuff.

Even if it was clear *Ms. Ryan* was only resting her eyes.

Yeah, this wasn't his finest moment. And now he had no way to backpedal from it.

Then, there was her insane word vomit. That was the only thing he could call it.

Spencer had to admit though, if it were any other time, he would have laughed. It was adorable in some weird, she doesn't know when to stop talking, sort of way.

Maybe he made her nervous?

He kind of liked that idea.

Hump day, really? He had to hold back his smile.

However, as he was fighting the urge to wrap the curvy woman in his arms and tell her it was okay his brain started working again.

Spencer *had* to make sure this teacher wasn't like Belle's last. So he did the asshole thing and accused her of being a shit teacher without any proof.

Yeah. He was a dick here.

And Ms. Ellie Ryan seemed to call him out on it. Especially, if he heard what he thought he heard her mumble.

His eyes went to her mouth.

Thick, pouty lips...

No. What the fuck, dude? Where the hell did that come from?

Shaking his head Spencer tried taking a step back mentally. He was here for Annabelle. And, being rude and obnoxious with the teacher isn't going to help anyone.

Despite his reasoning, Spencer's eyes scanned her frame.

Belle was right. Her hair was in a messy bun on her head, and it did seem as though she didn't brush it. But there was something about it that was endearing.

She was a classic beauty, other than her hair.

Her clothes showed off her natural thick curves.

Spencer would know since her skirt was a tad too tight for his liking.

Not because she couldn't pull it off... quite the opposite. It made *him* want to pull it off. This only frustrated him more. He wasn't supposed to be thinking like that. And yet...

Ellie Ryan was attractive.

Not someone he would've normally been attracted to, but then again, his preferences had changed drastically since Belle's mother.

He blanched.

What the hell? Why was he even thinking like that? Sure, he appreciated women, but since the disaster of his past he'd sworn off them.

The *only* woman he cared about was his daughter. And right now, if Ms. Ryan couldn't prove to him that she was in fact, everything the principal stated, there was going to be an issue.

"Please, have a seat, Mr. Hurley."

Spencer's eyes went to her face, snapping him back to reality. *Good God, get a grip. You see a sexy lady and you fucking lose your mind. What are you, ten?*

Spencer studied her face, trying to stop his brain. Her eyes had hardened, almost in a guarding way. She seemed cold, her features stone.

He wanted the bubbly hump day talking Ellie back. Not this one.

Like a lightbulb going off, her voice registered in his head. He swallowed. Holy shit. Was it normal for a voice to turn someone on?

Stop it! Get your shit together numb-nuts. Yeah, it's been a while but, fuck, dude. I'm running so hot and cold I can't keep up with my own shit. For fuck's sake.

Let's take a gigantic step back and remember why you're here.

Your daughter. Spencer let out a breath he hadn't known he was holding. *Don't let the first chick to get you going again be your downfall.*

Spencer straightened his back. Let's get through this meeting intact. With his walls back in place and his focus fully on Belle, he looked at the teacher. "Please, call me Spencer."

Ellie gave him a leery look before she nodded once. "Fine, Spencer, please have a seat."

While he sat, he watched her from behind the desk. Gone was the fight in her eyes. It was almost as if she resolved to get this over with as fast as he did.

Interesting.

Everything about her now was professional. And why in the hell did that make him angrier?

He really wanted the playful Ms. Ryan back.

"I had Annabelle take her assessment after school today, as you know. I'd just finished going through her scoring before you walked in."

"So, you weren't sleeping?" *The fuck?* He sat back shocked at his own words. Why did he say that? He knew damn well she wasn't sleeping, so why did he put his foot in his mouth?

Is this what being insane felt like? An attractive woman looks your way and you lose all conscious thought.

Ellie's eyes narrowed dangerously on him, and fuck him if that didn't get his blood going even more.

She calmly placed the papers on her desk. "Fine. We are going to do this. Just like when my students get in temper tantrums and won't let them go. Let's have it out, so we can get back to what's important here. You know, your daughter."

Whoa, it was like she poured cold water on him and scolded him like an errant child all at once. And fuck him if he didn't like that also.

"What exactly is your problem, Mr. Hurley? You and I both know I wasn't sleeping. Besides, who sleeps sitting up? It's not like we're in some apocalyptic world and we've got to always be on alert." Her shoulders went back pushing out her chest in a defiant pose.

Fuck him for his eyes going directly there as she continued to berate him.

"Now, that we've got that little tidbit out of the way, let's get something straight. I am here and here for one reason only. That's to help *my* students succeed in every way I can. Seeing as you've only known me for what? All of five minutes. You're going to need to take a giant step back there, hotshot. The attitude pouring off of you is nauseating and I would prefer to keep my lunch down. Now, you either need to desperately get laid, or explain to me what the hell crawled up your ass and died?"

Sexy.

What. The. Fuck? No seriously, what the ever-loving fuck?

"Frankly, Mr. Hurley, I don't give a damn if you like me or not. The only thing I care about is Annabelle and her education. I'm here to provide her the tools she'll need to survive in this world. And if you speak to me like that again, or look at me like you're better than me, I do not give a shit if you are the parent of one of my children. I will take this stapler and shove it up your ass. Now, are you ready to put your tude away so we can get back to business, or do we need to meet out in the parking lot for a showdown?"

Spencer stared at her, do not mess with me face, in awe. He couldn't remember the last time someone other than his dad had talked to him like that.

Fuck him.

And fuck his dick, too, because sure as shit that fucker took notice.

Besides, if her speech had anything to show, it was that she had his daughter's back. And fuck him again, that made his dick *even* harder.

"I see you're speechless. Good, keep it that way while I explain to you what your daughter will need going forward." She picked up the stack of papers like she hadn't just ripped off his balls and made him eat them.

Spencer should've been embarrassed. He should've yelled at her. He should be walking out of this room, grabbing Annabelle and leaving, but instead, all he wanted to do was bend her over her desk and fuck her.

Hard.

It's like the part of his brain that formed words stopped working and instead rushed all his blood down south.

"*Belle* is extremely intelligent. She's already grasped the concept of having to learn something a new way. I've had students for a few years that still struggle with that. She has no issue picking apart a problem, and finding the solution that fits her needs. That being said, although I am hopeful within a year or two, we can move her to regular classes. She has a long road ahead of her. But she can get there." She placed the papers down. "And when she does, I'll make sure she'll get the accommodations she needs, like extra time on tests, notetakers, people to read her the work if needed. I will make sure she has every useful tool at her discretion."

He stared at her begging for his brain to start functioning.

"I will stop at nothing to make sure she gets the education she deserves. Do you have any questions for me?"

Questions? What are questions?

After a moment his brain finally worked. Awe was the only thing he could come up with. He came in here ready to fight for his daughter's education. Instead, he got shit on and told *she* was there to fight for Belle's education and he could fuck off for all she cared. Damn, if that didn't do something to his heart, though.

Right now, Ms. Ryan was offering to help Belle more than anyone else had. And she was genuine about it.

Before Spencer could fathom words, or wrap his head around the fact someone other than his dad or him would be there for Belle, Ellie looked at the clock on the wall and stood.

"I do hate to cut this meeting short." The sarcasm coming off her was intense. "But I have students I need to tutor in the library. If you come up with anything please do not hesitate to reach out."

As Ellie walked through the room, she turned back to him. "Belle's in Room 108, the art room with Ms. Sally Johnson. It's down the hall to the right." She popped her right hip giving him one last glare as she turned back and walked out of the room.

Spencer's mouth hung open. What the absolute fuck just happened, and more importantly, why the hell did he want to run after her?

CHAPTER EIGHT

"WELL, HE WAS A FUCKING DICK," Ellie grumbled as she stormed into her house. "Smoking hot, but still a dick."

Her annoyance was sky-high. Normally, when it came to her after school tutoring, her kids had her undivided attention.

Not today.

Nope. Prick, McPrick's face kept popping up. It was hard to get through the session without every five seconds wanting to break his neck. Which only served to piss her off more. Her kids deserved her full attention.

Hell, even the pencil she had in her hand at one point snapped in two. Not unlike what she wanted to do to Fuck-face McGee.

Gahh. Calm down there, Ellie. No need to seek violence. It's done and over with. Time to move on. She rubbed her forehead trying to ease the frustration of the day. *Could moving on consist of fantasies of punching him in his perfect face, while the other wanted to kiss him in said perfect face?*

No.

Bad, Ellie.

Stop it. Bad.

Before Ellie could stop herself from completely losing her mind, she heard the distinct sound of paws running toward her.

Her mouth curved into a smile. It was like the whole world melted away as Roxy turned the corner into the hall and ran full speed at Ellie.

"Hey, pretty girl." Ellie's smile spread across her face, as her oaf of a dog tried skidding to a stop.

Tried was the keyword there.

Before Ellie could brace herself, as she usually did, Roxy plowed into her knocking Ellie straight onto her butt.

"Roxy, really?" Her dog kissed her face trying to jump into her lap. "I'm blaming jerkface for this, too. If I wasn't distracted, I would have been prepared for your daily collide."

Roxy barked making her laugh. "Okay, I get it. I do. You missed me." Ellie kissed between Roxy's eyes. "I missed you too, Roxy Foxy. I'm sorry I didn't greet you the moment I came in. Will you ever forgive me?"

She barked at her again.

Then on the turn of a dime, Roxy jumped from her lap before darting directly to the kitchen.

Ellie shook her head. Leave it to Roxy to always entertain.

Quickly she stood and fixed her clothes. *Silly Rox.*

Then, as fast as Roxy disappeared, she returned with her dog food bowl in her mouth which she promptly threw at Ellie's feet.

Hard.

"Roxy! What the fuck?" Ellie's eyes narrowed which only caused her dog to bark again. "I'm not going to let you bully me." She forced herself to be stern, all the while fighting her laugh.

Ignoring her, Roxy picked up the bowl and threw it at her feet again.

"Roxy-Ann Ryan, how dare you? I come home from a grueling day and all I want is love from my pup but you only want food. You act like you didn't have a three-course meal for breakfast."

Roxy picked up the bowl again before tossing it at Ellie's feet once more.

"My heart!" She placed her hand over her chest. "This hurts."

Roxy jumped into the air before doing a twirl.

"Roxy-Ann, it's not even dinnertime!"

Her demanding devil-dog picked up the bowl and tossed it for what seemed like the hundredth time.

"No more whipped cream treats for you!"

That caused her dog to halt in place for a second before she then picked up the bowl. This time however, instead of tossing it at Ellie's feet she gently placed it on the ground and laid behind it. She looked up at her mother with her tongue hanging out of the left side of her mouth, a huge smile on her face.

"Don't you dare try to butter me up there, missy. I know the game you are playing. I wasn't born yesterday."

Roxy rolled over onto her back, kicking her feet in the air being as playful as she could be.

Stay strong. She does this every day. You are her Alpha, not the other way around. Roxy's tongue flopped out of her mouth and landed on the floor. It was the cutest thing Ellie had ever seen, okay, well... it was the cutest thing the first time she'd done it almost five years ago, but how could she resist that sweet face? *Oh geez, I'm such a pushover.*

"Every single time." Ellie walked past the menace and headed to the kitchen. "I want you to remember this the next time I ask you to do something." She took the food out of the fridge. When she turned back, her dog was now in the kitchen bouncing on her two front feet. "See, I'm a good mom. I'm feeding you early."

Roxy barked.

"You seriously act like I never feed you." Ellie placed the food on the ground and watched as Roxy ate it while her butt danced in the air.

"In an hour when it's real dinnertime don't come crying to me." Her dog gladly ignored her, as Ellie turned back to the fridge and returned the dog food. "No respect. I swear."

With a shake of her head, she turned back to look at Roxy before leaning on the counter. "My dog might walk all over me and demand more food than she needed..." Ellie turned her glare to a happy pup still munching away at her food. "At least I've got Sally coming over tonight. Maybe I'll actually get some respect in this house."

Ellie *really* needed Sally right now. Talking to her might clear her head. Even now her mind kept going back to Belle's father. He'd somehow gotten under her skin, and for as long as she could remember, that hadn't happened in years. And then her word vomit to him about hump day.

She banged her head on the counter.

What was wrong with her? And even after the disdain in his eyes when he looked down at her, she still found him attractive.

Most of the time when people treated her differently, she shrugged it off. Or told them where they could shove it. And never thought of it again. But with him...

"Ughhh," she let out an annoyed groan. "Get your shit together, Ellie."

Just because you were attractive, did not give you the right to treat people like shit. Her anger came back. *Jerk.*

Ellie's eyes moved to Roxy who was gobbling down her food oblivious to Ellie's meltdown. Thank God Sally was coming over. Ellie needed some serious girl talk, or boy talk, or who the hell knew talk.

Wine talk would be fine at this point.

She placed her fingers to her temples again hoping it would fix whatever hell her life had ended up in.

However, just as she felt some of the pressure leave, her phone rang. With a strained huff, Ellie blindly reached for her phone in her pocket answering. "Hit me with it."

"Is that how you answer the phone now, Ellie? I thought your mother and I brought you up better than that?" Her father, Dean's voice bellowed through her phone.

"What could be better than my greeting, Dad?" Ellie placed the phone on speaker, before tossing it on the counter.

"Ellie Mae..."

"Blahh. Do not use my middle name like that." She shuddered.

"How about Ellie Mae Ryan, what the hell was this about you telling your students you came into this earth in a backseat of a car?"

She looked around the room. *Where can I hide? Oh crap.*

"Ellie..."

"It's true!" Ellie screamed.

"And the back of my '67 Cadillac was never the same since." She heard the laugh in her father's voice. *"Still that wasn't something you should be sharing with elementary school kids."*

"Bob's overreacting. It didn't happen the way he made it seem."

"And how did Bob make it seem?"

Uhh, let's not go there. "Why'd Bob call and tell on me?"

"Because he's my best friend and it's either he call me, and I try and knock some sense into you or him fire you. Then you and Roxy will end up living back at home."

Over her dead body. "Did you know Bob said the word ass today? He did. I was there. I saw it and heard it." What was she, five?

"I've also heard him say the word fuck, your point is?"

"He does not!"

"Where do you think you heard it from? Back in the day, he had a mouth on him like a sailor. You should hear the stories he told before he met his wife."

Ellie jammed her fingers in her ears. "I'm not listening. I'm not listening!"

"Are you done?"

She pulled her fingers out of her ears when she heard her father's heavy sigh.

"I swear I am surrounded by children. You and Bob."

"You are, dear." Ellie heard her mother, Shannon's voice in the background.

"Tell mom I said hi."

"Ellie says hello." She heard some muffled noises before her father continued. *"Now, back to this nonsense. Your distraction won't work on me anymore. You're not sixteen. What the hell was Bob going on about?"*

Ellie groaned. "Fuck if I know, Dad. Sometimes I think Bob's got a screw loose. I'm nothing but a perfect employee."

"Somehow, I doubt that."

She gasped. "Rude!"

Ellie was sure her father rolled his eyes. *"You win for now, El. I'm too tired to deal with it. How were classes today, sweetheart?"*

"Good." She shrugged. "For the most part. I met with the parent of my new student."

"Yes, Bob said you had someone new. That's how he found out you were giving your kids sex-ed lessons."

"For fuck's sake. Really? Is that what he told you?"

"For someone that claims she's innocent you protest an awful lot."

Ellie didn't know why she expected anything less than this type of conversation with her parents. Deciding it was best to ignore him, she continued, "Yes, I've got a new student, she reminds me a lot of me."

"That so?"

"Yeah. At one point today, I could swear I was looking at myself when she took her assessment."

"How'd that go over?" he asked.

"Same as it always does. I want to help them in every way I can. You know, like how you, mom, and Bob helped me. I want to be what you three were to me, for my kids."

"You are, Ellie."

"Sometimes I don't think so. Especially, when their parents get involved that think I don't know—"

"Did something happen I should know about?" His voice hardened. *"Ellie Mae, you tell me right now, did some asshole say something? You know I'll go right back to when I did when you were younger. All you have to do is say the word. No one messes with my little girl—"*

"Down, Dad." The corner of her mouth rose. All these years later and her parents were still there ready to destroy anyone that made her feel unworthy. Especially when it came to her abilities. "It's nothing I can't handle."

He grumbled on the other line. *"Fine. Don't tell me. I'll have Bob —"*

"It's not a big deal, Dad. Anyway, I'm gonna help her the best I can."

"I know, sweetie." He sighed. *"You will do everything in your power."*

"Always."

"We'll see you this Sunday for dinner, right?"

"What if I said I was sick?"

"It's Tuesday, how do you know you'll be sick on Sunday?"

"Uhhhh..."

"Exactly, I believe Bob and his wife are coming to dinner Friday. That way I'll get all the juicy intel before you have a chance to deny it."

"Shoot me now."

"Don't forget to bring my little Roxy. See you Sunday, Ellie. Love you."

"Love you too, Dad."

The moment she disconnected the phone she felt Roxy's food bowl hit her foot before clanging to the ground. "You've got to be kidding me! You are not still hungry!"

Roxy barked.

"Are you just gonna stand there or are you gonna feed your dog?" Sally asked, walking into the kitchen.

"Do not let this little bitch fool you. She's been fed already. Her demands have been met." Ellie glared at her dog as her best friend betrayed her.

Sally dropped to her knees. "How's my Roxy Foxy? Are you a good girl? Do you want Aunt Sally to give you a treat? Yes, you do. Big ole mean mommy doesn't want to feed you."

"Do not enable her!"

Sally snapped her head toward Ellie. "*You* enable her!"

"No. You do!"

"I'm allowed to, I'm the favorite aunt. Duh. It's in my contract." Sally jumped to her feet before giving Roxy a treat from the treat container.

"For Pete's sake." Ellie threw her hands into the air. "You didn't even make her do a trick first."

"Do I make you do a trick before we eat?"

"Oh my God, it's like talking to a wall."

"Did you just call me a wall?" Sally glared at her.

"A very pretty wall."

Sally hitched her hip before tossing another treat to Roxy who was eagerly waiting. "Damn straight."

"Forget it." Ellie turned to the fridge grabbing the pizza menu. "Pizza?"

"I resent the wall comment, but accept the pizza offer." Sally's eyebrows pulled together as she gave Ellie the once-over. "Looks like you've had one hell of a day."

"I could say the same to you. You've got blue paint across your pants."

Sally shrugged. "A day I don't come home with paint on me, is a bad day."

A warm smile spread on Ellie's face. It was one of the things she loved most about Sally. She loved getting down and dirty with her students. No one could ever say her art projects didn't have heart and soul in them.

"Seriously, El, you look like you've been through the wringer. You okay?" She opened Ellie's fridge before grabbing a bottle of water.

"You could say that."

"Did it have anything to do with Mr. McHotPants?"

"Who?"

"Belle's father."

"How do you know what he looks like?"

"He came by the art room to pick her up after your meeting. Did his hotness cloud your memory?" She cocked her brow. "I don't blame you, though. Whoo-ee, he is nice to look at. Did you see his butt? I could bounce me a quarter off that thing."

"Sally..."

"Are you telling me he wasn't drop-dead gorgeous? Do I need to take you to an optometrist?"

"I didn't say that." Ellie pushed her hair out of her face, annoyed.

Sally's whole face brightened. "Ohhh, I think there is a story here." She wrung her hands together as she danced. "Oh, there is a story here. As soon as we order pizza, you're spilling."

"There is nothing to spill." Ellie grabbed her phone.

"I'd like to spill something on him... then lick it off." Sally looked away dreamily.

"Sally!"

"What?" She cocked her head. "Don't get mad at me for saying what you're thinking."

Ellie's eyes narrowed on her best friend. "Yeah, well too bad he's an asshole."

"What! There's no way? He was as sweet as could be when he picked Belle up. I mean he seemed a little distracted but he was nothing but nice."

Ellie turned away. She hated moments like this. Ones when she had to find the words to explain how someone made her feel not good enough.

"Babe?" Sally moved closer.

"Let's get the night started, then we can talk."

She didn't push it. "Fine, you win right now, but I promise you as soon as I can, I'm prying this out of you."

"I wouldn't expect anything less."

"Since you aren't willing to give momma a much-needed story time, movie it is. I can't wait to see Trevor McCain in his new role." She licked her lips. "Can you believe they cast his wife as his love interest?!"

Ellie smiled. "I heard he refused to do it without her."

"Gives me hope for us curvy girls. The chemistry between him and Maggie on-screen is electrifying." Sally got this faraway look in her eyes.

"You and me both, sister." Instantly an image of Spencer Hurley popped into her head.

Oh, heck no! No, no, stop that right now.

Pushing past her thoughts she focused on Trevor McCain and his wife Maggie. *Quick think of something else. Got it.* "He's apparently super protective of her."

"I want that one day," Sally remarked.

"We both do." Ellie tossed her phone to her best friend. "Now, order the pizza and let's get to feasting on some man candy. Nothing better than Trevor McCain with his shirt off."

"Sure, then we can get to talking about Mr. McHot-Pants." Sally turned on her heel heading out of the kitchen leaving Ellie alone.

Roxy gave a quick bark, before trotting right after Sally agreeing with her.

Figures.

CHAPTER NINE

Spencer walked into the local coffee shop after dropping Belle off at school one morning.

It'd been three days since his meeting with Ellie Ryan and he still couldn't wrap his head around it. So, he figured coffee and a sweet treat could help.

The meeting replayed over in his head more times than he could count. But that wasn't the issue. No, not at all.

Spencer couldn't get Ellie out of his head.

There was something about her that—

Spencer growled in frustration. Since that day, she'd been the starring role in every one of his dreams.

Dreams no man should have regarding his child's *teacher*.

Spencer wanted to punch himself right in the face.

Hard. And multiple times.

No matter how many times he replayed it, he couldn't figure out where everything went wrong.

And then there was the look on her face, the one that constantly haunted him. She was pissed at him sure, but no.

This was the look right before then. The one that looked like she'd been slapped.

Okay, Spencer knew he was rusty when it came to the opposite sex, but this was...

Before he could stop himself, an image of Ellie's body jumped into his mind. The same image that had him making a mess of himself every morning.

He groaned in annoyance.

Ellie was breathtakingly beautiful. Curves, he died to touch. Hair, albeit messy, he wanted to run his fingers through. Plump lips he wanted to taste. The same lips he wanted wrapped around his —

No.

None of that.

Nope.

We will not go there again. She's your child's teacher, to say the least. Not to mention, the fact you are staying away from women altogether. You, dumbass.

See, this is why he wanted to punch himself. Then there was the way she told him off. He never thought he was a masochist before, but the way she chewed him up and spit him out was enough to have him shoot his load right then and there.

Because of *her,* and well, it might have to do with the fact that he hadn't gotten laid in fucking years.

But it was mostly her.

Wasn't moving supposed to make things easier for them? Apparently not.

That's it, Spencer was putting a stop to his screwed-up brain and Ellie.

And now.

No freaking more.

He was better than this, and he for sure as shit wasn't going to complicate their new start.

That settled it, the only communication he'd have with Ms. Ryan going forward would be parent-teacher meetings.

Spencer stood taller and mentally patted himself on the back. See, everything was going to be fine. No more *Ellie* Ryan.

Now life could go back to normal.

With his new lease on life, Spencer abruptly stepped out of line to get a better look at the case of sweets to his right. However, in his quick movement he didn't see the person walking past him.

It happened so fast Spencer wasn't able to stop. His body plowed right into them.

"You have got to be kidding me!" the woman grumbled as her beverage drenched her top before falling to the floor.

Spencer's stomach bottomed out. "Shit. I'm so sorry. I didn't see you there. Please, let me—"

She faced him.

Fuck.

The woman who was now glaring daggers in his direction, was the same person he just vowed to never see again. "It's you!"

Ellie's lips pursed together as her eyes narrowed further on him. "Could today get *any* worse?"

What the hell? It wasn't like he did it on purpose.

She looked up to the ceiling. "Is this what I get for making the right today? Is it? You think this is funny?"

"Who are you talking to?"

"Mr. Hurley," Ellie responded as she attempted to brush the coffee off her now covered shirt.

Spencer's brain kicked in. "Oh shit, I'm so sorry. I

honestly didn't see you there." He reached to the napkins on the counter. "Here let me help you."

He started patting the front of her top before Ellie snatched the napkins from his hands pushing him aside. "It's fine, Mr. Hurley, and I'd appreciate if you wanted to grope me, you'd at least buy me dinner first."

"Grope you?" His hands snapped back.

As she continued to wipe the coffee from her shirt, Spencer's eyes widened. The sheer material was now almost see-through.

He couldn't stop his eyes from focusing on the swell of her breast peeking from the top of her bra. The same breasts he'd spent the last few nights fantasizing about.

"You can put your eyes back into your sockets, Mr. Hurley. They're just tits."

"I wasn't staring!"

"Tell that to the heat on your cheeks." Giving up Ellie balled the napkins in her hand before tossing them into the nearby bin. "At least nothing happened to you," she said, clutching the brown bag in her hands.

Spencer cocked his left brow. "Did you just talk to your food?"

"Did you just openly stare at my breasts?" she countered. "Besides, you would too, if you'd had the last croissant in your possession." She held up the bag. "These things are the best in the world. If you'd fucked it up, I'd have to wait until tomorrow to get another one."

"That seems a little obsessive."

"Trust me, you'd feel the same once you've had one." Her shoulders shrugged, not caring what he thought.

"Let me try it." *Who said that? He for sure knew it wasn't him.*

77

Ellie's gorgeous eyes widened as her mouth formed a tiny 'o'. "No."

"Come on. If they're as good as you're claiming, then prove it. Prove that it's normal to talk to your food."

"I do *not* have to justify myself to you."

"What are you, scared?" When her right eye twitched, he felt like he'd somehow won the lottery. Fuck, he loved this.

It only took Ellie another moment before she let out an annoyed huff. "Fine. Here." She reached into the bag and ripped off a corner. "I'm only doing this so you'll stop looking at me like that."

"Like what?"

"That. Never mind. Forget it, here!" She shoved it into his hand. "Now, if you'll excuse me, I need to get going."

No. She couldn't leave.

He wanted her to stay and spar with him more. Yep, it's official, he was a masochist now. At least where Ellie was concerned. "Don't you need another coffee? Let me buy it for you. It's the least I could do since I was the one that caused that." He waved his hand around her top.

Without thinking, he tossed the food she'd given him in his mouth. Just as he was about to go to the counter, he froze.

Holy shit this was good. His eyes folded as he fought back his moan. No seriously, holy shit, this was the best croissant he'd had in his life.

"Told you," her voice broke through his food-induced coma.

"This *is* delicious." His eyes went to the bag holding the rest of her pastry.

"Hell no! Get your grimy hands away." She held it out

of his reach. "You're out of your mind if you think you're getting the rest. This is *mine*. And, I do not share!"

"Neither, do I." His eyes honed in on her chest once again as the words hung in the air.

The moment her face heated, the gravity of his words hit him. *The hell, dude?*

When Ellie hugged the bag closer to her chest, his lust-filled words were forgotten as he looked at her food. "You just did, though. Share that is."

"Only to get you to shut up."

"There are other ways to get me to shut up."

Her cheeks brightened. "What is wrong with you?"

He'd like to know the answer to that as well.

Was he flirting? Is this what flirting was now? Holy shit he was flirting with her. What the *hell* was wrong with him? Shaking his thoughts out of his head and doing his best to tamp down whatever the hell was going on with him, he motioned to the counter. "Let me fix it. One coffee, and another one of those beauties."

"This was the last one. Didn't you listen to a word I said? Or were you too busy staring at my tits?" She held up the bag like a prized fighter holding her trophy. "Besides, it's fine. I'll make coffee in the lounge," she said the words with a twinge of annoyance that had him quirking his brow.

"No, let me make it right."

"There is nothing to make right, Mr. Hurley. Now, if you'll excuse me I have to —"

As she made a step toward the door, he sideswiped his movement, blocking her. "Please. I feel horrible about your shirt. Also, call me Spencer."

"No, thank you. I've got to go, I'm already late."

Before her words registered Spencer found his eyes honing in on her chest again.

"Oh, for fuck's sake." Ellie took a step around him moving toward the door.

Already late... Wait. He looked to the clock on the wall.

School started ten minutes ago. Why the fuck was she here?

Something snapped inside of him. This *woman,* the same woman that should be teaching his little girl right now, was instead standing in a coffee shop.

He fucking knew it. "Why the hell aren't you in your classroom?"

CHAPTER TEN

Ellie stopped only steps from the door.

Do not punch the father of one of your students in the face. Do not punch the father of one of your students in the face. Her fist clenched at her side. She didn't need to give Talley any more ammunition, so punching Spencer was out of the question.

Quickly, Ellie spun on her heel to face him. "What in the heck do you think I'm trying to do here? Powder my freaking nose?"

Fuck, this dude.

No seriously, who cares if he is one of the hottest men Ellie had ever seen? He really needed an uppercut to the chin.

"You should have been there ten, no twenty minutes ago." His eyes dangerously hardened on her.

Had she said it already? Well if not, seriously fuck him and his overly superior attitude. "If it wasn't for this little pow-wow here, I'd be on my way or I'd probably be there," she growled at him.

"Why the hell aren't you there now?"

"Who are you, my father?"

"If I were, you'd damn well be in school, and if you put up a fight, I'd turn you over my knee in a heartbeat."

The second the words were out of his mouth it was like the air was sucked from the room.

Ellie froze. She didn't know whether to slap him or let her mind run away with his words.

Too bad the latter happened.

Holy crap-a-molie. Screw her ridiculous mind for conjuring up images of just that. As Ellie did her best to push aside the feeling between her legs, she looked at him.

At least Spencer looked as shocked as she felt.

Good.

Although, his words brought a whole new meaning to her *hump day* mouth vomit.

Ellie watched him, not sure what to say next without saying something like *hump day* again.

His face turned red.

A deep red.

Wow, he looks kinda adorable with the blush going on. When he's not a raging asshole, he's downright adorable— NO! We will not go there. No. Hell no. Universe, I swear if you did this on purpose, I'm gonna be pissed.

Spencer, shocked by what he'd said, took a step back unbalanced.

Man, Sally's going to eat this up.

Then beyond any ounce of self-control Ellie had, and against her better judgment, she did the unthinkable. "Who said that would be a punishment?" She followed up with a wink. Sealing her fate in the Most Idiotic Things You Could Do Hall of Fame.

Spencer stumbled back again, but this time he lost his

footing, hitting the stand of cookies knocking them over as he stared at her with his eyes wide.

She chuckled.

One for Ellie.

Zero for McHotPants.

With her head held high, she turned on her heel and headed out the door. *See that, I got this. I'm Queen of the Universe now! Hear me roar.*

Ellie jumped into her car, with an extra pep in her step before she safely put her pastry in the seat next to her with a promise to devour it soon. She then put her car in drive and headed off in the direction of the school.

What started out as a shitty day turned into a marvelous one. Who said the world couldn't be on your side?

Looking down she caught sight of her shirt... Okay, well that still sucked. At least her shirt wasn't see-through anymore, just stained badly.

She looked at the clock in her car. There was no time to go home and change, this was going to have to do.

Maybe this will replace the green underwear thing? She thought about it for a second. *Nahh,* she knew her students. This will just be added to it.

Her students. Ellie's lips formed into a lopsided grin.

They were the best part about her day, even when she had a shit morning. Their smiles, their stories, their— *Holy shit!*

That's when it hit her. *That was Annabelle's father!*

Her car swerved as her mind exploded with what she'd done.

Oh my God! Holy shit. What did you do!! Her hands shook as she took the turn pulling into the school.

"Why couldn't you keep your mouth shut?" Once she

parked, she slammed her head onto the steering wheel causing her to jump when the horn went off. "Shut up!"

What in the hell was she thinking? Queen of the Universe her ass. Ellie should've made the left and gone to school in the first place rather than the stupid coffee shop.

She banged her head against the wheel again before her eyes darted to the pastry bag. After sending it an evil look, she went back to banging her head on the wheel.

She'd have to cancel all parent-teacher meetings with him, move to a new school. Crap, move to a new state.

Oh shit, what if Bob found out? Or her parents?

As she was waist-deep in her meltdown in the car, Ellie's phone went off. "Oh, shit crackers," she groaned. With her luck, it was probably the Universe sending her a "try me again" message.

Deciding it was best to face her death head-on, she grabbed her phone. Seeing it was only a message from Sally, she somewhat relaxed.

Where the hell are you, El? Talley is looking everywhere for you.

Ellie looked toward the roof of her car. "This isn't funny." Quickly she sent back a message.

I just pulled into the parking lot. I'm sitting in my car dying.

Ellie's eyes dropped to her top again. "Someone put me out of my misery."

Her phone buzzed.

Telling the cute coffee guy 'you too' after he hands you your cup and goes here you go, is not a reason for death. You do it every other day, you should be used to it. Now, get your ass in here. Talley looked pissed.

Damn it. Damn it straight to hell.

If only it was just that. Sal, this is bad, way bad. Like green panties bad. No. It's worse.

Sally's message instantly popped up.

Nothing is worse than green panties bad. Get your butt in here, Ellie. Once Talley's done with you, and you aren't fired, come tell me about it at lunch. I'll remind you how you shouldn't freak out about it. Get. Your. Butt. In. Here! Do not leave me with these kids alone.

Why wasn't Sally understanding this was the end of the world bad?

I can't. I ran into Annabelle's father and told him he could bend me over and spank me!

Ellie saw the bubble showing Sally's typing disappear. "See!!"

YOU DID WHAT?

Now she's getting it.

Told you. There is no way I can go in there. Ever. I need to change my name and go into witness protection. How easy do you think it is to apply?

Ellie slammed her head onto the steering wheel again as her phone buzzed.

Fuck you are. Get your ass in here right now, I need to know every detail and if you don't, I'm going out there and dragging you in. Don't make me tell Talley where you are.

Ellie's jaw dropped.

You wouldn't.

Sally's reply came in less than a second.

I would. Now, get in here. Your students are about to show up.

"Fuck me on a stick." Sally was right. Morning announcements will be over in a few minutes and then her kids would be in her classroom.

If she wasn't in there waiting who knew what Travis would do.

Screw this adulting crap. Ellie wanted her money back.

Okay, you can do this. You won't ever have to see him again. Nope. Never. You'll make sure of it. Everything is fine. Totally fine. You've got this. Just take a deep breath and forget you've just thrown your life off a cliff.

Grabbing her purse, Ellie unbuckled her belt. Before getting out of the car she took the brown bag. "I'm not forgetting you. I'll never be able to show my face there again. I've gotta make you last. On second thought, this is all your fault."

Great. Now she was being even more ridiculous.

As Ellie walked toward the front of the school, she took a deep breath. One moment at a time.

She could do this.

Now, to sneak in undetected and avoid Talley for the remainder of her life...

When Ellie reached the door, she carefully opened it, peeking in to see if anyone was in the hall.

No one was there.

"Thank fuck," she whispered under her breath.

"Language, Ms. Ryan. There are children here."

Ellie let out a yelp as she fell backwards into the door.

Bob Talley walked from around the corner with his arms crossed over his chest.

"Shit."

"*Language.*"

"Then don't sneak up on people, you jerk." Her hand went to her chest as she tried to stop from having a heart attack.

Oh no. Did I just call him a jerk at school? You know when he's not just your dad's best friend or a pseudo father to you, but your boss? Way to make a shit morning ten times shittier. Fuck a freaking duck.

"Ellie..." he warned.

"It's not what it looks like," she protested.

"It looks like, not only are you late, *again,* but you have coffee all over you." He raised his left brow. "I won't even mention the language."

"Well okay, so maybe it's how it looks, but—"

He held up his hand stopping her from continuing. "Any other day, I'd care about it, but not today."

Oh no... this wasn't good.

"Can you tell me why I just got off the phone with Mr. Hurley and why he was—"

"He told on me?" That fucking prick. "Are you kidding me that ass— I mean, butt wipe called you to tell on me?"

What else did he say?

Spencer: one.

Ellie: zero.

Talley: five-hundred and twelve.

Shit.

"Tell on you?" Bob looked at her like she had two heads. "Like I wouldn't have realized you were late?"

"I didn't—"

"He wants to meet with you today after school."

Ellie's eyes bulged. *What? Why?*"

Bob shook his head. "If I have to file paperwork because he lodges some complaint about you... I swear to God, Ellie, your father will be the least of your worries. I can't look past a filed complaint."

File a complaint! Oh, hell no! She should file a complaint against him. After all, he was the one who started it! He said he'd spank *her*.

Anger coursed through Ellie's body. Forget it. It seemed as though she was going to have to deal with Mr. I-tell-on-people-and-then-ruin-a-perfectly-good-day herself. "I'll deal with this."

"I expect you to." He thinned his lips. "Don't make me come looking for you again, Ellie. You know how much I *hate* paperwork."

"Yeah, yeah. I get it." She waved him off as she walked past him. "I'll shoot you an email."

"You drive me up the wall, Ellie Mae. You know what, I'm calling Dean."

Damn it. He used her middle name. That was *never* good.

Great. Now, she was going to get the third degree

from her father. Son of a bitch. She groaned as she made her way into her classroom. What a perfect freaking day. And to think, she gave that jerk-face a piece of her croissant.

Ellie looked at the clock on the wall. She had exactly three minutes before her students showed.

Her students...

That was still the most important thing to her. Taking a deep breath, she tried to calm herself.

She knew what she had to do. Logging into her computer, she pulled up Belle's file and grabbed the contact information. Before she could stop herself, she was dialing Spencer Hurley.

Universe, if you don't give me brownie points for this, I swear to all things, we are done. You hear me?

"This is Spencer." For a split second, she was stunned into silence.

How the hell did his voice sound like honey?

"Hello? Is anyone there?"

Shit. "Yes, hello. Mr. Hurley?"

"This is he."

"Hi again, this is Ellie Ryan, Annabelle's teacher."

"Ms. Ryan—"

"I'm not sure what game you're playing here, Mr. Hurley, but I can assure you it is one you will not win. That being said, I apologize for my remarks this morning. It was inappropriate. And despite what it looks like, I am always on time for my students in the morning. Now, if we could just put all of this behind us, we can focus on getting your daughter the best education she deserves."

"Ellie—"

"How about we start over?" *And not get me fired, or arrested on murder charges.* "What if we agree to stay out of each other's hair, unless it's regarding Annabelle." So professional. Point for Ellie.

"Are you done?"

She bit her tongue. Ellie could look good in orange if it came down to it. "Yes," she growled.

"Good," his voice purred. *"Belle should and will always be the top priority."*

"I agree —"

"But there is one thing you should be aware of, Ellie..." his voice dropped an octave. *"It doesn't always have to be a punishment."* He disconnected the call leaving her frozen as she clenched her thighs together.

Oh, my —

"Yo, Ms. Ryan what's all over your shirt?" Travis asked as he looked her up and down. "Did you finally follow through with Mr. Douglass and he spill coffee on you?"

Ellie's eyes snapped to him, before she looked down at her shirt, still unable to form words.

"Doesn't matter." Travis shrugged. "How about that movie?"

"Ms. Ryan!" Belle ran into her room. "Principal Talley told me I get to come to your class after school today. My dad's picking me up from here!"

Fuck. Me.

CHAPTER ELEVEN

Spencer stared at the phone in his hand like it was a snake about to strike.

Maybe, just maybe, if he stayed absolutely still the world would stop turning and he could pretend he didn't fuck up not only his, but his daughter's life.

It was as if some possessed demon had taken over his body for the last twenty minutes and decided to play the "how bad can I make this" game.

It was safe to say: pretty bad.

His heart was seconds from exploding out of his chest. Which was great, now he'd end up at the hospital trying to explain how he told his kid's teacher he'd bend her over and spank her ass. *That* was going to go over *really* well.

Spencer squeezed his eyes shut replaying his demise.

First, his clumsy ass knocked into her making her spill coffee down her top... although, seeing the swell of her breast did... *No*.

He would not go there again.

Those damn breasts were the thing that kicked his body into overdrive to begin with.

He got one glimpse of a chest and he became some deranged teenager that'd never seen a tit before.

Hell no. That wasn't him.

He'd been around the block long enough to know seeing a pair of tits wasn't supposed to ignite him.

He wasn't some fucking creep.

But then again, they were *her* breasts. The same breasts that had been starring in his even more fucked up fantasies.

He closed his eyes as an image of Ellie bent over his lap with her rounded ass in the air popped into his mind.

No!

Stop it! It was all just a dream. Yep, that was it. I'm still asleep in bed. When I wake up, I'll laugh all this off and then pack up our house and move across the country. Yes, that is exactly what is going on... See, I figured this out.

A notification on his phone chimed causing him to open his eyes. "Fuck!"

This all happened. Every last bit of it.

"Fuck me."

Why in the hell had he called the school? Why? Please dear Lord, someone explain to him why he called and *told on her*, like some snot-nosed kid trying to get someone in trouble.

Yeah, real winner here.

Spencer could have left it all alone like Ellie said. Pretend it never happened. Move on with their lives and focus on Belle.

But no...

It doesn't always have to be a punishment... He mocked himself. Who the hell even says shit like that?

Apparently, him.

And the tiny gasp he heard from Ellie's mouth right before he disconnected the call went *straight* to his dick.

Fuck him.

He glared at his lap. *This is all your fault. All of it. You see a pretty girl with curves that you want and you fucking lose your mind.*

Spencer wanted to bang his head against the wall to get the images clouding his mind out of his head.

Her on her knees in front of him.

Her on her back beneath him.

Her on her stomach with her ass in the air.

"Enough!" he growled as he tossed his phone onto the passenger seat of his SUV.

Besides, what happened to his motto of no more women, anyway? Since the fiasco with his ex, he'd sworn off them completely.

It was safer that way.

Safer for his little girl. He refused to have her grow up with random women coming in and out of her life. No.

Plus, if he was honest with himself, this was safer for him too.

If you kept people at a distance, they couldn't destroy you.

It was as simple as that.

And yet, when it came to Ellie Ryan, everything was forgotten. It was as if when she was around him his logic disappeared and someone else took over.

Seeing her at the coffee shop sent a wave of, he had no fucking idea, through him... Excitement? Thrill? Lust?

Her lips, her curves, her everything. They all called to him.

And for fuck's sake, she's his daughter's *teacher*.

Spencer pulled into his driveway with a raging headache.

See, this is why staying away from women was smarter. They made him lose his freaking mind.

As Spencer stomped into his house, his phone went off. For a split second his heart stopped. Could she be calling him back? What would she say?

What would *he* say?

Why did he like the thought of her calling again?

He answered without looking. "Spencer."

"Who crawled up your ass and died?"

Spencer let out his breath. Thank God it was just his dad. His whole body relaxed as his left hand went to his temple. "I don't know what you're talking about."

"Okay," Randal replied dryly. Spencer could hear the eye roll in his voice. *"Whatever lets you sleep at night, son."*

"What do I owe the pleasure, Dad?" Spencer winced at his tone. Even he heard the edge.

"Wow, something really did crawl up your ass. You'd think you'd be elated I even called your punk ass."

"Punk ass. Really?" Spencer shook his head as his hand went to his chest. "Oh, however could I forget, my father, oh father, how I am so over the moon you called. Let me take a seat so I can give you my undivided attention."

"Boy, I swear, if you hadn't given me that perfect grand-baby, I'd have beat your ass ten feet underground by now. You hear me?"

"You and what army."

"Moving away seems to have clouded your memory. Don't forget who changed your diaper every time you shit yourself."

The corner of Spencer's lip turned up. "And who's gonna change yours in a few years, Randal?"

"Boy... don't make me regret coming to see you tomorrow."

Spencer almost dropped his phone. "Tomorrow?"

"That's right. I figured you were getting too comfortable in your new life."

Spencer shook his head with a laugh. Geez, his father was dramatic. Now he knew where Belle got it from. "Sure thing, Dad," he replied drily.

He had to admit though, the fact his father was coming for a visit did ease him a bit. His dad always did. They might pretend to be at each other's throats most of the time, but his dad was his best friend.

His dad was the one that was there for him when Belle was born. He moved heaven and earth to help in every way he could.

Maybe with him here, he could figure out what to do. Plus, his dad would be good to talk to.

"Spencer..." His father's voice broke through his thoughts. *"You okay?"*

He leaned against the counter in his kitchen. Was he okay? No. Was he going to tell his dad that? Also, hell no. At least not right now. His dad knew him better than he knew himself. But he didn't want to talk about it. Not when he was still trying to piece together why Ellie made him lose his fucking mind. And why the more and more he thought about it, he liked it. Maybe he should explore what ever it was that was going on with him....

Spencer shook his head. He'll talk about it with his dad once he got there. This wasn't a conversation to have over the phone anyway.

"Yeah," he lied.

The phone was silent for a moment. *"You lying to me?"*

Busted. "No—"

"I can hear it in your voice, Spence. Reminds me of when you were having troubles with—"

"Dad. Don't."

"Since that bitch. I know I shouldn't talk bad about the mother of my grandbaby—"

"Dad..."

"Only good thing that came from her was our girl." That was something Spencer could one hundred percent agree with.

"Hold on...Son, you got girl problems?"

For fuck's sake.

Quickly, he backtracked. He could talk about it in person tomorrow. "What? No. Why in the hell would you think that?"

"That's pretty defensive there if you ask me."

"Dad."

"Somebody tickling your pickle?"

"Dad!"

"What?"

Spencer closed his eyes. He took it back. He was not talking to his dad about this and he was *not* his best friend.

"If someone's tickling your pickle, are you at least using protection? I mean I'm all for having another grandbaby. Especially, if they are anything like my Bella but I don't—"

"Holy shit, I'm hanging up now."

"You can't hang up. I have to tell you when to pick me up from the airport."

"Who said I'd pick you up?"

"I did. I'm still your father after all."

"And I have to listen to you?"

"You might be older now, but not old enough I wouldn't take you over my knee, young man."

Any other time his father threw down the gauntlet, Spencer would've gladly picked it up. But his dad's words had his mind going straight to the problem he was having.

Ellie.

Naked.

Bent over his knee.

Damn it. "This conversation is over."

His father chuckled. *"Fine. We can talk about your girly problem tomorrow. Flight lands at* 11:30. *Don't tell Bella. I want to surprise her."*

"Sure thing, old man."

"Old man me one more time and I'll knock your ass to the ground as soon as I'm off the plane."

"Keep telling yourself that, *old man.* Love you. See you tomorrow." Spencer hung up with a smirk on his face. Shoving his phone in his back pocket he looked at the clock.

Shit. He paled.

He only had about three hours to figure out what in the fuck he was going to say to Ellie when he picked Belle up *from her classroom...*

And yet, the thought of seeing her again had a wicked smirk appearing on his face.

CHAPTER TWELVE

Ellie had been in a full-on panic attack since the call with Spencer that morning, and it'd only gotten worse as the day went on.

Might she add, it didn't help that once Ellie finally got the chance to tell Sally everything, that bitch laughed so hard in her face she spit out her drink all over the place. Which promptly landed directly onto her shirt. The same shirt that was not only covered in coffee but was now covered in tea and Sally spit.

Wonderful.

Ellie would have liked to say that was the worst of it. Not by a long shot.

Before her afternoon students, Ellie ended up in the lounge to pour herself another cup of mud water only for Bob to walk in. Shake his head, mumble something under his breath and then leave, pulling out his phone in the process.

Mud water completely forgotten, Ellie hightailed it to her desk in a sprint, grabbed her phone and promptly blocked her dad's number, and then turned it off.

She might have also buried it in the back of her classroom, and for good measure piled anything she could find onto it.

See, Ellie was a problem solver.

When she turned back to the front of her room, Sally was there. As she held out Ellie's disgusting mud water, she had tears in her eyes from laughing.

Freaking Sally.

At one point, Ellie wasn't sure if Sally could breathe for all her ridiculous hooting and hollering. And to be honest, Ellie wasn't sure if she'd call nine-one-one if Sally ended up passing out.

That's what you get.

Was it normal to want to throttle your best friend?

No?

Well, then shit.

As Sally kicked her feet up on Ellie's desk, she wouldn't shut her face about McHotPants. And if Ellie didn't swear on her life, she'd spill every last detail after her and McHot-Pant's meeting, she was going to steal Roxy.

Joke's on Sally.

Roxy would never leave her... Unless she had treats. Okay, never mind. Sally could easily steal her dog.

At least Ellie got the last laugh.

When Sally danced out of her room singing songs about K-I-S-S-I-N-G, she kicked a workbook in Sally's path causing her to trip.

Ellie: one.

Sally: zero.

It might have been mean, but she deserved it. Although, Ellie's glory was short-lived when Sally caught herself before sending her a death glare with the promise to get her back and soon.

Damn it. Today had been nothing but a mess.

A full-on freaking, might as well give up, mess.

Screw it.

She was putting all the blame on that damn croissant. If she hadn't gone there in the first place, *none* of this would have happened. That stupid, flaky, delicious, devil croissant.

Ellie sat at her desk as she waited for her impending doom. Spencer's words rang through her head for the millionth time causing her skin to tingle.

Why couldn't her body understand Spencer was a bad idea? A very bad but also delicious idea.

She blanched.

No.

What the hell was wrong with her?

What happened to Ellie hating him? Huh? Twice now, he'd been an asshole to her, but try telling that to her va-jay-jay.

Stupid body. Can you not get on the same page as our brain?

"Ms. Ryan!"

"Ahhh!" Ellie jumped out of her seat as Belle scared the living crap out of her. "Warn a person, kid. I think you just took ten years off my life."

Belle smirked, sending her a wink. "Ten years isn't that long."

"Dang, what is it, Pick on Ellie day?"

"According to Travis, that's every day."

"Understatement of the year." Something inside Ellie relaxed as she joked with Belle. Maybe Annabelle had some weird psychic gift, one that specifically said, *will calm Ellie Ryan when having a meltdown.* Come to think of it, Sally would kill for that.

Ellie shook her head banishing the thought, Sally could screw off, she was still mad at her.

"How were your other classes today?" Ellie asked as she adjusted herself in her seat.

"Okay, I guess." When Belle's face fell for a second, Ellie watched her. *That was weird.* "You sure, Belle?"

Belle forced a smile as she answered, "Yeah."

Instead of pushing it, Ellie pulled the chair from behind her to her desk. "Come sit."

"With you?"

"No, with the Pope. Duh. Of course, with me." Ellie laughed. "Come see what it's like to look down upon the endless rows of empty seats. Whatever the dust touches will be yours one day," Ellie said in her best *Mufasa* voice.

"Since everything is dusty, that's a lot of stuff." Belle giggled.

"You've been hanging around Travis too much." *Figures.* "Get your butt over here, chickadee."

"Yes, ma'am." Belle danced to the seat before plopping her butt down. "Oh wow, you can see everything from here."

"It's a teacher's secret."

"It's not a secret anymore since you told me." Belle sat further into the seat kicking out her feet. "I like it in here, Ms. Ryan."

Warmth radiated through Ellie as she looked at the girl next to her. "Me too, sweet pea."

Ellie took in the sight of Belle as she looked around the classroom. She couldn't help the feeling of something being off... Maybe it was just her and the parallel universe she jumped in dealing with Belle's dad. But then again Ellie didn't know why, but it felt like something else.

Deciding it was best to leave it alone for now, Ellie

opened the left drawer of her desk. "I usually have a snack right now, wanna split it with me?"

Belle's eyes widened. "Twix! They're my favorite."

"Me too. Good thing there's two of 'em, right?" *Chocolate always makes everything better.* Ellie did a little dance in her seat as she opened the wrapper. *Yummy.*

Belle held out her hand grabbing the bar from Ellie before taking a huge bite.

"How was Mrs. Grady's class after art?"

Belle stopped chewing. "Uh, it was okay I guess." She turned toward Ellie, her last bit of the candy bar left on the desk. "I really wish I had you all day."

"If that was possible, I'd like that." Her face softened as she looked at the girl.

"You'd want to have us all day?"

"Of course, I would. Don't tell anyone, but you guys are my favorites." She smiled before sending her a mock glare. "If you do, I'll deny it."

"Having us all day means also having *Travis* all day." A smirk appeared on Belle's lips.

"True," Ellie sighed. "Ehh, he's not all bad, just misunderstood. We'd probably end up watching a movie once a week, so I didn't have to hear him, though."

Belle giggled picking up the rest of the candy bar before she shoved it in her mouth.

"What do you think about Mrs. Grady's class?" Ellie asked again. "None of my other students have had her. She's new this year." Ellie popped the rest of her candy into her mouth.

"I've only been there a few days. I can't really decide yet," Belle replied diplomatically with a shrug.

"And, yet you have."

As Belle stopped talking, Ellie realized it was best to

leave it alone for the time being. No use in pushing someone that didn't want to talk. Ellie hoped Belle understood she could always come to her. No matter what it was. She decided to change tactics. "While we wait for your dad, how about we go through some worksheets? We can do them together."

Belle's nose scrunched like she smelled something bad. "What's in it for me?"

"You *have* been hanging around Travis too much."

"Maybe." A half-smile appeared on her face as she looked at Ellie eagerly. "Can I try on my own first?"

Ellie loved Belle's go-getter attitude. *Hell yeah.* "I expect nothing less from you, Annabelle Hurley. How about we do this..." She gestured around the empty room. "I know you said you don't like reading out loud, but no one else is here. What if we took turns reading to each other?"

Belle bit her bottom lip.

"When I was younger, I hated reading out loud. Actually, it terrified me. I'd go completely white. My palms would sweat and shake and I'd feel like I was transported into a different world. Or, that I was about to vomit. It was usually the vomit."

Belle's eyes widened as she nodded. "That's me! That's exactly how I feel too."

"But," Ellie continued, smiling sweetly at her. "As I grew up, I learned when I *hear* the words rather than just reading them, I understood them better."

"Really?"

"Yes, really. It's only you and me here, so even if we find a word that we struggle with we can work through it together. How about we give it a try?"

"Oh— umm, okay." Belle looked down at the paper that

had a few paragraphs on it before snapping her head back to Ellie. "I changed my mind, you go first."

"Only if you go second." Ellie winked causing Belle's toothy smile to reappear.

As Ellie began reading the first paragraph, she went slow, precise, and made it easy for Belle to follow along. She made sure to keep an eye on Belle to see if there was anything she struggled with. Once Ellie reached the end of the paragraph, she pushed the paper over to her. "Your turn, sweetie."

As Belle looked up at her, her whole face brightened at the endearment. "Okay." Slowly but surely Belle read the words with ease.

Ellie continued to watch her as she read.

Belle was smart, resilient, and damn well determined. When she came across a word she didn't know, she'd stop and stare at it trying to piece it together in her head.

Sometimes she'd figure it out within seconds; other times she kept trying.

Just like now.

"Try sounding it out loud. It might be easier," Ellie encouraged.

Belle worried her bottom lip looking at the paper.

"It's okay. Take your time."

Belle took a deep breath. "Ow-owkay-owkaysi-on-ally." When she didn't get it, Belle looked up at her for guidance.

"Try it one more time."

The sweet girl focused her attention back on the word. "Owkayshy-on-ally."

Seeing that Belle was still struggling, Ellie moved her finger to the letters that formed the word 'on'. "Sometimes when we know or see a word we recognize buried in another word we focus on that. Try putting the 'on' with the beginning part instead of on its own."

Belle nodded taking her direction. "Oksayshon..." She stopped for a second to think.

Keeping quiet Ellie could see the wheels turning in Belle's head.

"Occasionally!" Belle's whole face beamed like she'd just witnessed fireworks for the first time.

"That's right!" Ellie gave her a high-five. "See, sometimes we need to break the word up differently."

"I got it! And, all on my own."

"That you did, sweet girl." Ellie reached into her desk, taking out another candy bar. "This calls for a celebration."

However, Belle ignored the candy as she continued to stare at her, her smile spreading across her whole face. "I got the word."

"That you did, honey." Pride swelled through Ellie's chest. "You're very smart, little one. Occasionally was one of the hardest words to read when I was your age."

"It was?"

"Yep. But I learned when I came across words I didn't understand, sounding them out helped me hear it." A lopsided grin spread on Belle's face as Ellie talked. "It's kinda like learning something two different ways at the same time."

"My dad does that with me."

"Then your dad is a very smart man. The more you practice the better you'll get. Before you know it, you'll be reading novels like this." Ellie reached into her bag and pulled out a book.

"Whoa. You can read all that?"

"Yes ma'am. I love to read."

"You don't get hung up on any of the words?"

Ellie's head cocked to the side. "Sometimes, I do. But I don't let it stop me. This book's all about wizards and were-wolves. There are times I'll come across a word, especially if the author used a complex word and I have to take a moment to figure it out."

"But you're supposed to know everything."

Ellie pushed back in her seat surprised. "I am? Who told you that? If I'm supposed to know everything, we got some issues there, sister. I forget to put on my pants some days." She then pointed at her shirt. "If this looks like someone that has everything figured out then we got big problems."

Belle laughed. "You do look like a mess today."

"Thanks." Ellie's eyes rolled. "Appreciate the honesty there."

"My dad said you should always be honest, even if it could hurt someone's feelings." She gave her a worried look. "Did I hurt your feelings?"

"Nah," Ellie reassured her, shaking her head. "I know I'm a mess. So, no harm, no foul."

"Good. I don't want to hurt my favorite teacher's feelings."

Ellie's heart almost burst. *You're becoming my favorite also, kid.*

"I really like reading too," Belle announced with a small smile.

Ellie chuckled as Belle continued, "My dad used to take me to the library and let me pick out books. We'd read them together, or if I wanted to try on my own, I'd read them in my room until I came across a word I didn't know. I'd try but if I still didn't get it, I'd ask my dad or grandpa."

"That's a smart thing to do."

"I want to read books like you do with mythical creatures and stuff."

The corner of Ellie's mouth turned up. "You can do that." Although, Belle wouldn't be able to read the book Ellie had in her bag, right now. The love triangle was a little too mature for her. "Are you reading anything right now? I did mention about a book report coming up."

The color drained from Belle's face.

"Don't worry, sweetie. It's only a summary of what you liked and didn't like."

"Oh, okay. You hadn't really mentioned it in class again. I thought you'd forgotten."

"Did Travis tell you that?" That kid was going to cause Ellie to drink.

"No, but you never said anything else. I figured if no one asked, then we wouldn't have to do it."

"If only the world worked that way." Ellie watched as panic flashed across Belle's face. "I'll help you if you want me to. We can even read it together. Exactly like we did now."

"Really?"

"Of course. We can take turns. We can work on it during class or even after if you want me to tutor you?" The joy radiating off Belle was exactly the reason why Ellie did this. Sometimes kids just needed a little extra encouragement.

"I'd like that."

"Then it's settled." Ellie picked up the paper from Belle's hand ready to start the next paragraph.

"I'll always help her with her reading," a deep voice echoed through her empty room causing Ellie to jump, screaming. "Ahhhh!"

"Give a person a warning!" Ellie placed her hand over her heart. "I might have just peed a little."

At her words, Belle burst into giggles as Ellie tried to control her erratic heart. "Man, between you and Belle who needs a gym membership? My poor freaking heart." She looked to the door to see Spencer Hurley leaning against the frame with his arms crossed over his chest. *Again.* What? Is that the only mood this guy knew?

Give her a break.

Before Ellie could roll her eyes though, Spencer gave her the once-over before stopping at her face.

There goes any thought of her controlling her heart. Ellie's cheeks heated as he stared into her eyes, almost like he was staring into her soul.

Shit a freaking brick.

"Daddy!"

Daddy? What? Who is calling someone daddy? Did I just call him daddy? Her brain short-circuited.

From the corner of her eye, Ellie saw a brown-haired ball of something run through the room catapulting itself into the Greek god's arms.

Her first instinct was to jump back thinking a human-sized rat got into her classroom, but then her brain finally started working.

Annabelle. *Get a grip, Ellie.*

Spencer held his daughter close to his chest as he kissed her forehead. "Hey love, did you miss me?"

"Always." The girl clung to her father, not unlike how Ellie wanted to do.

No. Bad, Ellie. You do not think that way, even if he was the one that threatened to spank you— She stopped as the reason why Spencer Hurley was standing in her classroom came rushing back to her.

Crap.

Uh. Universe, any second now, I'd really appreciate a hoard of wildebeest stomping in to kill me off, please.

"Good afternoon, Ms. Ryan."

Oh God, why was his voice so deep? That shouldn't be healthy right? Maybe he had something wrong and should go see a doctor?

Ellie wanted to slam her hand on the table as she figured it out. Her mom was a doctor. Okay, she was a woman's health doctor and sex therapist but it was close enough. She'd make him an appointment, and Spencer would be so grateful, he'd forget any of this happened. See, problem solved.

Make Spencer an appointment at her mother's women's health practice.

Hell yeah!

"Ms. Ryan helped me figure out a word." Belle bounced on her feet as she grinned at her father then back to Ellie.

"I saw that." Spencer smiled down at his daughter.

He saw that? How long had he been standing there?

Spencer artfully cocked his brow toward her. "Ms. Ryan."

She blankly stared at him for a moment until he cleared his throat.

"Uhh, yeah. Pretty sure that's me unless you want to speak to another Ms. Ryan." Ellie pulled out her phone, which she'd unburied after the last bell. "Oh wait, that's a great idea, let me call my mom. She'll set you up with an appointment."

Why did he look so shocked? Hadn't she explained how she was going to get him to the doctor and he'd then forget— Oh no, she'd only thought that.

"Appointment?" Both of his eyebrows rose.

"You know what?" Ellie dropped her phone in her bag. "Ignore me. I'm on some sugar high, or maybe the chocolate was laced with arsenic and I'm poisoned."

Belle snapped her eyes to her dad. "Ms. Ryan gave me one of the chocolates, Dad. And I didn't have any dinner yet."

Ellie waved her hands between her and Belle. "You're not supposed to rat me out. Sharing one's chocolate is a sacred act. Are you trying to throw me to the wolves?"

"Dad isn't a wolf." Belle looked at her father. "Are you?"

Spencer's hot expression turned toward Ellie. "I'm not a wolf, but I've been known to bite."

Was she sitting? Holy moly, Ellie hoped she was sitting. If not, she was going down because her knees just wobbled.

"Ms. Ryan said she's reading a book about werewolves right now."

"That so?" Spencer kept his eyes on Ellie. "I'm sure she's read about biting then."

"I don't know." Belle turned to her. "Is there a lot of biting in your book?"

Ellie squeaked as she felt her throat close.

"Maybe you can help me find a book like yours to read for my book report, Ms. Ryan. That way I can be just like you." Belle sent her a toothy smile before her whole face lit.

Arrow right through my heart. "You name it." Thank everything, Ellie found her voice.

"Belle, can you do me a favor and wait outside? I want to talk to Ms. Ryan alone."

"But I want to say goodbye to her?" she whined.

Spencer nodded his head, giving Belle the go-ahead to run back to Ellie and give her a hug. "Thank you for your help. I'll see you tomorrow."

With Belle in her arms, even for that split second, it

seemed like everything melted away. "I'm looking forward to it."

Belle smiled before looking back at her dad. "I'll wait outside."

No! Ellie stared at her begging Belle to read her mind. *You can't leave me, you're my human shield!*

Just like that, the traitor ran out of the room, leaving her and Spencer alone.

Oh, shoot.

Spencer took a few steps toward Ellie's desk. "Thank you for helping Belle. I've been trying to get her to read words she doesn't understand out loud for years."

Ellie nodded trying to push past it. The look he was giving her was doing weird things to her downstairs land. "Think nothing of it."

"It's not nothing to me." He took two more steps closer to her. "I don't know what it is about you, Ellie, but you make me forget all my rules."

"Don't forget your rules. Rules are there for a reason," she rushed out.

"Rules are meant to be broken."

Ellie's eyes shifted around the room. She definitely felt like she was back under a microscope again, but this time it was different.

No. That's it. This has to stop. Remember how he made you feel, Ellie? She clenched her thighs together. *No, you stupid body, the first time you met him. People like Spencer Hurley are all the same. You need to stop this now. Get your-self together, you dumb-dumb.*

She took a deep breath before straightening her back. "Spencer, this morning got a little out of hand on both of our parts. Let's just agree to never speak of it again, and we'll move on."

Spencer's eyes darkened as he stared down at her. "I like when you say my name."

"Th-that's not appropriate." Ellie almost fell out of her seat.

"Slip of the tongue," Spencer purred. "Slips of the tongue, they can be bad or *good* depending on what the situation is and where the tongue may be."

Is it hot in here? I think it's hot in here. Stop this. Stay strong. You are in control of this ship not him and definitely not your stupid va-jay-jay.

Spencer towered over her desk putting his hands on either side closing her in. "Wouldn't you agree?"

Was she supposed to answer that?

"You fire me up, Ellie, and I can't figure out why. One moment I want to throttle your neck, then the next you're helping my daughter like she's your equal. And I want to kis—"

"No one should be made to feel less," she interrupted. Ellie scolded herself. That was exactly how he'd made her feel.

See, this was ridiculous. He was already playing with her, even after making her feel like she wasn't good enough, her body had lost its mind.

"And when I see that fire in your eyes, like the one you're shooting my way right now all I want to do is see exactly how good those lips taste." He straightened. "I'll be seeing you soon, Ms. Ryan." He looked up and down her again. "Very soon."

With that, he turned and walked out of the classroom. "Come on, kiddo, time to go."

Belle stuck her head in the room and waved. "Bye, Ms. Ryan. See you tomorrow."

Ellie sat there at her desk for what felt like an eternity

after they left trying to wrap her mind even remotely around what happened.

She tossed her head onto her desk. What the hell had she gotten herself into? People like Spencer Hurley were nothing but bad news, and she needed to remember that.

Now, if only she could get her lady bits to understand.

As she banged her head once more for good measure on her desk, his words popped back into her mind.

Ellie lifted her head as her eyes widened. "What the hell did he mean he said he'd be seeing me soon?"

CHAPTER THIRTEEN

"GRANDPA! You're doing it wrong! You have to dance like this..."

Spencer smiled hearing his daughter's scream throughout the house. It didn't hurt he knew the exact dance Belle was trying to teach his old man. He had to learn it last week.

A wicked smile spread across his face. He'd make Belle force his dad to perform it later. How he was going to keep from busting a gut at his father trying to prove he could do it, he didn't know, but he couldn't wait.

Damn. Spencer was grateful his dad was here now. He'd only been here a little over a week and Belle's mood, and his, had improved drastically.

They'd missed him, more than he realized.

He'd never forget when they pulled up outside of the school and Belle saw who was in the front seat with him.

Thank everything his dad was fast and could catch. Before Spencer could put the SUV in park his dad was out of the door, his arms ready as Belle catapulted herself through the air.

She'd screamed her excitement before bursting into happy tears, her grandpa was there.

That night, after getting Belle to bed, his dad had walked into the kitchen and threatened bloody murder if Spencer didn't spill his guts.

A scowl appeared on Spencer's face as he remembered what happened after he told his dad everything. That asshole burst into laughter causing him to keel over and hyperventilate.

Fucker.

He thought it was the most hilarious thing he'd ever heard.

Why Spencer told him about the meeting after school, he didn't know. He was almost positive his dad almost pissed himself laughing.

He sat back in his chair, as Ellie popped into his mind again. There was something about her, and like his dad said, maybe that pull was there for a reason.

You did pretty much threaten to bite her. Spencer crossed his hands over his stomach as he leaned back. His smile morphed into a wolfish grin as the look of Ellie's face when he'd said it came into his head.

He would never forget that. The shock was priceless. So was the lust in her eyes.

Now, if only he could get past her being Belle's teacher. That's bound to cause a lot of problems. Problems he should be taking one look at and running the other—

"Grandpa, what the heck took you so long?"

"Geez Bella, I was taking a leak, when you get to my age you pee all the time. Give me a break."

"Eww."

"Blame the human body not me. You got me moving muscles I didn't even know I had anymore. My body's so confused, it doesn't know if it needs to pee, or have a heart attack."

Spencer barked out a laugh.

"Grandpa, can we get a dog?"

Fuck! Spencer jumped from his chair, causing it to hit the wall with a bang. He then took off running toward the living room. *That little shit.*

He should've known better than to leave her alone with his dad. Randal was probably halfway to the door to take Belle to the shelter.

"No!" Spencer shouted through the hall before rounding the corner where his father was clearly about to say yes. "Don't even think about it, Dad."

"Why not? She's old enough." Randal squared off puffing out his chest trying to intimidate him.

Oh, for fuck's sake. How was *he* the normal one in the family?

Spencer matched his father's stance, staring down his dad's narrowed eyes and thinned lips. *Bring it on, old man.*

From the corner of Spencer's eye, he could see Belle dancing on her feet. "Please, Dad. Please, I promise I'll be extra good. I won't ask for any help ever again."

Spencer's body jolted at her words. Breaking the trance with his father he took the giant step toward Belle and dropped to his knees. "Baby..."

"Please, Dad. I promise I'll never ask you to help me with my schoolwork or reading, or anything again. I'll do it on my own."

Spencer pulled her into his arms squeezing her tight. "Sweetie, no. Don't ever think you need to bargain like that." He didn't know what to say. Had he failed her so much she thought asking for help was an issue for him?

"Bella..." His dad moved to his side.

"Baby girl," Spencer continued. "We love helping you. Both of us. It's *never* a problem when you need to ask for help. That's what we're here for."

Belle pulled back to look at him. "I know, but I thought if maybe I stopped, we'd have more time for a dog."

His heart broke. "Belle, I will *always* have time for you, dog or no dog. You need help, I'm here."

She smiled at his dad. "And Grandpa?"

"Yeah, Bella." His dad put his hand on Belle's shoulder, giving it a squeeze.

"And, Ms. Ryan?!"

Spencer heard the stifled laugh come from his father, causing him to shoot his dad a death glare. He turned back to Belle. "Yes, even Ms. Ryan. And, I promise, Annabelle, as soon as we're more settled, we'll get a dog."

"When will we be settled? Tomorrow?" She smirked, as a sparkle appeared in her eye.

Oh, for fuck's sake. "Annabelle..."

"What? It's a valid question."

Spencer shook his head as his dad laughed. "How about instead we take Grandpa to the park we found on the way to school?"

"The park?" Belle's face lit.

"Yeah, the one you've wanted to check out."

Belle's eyes narrowed on him, immediately. "I know what you're doing."

"What's that?"

"You think if we take Grandpa to the park, I'll forget about the dog." She looked at his dad. "Is he serious?"

Randal nodded. "Afraid so. I don't know where you got your smarts from, Bella, it sure ain't him."

Why am I always the butt of their jokes? He wanted to

shake his head, but if it broke the tension, then he was all for it, even if it did drive him up the wall.

Instead of taking their bait, Spencer quirked his brow at his daughter. "Park or no park?"

"Park!" Belle screamed before rushing to look for her shoes.

"Son, one of these days she's gonna outsmart you."

"She already does."

"Good."

Spencer walked toward the front door. "Go get your shoes on, Randal."

"*Boyyyy.*"

CHAPTER FOURTEEN

"Oh, my freaking word, shut your mouth hole. I cannot believe effing Bob is a snitch. I really thought he was better than that, Dad." Ellie crossed her arms over her chest as her father glared at her.

"Bob's the one who keeps tabs on you for me."

"I'm not a possession that needs to have tabs kept on her." She was going to murder her father, then Bob, or maybe Bob first and then her father.

Either way, someone was dying.

"I've been telling him that for years, sweetie," Ellie's mom remarked walking into the kitchen, Roxy following behind.

Ellie's attention snapped to her dog.

Of course, her mother had a bag of Roxy's favorite treats in her hand, as she stuffed more into her pocket. And by favorite, she meant any. Roxy never met a treat she didn't love. That damn dog would follow a burglar around if they offered her food.

Traitor.

Roxy then had the gall to look at Ellie and wink before

nudging under her mother's hand. The same hand that reached into her pocket and pulled out a dog treat to give her.

Ellie growled giving Roxy the look they'd be talking about this later, before turning back to her dad. "It's fine. Don't listen to everything big ole annoying *Robert* has to say."

"Sure thing, El." Dean turned away ignoring her. "Tell me more about the father that's been giving you issues. After Bob's call, I thought there was gonna be paperwork involved."

For Pete's sake. I'm sending Bob dead flowers in the mail, or hiding his favorite coffee cup. "It's nothing, I just ran into my new student's dad at a coffee shop. Then we had some words." Words that still played over and over in her mind.

"When you should've been at work..."

"I had ten extra minutes!" she defended as her mouth fell open. *The nerve.* "I'm not late for my students."

Dean sighed as he shook his head. "I'm surprised Bob hasn't fired you."

And there went her migraine. "Lunch is over. Come on, Roxy Foxy time to leave."

"No, ma'am, you will not," her mother protested. "Roxy *always* gets a walk once we're done. It's tradition." To make matters worse Roxy huffed. Then to add to Ellie's annoyance her mother reached into her pocket tossing Roxy another treat.

Oh, for the love of... "I walk her every day, *mom*." Ellie's eyes narrowed at her mother who once again tossed Roxy another treat. Ellie didn't know whether she wanted laser beams to shoot out of her eyes and maim her mother, or Roxy since that she-devil gladly did a circus twirl on her hind legs begging for another scrumptious treat.

"But, I don't. You don't come around as much as you should." Shannon placed her hand over her chest. "It breaks a poor mother's heart her daughter doesn't love her enough to come by more often."

Barf... Ellie was about to choke on the guilt trip. "I'm here every weekend!"

"Sometimes you forget Roxy." Shannon's eyes saddened before she tossed another treat to Roxy.

"No, I don't!"

Shannon scratched behind Roxy's ears.

"Ohh, now I get it, this is about my dog, not me. Figures." Ellie turned to her pooch. "Ready to go for your walk with your guilt-tripping, should be placed in a home by now, makes me question if they really are my parents, treat giving even when I ask them not to, grandparents?"

Roxy barked her tongue flopping out of the left side of her mouth.

"We have to give Roxy everything she wants including treats. You won't give us any grandchildren to spoil. Whose fault is that?" Shannon cocked her head at her daughter.

Roxy barked in agreement.

See, traitor.

"You know, dear, you aren't getting any younger. Sooner or later you're going to be all dried up and all we'll have is Roxy to spoil." Her mother tossed the menace another treat. "Now, I'm not saying it's impossible to conceive children when you're older, but it can be harder. There are more complications involved. Of course, you'll have me to make sure everything goes as smooth as possible, but with the way you're going, we'll never see a baby."

"Please stop talking."

"Why?"

"I didn't know today's lunch involved me being roasted."

"Sure, you did, El," her dad remarked with a laugh. "That's where all our conversations end up."

"Is it too late for me to turn you two in and get new parents?"

Dean pulled out his phone. "I can call Bob."

Ellie's eyes widened. "No!" The last thing she needed was her dad to call Bob and say Lord knows what. It was already bad enough he was a part of all this.

Roxy barked as she danced in a circle at Bob's name.

"I believe Roxy thinks that's a great idea." Dean walked over to his wife before putting his hand in her pocket pulling out a treat to toss to the traitor.

"There's a bag on the counter. You didn't have to grope her in front of me." Ellie threw her hands over her eyes.

"Your father didn't grope me, dear. He was about five inches too far to the right." Shannon cocked her head at Ellie. "Has it really been that long since you've been felt up, sweetie?"

Ellie gagged louder as she dry heaved.

"Don't be such a prude, Ellie." Shannon tossed Roxy another treat, before patting her on the head.

This made Ellie jump for the bag of dog treats on the counter, of course it caused Roxy to switch loyalties and stand beside her. When Ellie reached into the bag grabbing a few treats she held them out for her dog. "Make sure you pee in one of their shoes." Ellie turned her glare toward her parents.

"She would never!" Dean yelled, appalled.

"Her loyalty goes only as far as whoever has the food." Ellie picked up the bag and placed it under her arm. "Now, come on, Rox, the sooner we get this over with, the sooner I can get home and wallow in self-pity that my parents are the way they are."

"You're very overdramatic, dear."

"I wonder where I got it from." She glared at her mother. Plus, she wasn't being overdramatic, her parents were ridiculous, her dog was a food loyal pain in her ass, and then well... then there was Spencer Hurley.

Even thinking his name did something to Ellie.

One second, she was fine and dandy sneaking into her class each morning like nothing had happened and then boom...

This dude walked into her life and just fucked everything up.

His words... oh man, his words.

Shaking the thoughts from her head, Ellie put Roxy's leash on before walking out the front door. The park was only around two blocks away from her parents' house, so it shouldn't be that grueling.

Besides, fresh air would do them all good.

Or maybe she could use this as her getaway and make a run for it...

Nahh, your luck, they'll end up chasing after you. Then people will wonder why you're running and think that these two people were trying to kidnap you, or that you stole their dog or something, and that would cause tons of problems. And, I really don't need that added to my list of shit I'm dealing with.

As they walked through the streets her father and mother started blabbering on about who knows what.

It was better for Ellie to ignore it.

Then out of nowhere, just like he had since the *biting* remark, Spencer popped into her head again.

Crap on a stick, why did he have to say that to her? Then there was the way his arms closed her in.

Those arms, her body shuddered.

Oh, and those hands, how could she forget his hands? They gripped the sides of her desk as he stared her down, and those fingers... She wondered what he could do with fingers like—

"Ellie, why's your face all red?"

"I'm not red," she blurted.

"Yes, you are," her mother announced. "Your face is all flushed and if I'm not mistaken—"

"I'm walking," she quickly interrupted. "Duhh. It takes a lot to haul this butt around." Her laugh sounded forced even to Ellie.

Stopping, Shannon gave her the once-over. "There is exertion from walking, but you're red all the way down to your neck."

"Hot flash. I'm having a hot flash!"

"You're too young for that, dear."

Please don't, please don't.

"If I didn't know any better, or if you were one of my clients, I'd say you have an excited flush."

No! Oh, my God. Why was she like this? WHY! "Mother no, we are not having this conversation."

"Suit yourself, dear." Shannon's eyes studied her. "But if you *were* one of my clients, I'd say you should explore what has your mind and body reacting—"

"Didn't we have enough of this talk in the house!"

Ignoring her, Shannon continued. "A healthy sex life is imperative in human culture. Even if you don't have a partner there are many toys —"

"That's enough talk!" Ellie screamed, walking faster trying to get away from her mother. Why couldn't she be a normal mom? You know the ones that *don't* talk about this kind of stuff with their children. Okay, she was the best women's health doctor in the state and had won countless awards for her intimacy therapy but that is not something someone wants to talk about with their parents.

Kill me now. No, seriously, Universe, if you're listening, can you please send a freak storm and shoot a bolt of lightning my way? I'd appreciate it. If that's too extreme I'd also be willing to trade. I've got some kick ass homemade ice cream in my freezer. She waited a second. *Okay, if ice cream isn't your thing, I'll give you my cell phone... Wait no, I'll give you Sally. You can have her. Scratch that, you have to give her back. I still need her help on figuring out how the hell I'm supposed to survive all this. You know what, never mind.*

"Don't embarrass her, love. She's trying to get away from us. Remember last time she ended up tripping on the sidewalk and then you had to patch her up."

"You're right, Dean. Last time Roxy tripped her, she bled all over the place."

Ellie's brows furrowed together. That's right, she snapped her eyes to Roxy with a glare. How had she forgotten about that? Roxy had purposely tripped her and she'd ended up cutting up her knees and hands. Of course, her mother was over the moon she got to take care of her little baby again. Which was another thing she'd yet to live down, case in point, right now.

New game plan, let's pretend this was all some screwed up dream. Maybe if Ellie focused on how beautiful of a day it was, she'd wake up and this would all be over.

She smiled to herself. *Job well done there, Ellie.*

Deciding to increase her speed regardless, she rounded the corner of the block to walk into the park. She'd had to admit this little park always brought a smile to her face. She used to come here when she was a little girl.

Hell, she remembered Bob tutoring her in math on the park benches over in the corner.

Ellie loved this park. In a weird way, it was like coming home to her. It was her happy place. When she was here nothing ever went wrong.

Her smile spread from ear-to-ear as each step she took into the park melted away the migraine her parents caused.

As her world finally felt lighter, Ellie ignored the commotion coming from the opposite side of the park.

Although, for some odd reason, that commotion sure sounded like it was coming closer...

"Dad! Look! It's Ms. Ryan and she has a dog!"

CHAPTER FIFTEEN

Before Ellie could grasp what happened, a little girl, who she now realized was Belle, ran full speed toward her.

"Ms. Ryan, Ms. Ryan. You have a dog!"

Ellie didn't have time to react as Belle ran right at her like she was being chased...

Oh shit, she was.

Ellie's eyes went from Belle to the older gentleman running behind her. That wasn't what had her heart jumping out of her chest, though. No, it was the man running behind him.

Was this what a heart attack felt like? Is that pain in my left arm? Universe, is this you getting back at me for offering to give you Sally?

"Annabelle, stop!" Spencer hollered at Belle who was now only inches from Ellie and Roxy. The same Roxy who was eagerly wagging her tail and pulling toward the child begging for attention and kisses.

It was like everything was now in slow motion.

Spencer Hurley. The same Spencer Hurley that had been screwing up her head, was now running toward her.

Effe me.

"Can I pet your dog? Please, Ms. Ryan?" Belle skid to a stop right in front of her before she bounced on the balls of her feet waiting for an answer.

With a nod of her head in a complete daze, Ellie managed to pipe out a small yes.

This was all some weird screwed up dream as the man who invaded her fantasies ran with such grace she hadn't even known existed toward her. His muscles showcased by the sun illuminating his physique, the long arms, those hands, his fingers.... Not the fingers again!

Oh, shit. Oh shit, on a bunch of bricks.

"Dean, look there's that flush again."

"I believe you're right, Shannon."

"Now, we know exactly what she was thinking about on the way over. And, here I was worried our little girl wasn't getting all her needs met." The amusement in her mother's voice made Ellie's teeth grind together. "*Mother...*"

"Somebody's defensive." The corner of Dean's mouth turned up.

"I will murder you all right now, cover you in peanut butter and let Roxy eat you. No one would ever find your bodies."

"You should use some of that aggression toward that man running our way, dear. The coitus would be fantastic."

Before Ellie could die, the older gentleman was there.

"Look, Grandpa, a doggie!"

"I see, Bella."

"Annabelle, never take off like that again, you hear me?" Spencer yelled as he came to a halt in front of them.

"But it was Ms. Ryan!"

"I don't care. What if something happened to you? Don't do it again."

"I'm sorry, Dad." Belle's face fell. "I saw Ms. Ryan and then her dog–"

"She's fine, everything is fine, we're all fine!" Ellie blurted. "It's not like I'm some stranger that would grab her and toss her in the back of a van and sell her to some creepy old man down the street—" Ellie snapped her hand over her mouth as she groaned. *What the hell is wrong with you, Ellie Ryan?*

Spencer cocked his brow at her.

"I have no idea why I just said that."

"It's because you find him attractive, dear," her mother interjected. "You always do this when someone gets you hot and bothered. Remember when you met Doctor Richman when you took Roxy to the vet the first time? I'm glad I was there to witness it. Never heard you spew nonsense like that before."

"You do bring up that story of her saying it's nice to do you too, when he said nice to meet you, a lot." Dean let out a belly laugh.

"I will strangle you both."

"Ms. Ryan." Spencer looked her up and down causing Ellie's body to tingle. When his eyes met hers again a smirked appeared on his face.

"Oh, sweetie, I approve." Shannon looked him up and down before turning back to her daughter, winking.

Ellie was going to murder her mother. Add her to the list right before Bob, and her father.

"Ms. Ryan, what's its name? Can I play with him? How old is he? Will he chase me if I run? I've always wanted a dog that will chase and play with me."

Belle's words snapped Ellie's death glare from her mother back to the little girl on her knees playing with Roxy who was gladly lapping it up.

129

Ellie tried to jump-start her brain. "He is a she, and her name is Roxy. I call her Roxy Foxy. She's a pain in my as— butt. Yes, you can play with her. She's seven years old. She loves to play chase. She doesn't get to as much anymore, 'cause my fat butt ain't running around so she can make a game trying to trip me."

A deep possessive growl came from her side causing Ellie to jump. *Did that sound come from Spencer?*

Ellie swallowed hard. "Here go play." She bent unhooking Roxy's leash. Within seconds both Belle and Roxy were out in the field running around.

"Ms. Ryan?" the older gentleman began. "As in the same Ms. Ryan teaching my grandbaby?"

Ellie held out her hand. "Please call me Ellie. And, yes I'm one of Annabelle's teachers."

I guess this is happening.

The older man shook her outreached hand. "Well, shit. Call me Randal." Still keeping a hold of her hand, the man turned to Spencer who hadn't taken his eyes off Ellie. "Is this the same teacher that's got your panties in a twist? The one you haven't shut up about?"

"Dad!" Spencer's attention snapped from Ellie as he glared at the older man.

"Don't dad me, son. You spent the better part of two days telling me how you couldn't think of anything else but bend—"

"I will take you back to the airport right now. Don't think I won't."

Ellie snatched her hand from Randal's placing both her fists on her hips. "Don't talk to your father like that," she scolded him like he was one of her students.

Spencer's brows shot to the sky. "Didn't you threaten to strangle them?" He pointed toward her parents.

"Whoo-we..." Shannon fanned herself. "You could cut the sexual tension with a knife. Dean, remember when you used to look at me like that?"

"Mom!"

"What? When a man looks at you like that, you *know* he's picturing what you've got under your clothes."

"Mother, so help me, I will do it. I will bury you in the backyard."

"You won't, dear, it's too much work."

Ellie's jaw hit the ground. "I would too!"

"No, you wouldn't," her dad laughed. "You'd give up two minutes in."

Ellie narrowed her eyes at her backstabbing parents. "A lot can happen in two minutes."

"Oh, honey, I hope that's not true, any man that can only last two minutes is *not* good enough for my daughter."

"Shannon, stop embarrassing her," Dean spoke. "But I agree, two minutes is a joke."

"Like you aren't itching to call Bob?" She glared at him.

Dean's face morphed into a sheepish grin.

"Holy crap on a freaking million crackers. Just kill me now and put me out of my misery. Do not bring Bob into this. I swear to all things, Dad, I will—"

"Ignore her squawking." Her father held out his hand. "I'm Dean Ryan, and this is my lovely wife Shannon."

Randal looked at Spencer. "I like these ones. You did good, kid. Now I know why you can't keep your head on straight."

"Dad..." he warned.

Randal still holding Dean's hand, pointed to his son. "Kids. They think we don't know."

"I have to agree, they always think they know more than us, but they forget we were once their age." Dean held out his hand to Spencer. "Nice to finally meet the man that's gotten my little girl's heart a-racin'.'"

Spencer took his hand firmly, clearly trying to hold back his laugh.

Bastard.

"It's nice to meet you both. Or should I say, *do you* both?" Spencer's face lit in a gorgeous smile as he turned back to Ellie, mocking her own words.

To her utter horror, it made her heart race as her cheeks heated.

"Do you see that, sweetie? He can't keep his eyes off her. And look at the blush again on her face." Shannon clapped her hands together in glee before holding out her hand to Spencer. "We might actually get grandbabies. I'm Ellie's mother, a certified sex therapist along with my Women's Health practice. I've got to say some of my clients dream about their partner's looking at them the way you're looking at my daughter right now."

Spencer returned her handshake before looking back at Ellie. "She's beautiful, I can't help it."

That's it. Ellie threw her hands up and walked away from the group. "I'm out."

"Where are you going?"

"Away from you lunatics."

Ellie stormed toward Belle mumbling about ways to sacrifice her parents to some god.

Screw this. Belle would be better conversation anyway than hanging out with the *adults*. And she used that word very loosely.

As Ellie walked toward the girl racing around with Roxy, something in Belle's laugh instantly calmed her. She couldn't quite figure out what it was, but hearing Belle's joy melted her heart. "If you find a stick, Roxy loves to play fetch."

"She does?"

"Yep."

Belle's eyes widened. "That's so cool." She started looking on the ground for a stick. "I didn't know you had a dog, Ms. Ryan. You really are my favorite teacher now."

Ellie laughed before bending to pet Roxy on the head. "Glad to hear it. I need to be someone's favorite. Lord knows I'm not my parents'."

Before Belle was able to find a stick, Ellie took off one of her shoes and waved it around the air making Roxy lose her mind. Belle burst into a fit of giggles.

Ellie fell to the ground when Roxy jumped on her. As they started wrestling, Belle jumped in playing along.

See, this was better company.

As Roxy and Belle climbed all over her trying to grab her shoe, for the first time in a long time Ellie felt like everything was finally right in the world.

At least for a moment.

Spencer couldn't keep his eyes off them. No matter how hard he tried to focus on what the others were saying, his eyes were glued to the woman on the grass playing with his daughter.

It's like he was living in a dream.

As their laughter echoed through the park, his heart skipped another beat. His dad was right.

"What are you waiting for, Spence?"

His dad's voice brought his attention back to the group. "Huh?"

Randal shook his head. "Boy, I swear sometimes it would be easier to slap you upside the head." Randal stared at him. "Better yet..." He smacked Spencer on the back of his skull.

"What the hell?"

"Stop pussyfooting around staring at them *wishing* you were part of it, and go."

He wanted to. More than anything Spencer wanted to. He wanted Ellie, and the more he thought about it the more he couldn't fight it.

But she was Belle's teacher.

That alone should make him stop. Then why hadn't it? Why was Ellie all he thought about?

"Wow, you can actually see the gears turning in his head." Dean laughed as Shannon nodded at him.

"I love him, but sometimes he lets his brain do all the thinking instead of going for it."

"Most men do," Shannon added.

With an irritated growl, Spencer turned back to the field watching as Ellie and Belle played and laughed.

His heart did that thing again.

You know what? Screw it. He could deal with the fact she was Belle's teacher later.

He wanted Ellie Ryan and nothing was going to stop him. Spencer took off running toward the field.

"Took you long enough!"

CHAPTER SIXTEEN

THIS WAS EASY.

Really easy, and that scared Ellie. As the three of them, well four including Roxy, played, everything felt right.

There wasn't any fighting, any arguing, any inappropriate comments, and most of all there weren't any remarks making her feel like she wasn't good enough.

It was just playing.

Two adults playing with a girl that had captured Ellie's heart and her dog.

Nothing more, nothing less.

Although, a few seconds ago Ellie had to stop herself from reaching out to tickle Spencer. Why her mind thought that was a good idea, she had no clue.

But as he laughed along with his daughter, Ellie's heart softened. Seeing them together was beautiful. The love they had for each other was undeniable.

Ellie's heart tightened again.

She'd be lying if she said she didn't like being part of it. And that bothered her.

Ellie jerked back. What the hell was she thinking? This

wasn't right. Belle was her student and her dad was someone Ellie needed to stay away from.

This had gone on long enough.

Ellie jumped to her feet. "It's time for Roxy Foxy and me to head home. I've got stuff I've gotta do tonight." Ellie pulled the leash from her back pocket before clipping Roxy to it.

"Can't you stay a little longer? We're having so much fun!" Belle cried as she got to her feet.

"I'm sorry, sweet pea. But Roxy Foxy and I have to go. I'm sure you'll play together again soon," she lied.

Belle's eyes widened as her toothy smile appeared. "Really?"

"I can guarantee it," Randal announced as he and Ellie's parents walked up to them.

Oh no, why do my parents have that look in their eyes?

"Dad?" Spencer asked, brushing off his jeans with his hands.

"Are you for real, Grandpa?"

"Sure am, Bella. You see Mr. and Mrs. Ryan here? They're Ellie's parents. We've agreed on a playdate between you, me, them, and Roxy tomorrow."

Ellie's mouth flew open. "You what?"

"Close your mouth, dear. You're asking for bugs to fly in or someone to put something in it." Shannon winked at Spencer.

Spencer barked out a laugh while Ellie looked for the closest rock to throw at his head, or her mother's.

"I like you," Spencer said, winking back at Shannon. "I've always liked people that shoot from the hip."

"Sorry, stud, but you're a tad too young for me, besides I think Dean would fight you."

Dean puffed out his chest. "I'd win."

Spencer let out another hearty laugh.

"Mother!" Ellie growled. "You do not say things like that. Especially to me. Your offspring. Do not talk about what can go in a mouth or any other part of the body for that matter."

Shannon crossed her arms over her middle as her brow quirked. "How do you think you got here?"

"Mom! Oh my God, I've walked into a nightmare. Dad, control her."

"I can't control your mom, El. You know she says what she says." He shook his head. "Lord knows I've tried but why bother when most of the time she's got excellent tips and tricks to try."

"Oh, for fu- Pete's sake. I'm done. I'm leaving you children." Ellie took Roxy's leash and started power walking away.

To her dismay, though, Roxy wasn't having any of it. "Come on, girl, don't do this to me now."

Roxy barked looking back at Belle.

"I know you love her, I get it, I do, but right now we need to go."

Roxy huffed before glaring at her. "Fine. I promise you a steak when we get home."

And of course, that had Roxy jumping to attention trotting up to Ellie's side. *Figures food would get you going.* Ellie glared down at her dog. *You're such an asshole.*

As if Roxy could hear her thoughts, the jerk growled at her. *No steak for you!*

Ellie did a quick wave behind her saying goodbye to Belle, as thankfully Roxy gave in and agreed to leave.

"Wait!"

Nope. Not going to happen. Ellie walked faster.

"Hey, wait!" Spencer caught up to her grabbing her arm.

"Nope. I think it's best if we go home."

"I don't agree," he said, stepping closer into her personal space. Ellie swallowed as she fought to take a step back. *Always stand your ground.*

Before she could stop herself, Ellie's eyes glanced at his arms. When she heard a deep chuckle come from Spencer her eyes snapped back to him.

"That proves it."

"Proves what?" she asked, getting defensive at being caught.

"Proves we both know something is going on between us."

"Demons."

His face scrunched. "What?"

"It's demons," Ellie repeated. "That's what's going on here."

"Ellie..." he laughed.

"What?" It could be, he had no idea.

Then Spencer Hurley shocked the crap out of her. "Go out with me, Ellie Ryan?"

"Insane man, say what!?" She let out a small scream.

Spencer laughed again while sporting that stupid smirk. "Our parents have already arranged a playdate. Just say yes."

She crossed her arms over her chest. "Since when do parents plan their children's dates? That doesn't sound very healthy to me."

"Normally, I would agree, but your mother is something else."

Ellie looked past Spencer to shoot her mother an evil

eye. When Ellie received a small wave back, she sent her the finger. "Something else is right."

"Say yes, Ellie." When Spencer rolled his eyes at her, it took everything inside of Ellie not to kick him.

"I'm sorry, but no. I can't even begin to list all the reasons why that would be a horrible idea."

"Give me a chance, just one." He looked down at her, his eyes heating. "Maybe we can finally get to the bottom of whatever I do to piss you off."

That made Ellie's eyes almost pop out of her head. "You don't piss me off," she lied.

He cocked his brow at her.

"Okay, at least all the time. You didn't seem to put your foot in your mouth while we were out playing with Belle and Roxy."

Why was she even contemplating this? She needed to stay as far away from Spencer as possible. It didn't matter how good he was with his daughter, or that he seemed to light a fire in her. He did the one thing that had always gutted her.

Spencer Hurley made her feel like she wasn't good enough....

"I don't know what passed through your head just now, but I didn't like it." He brought his finger under her chin making her look him in the eyes. "Let me fix it, Ellie. Or at least try to."

"I'm not someone who needs to be fixed, Mr. Hurley." She had to guard her heart. She couldn't do this. She would never go back on the promises she made to herself when she was younger. Ellie would never feel like that again.

"No." He angrily shook his head. "Don't. Don't go back to the Mr. Hurley shit. It's always Spencer to you."

"Fine. *Spencer—*"

"Let's at least talk it out. Just one date. That's it. If you still hate me after, I'll make sure to never bother you again." He took another step closer to her, only leaving an inch of space between them.

"And what if I say no?" Her breath hitched as Spencer's face leaned closer.

"You don't want to say no."

"How are you so sure about that?"

Spencer brought his lips down to hers.

For the first time in all of Ellie's life, everything stopped around her.

Spencer pulled back, pure lust in his eyes, as he looked down at her. "That's how."

Before Ellie could say anything or wrap her mind around it, celebrations erupted from behind them.

"That's my boy!"

"Yes!"

"See, dear. I told you! That's how your father kissed me on our first date!"

Ellie leaned around Spencer waving her middle finger in the air at the cheering *adults*. "All of you are on my murder list now. Even you..." She pointed at Randal. "You're first."

Randal turned to Dean. "She's an angry one, isn't she?"

"Leave her be." Shannon gave Ellie a thumbs up. "Think about all that passion once they finally put it to good use."

Ellie pushed Spencer out of the way as she made a lunge to throttle her mother. To her disappointment, though, his hands wrapped around her waist stopping her. "Let me go, I need to kill her."

Spencer let out a deep belly laugh. "I think keeping her around will help me."

"You can't use my mother against me." Ellie stopped fighting and stared at him in shock.

"I won't if you say yes." That stupid smirk appeared on his face again.

Blame it on the adrenaline or the fact his hands were on her waist, but against all Ellie's better judgment, she couldn't stop herself. "Fine. One date that's it. And I'm only agreeing to this, so I won't have to hear my parents for the next twenty years."

Spencer chuckled cupping Ellie's face in his hands. The heat in his eyes made Ellie swallow. "I'll see you tomorrow. Okay?" He kissed her again. "Oh, and we're all having dinner together tomorrow at your parents'. Apparently, they decided that too."

Spencer took off in a run back to the group leaving Ellie with her mouth hanging open.

"Close your mouth, dear. Remember what I told you!"

Then to add salt to her wound of what the absolute hell just happened, Belle jumped up and down drawing Ellie's attention to her. "Bye, Ms. Ryan, I'll see you tomorrow!"

Oh my God, how could she have forgotten about Belle being there? Her father had just kissed her!

And what the hell had she just agreed to?

Fuck. Me.

Sally was going to have a field day with this.

CHAPTER SEVENTEEN

ELLIE LOOKED DOWN at her outfit and groaned.

Am I really doing this? I shouldn't be doing this. I should call Spencer, tell him everything is off, pack up and move states. Yep, that's precisely what I am going to do. Ellie smiled at herself with her brilliant plan figured out. *Wait, but what about my kids? I couldn't do that to my students. What if no one stood up for them....*

"Ellie, why'd you stop talking?"

Ellie snapped out of her panic attack to look at Sally. The same Sally who was munching on a bag of chips, judging her.

"You look like you swallowed a baseball, then you had to throw it up but it got stuck." She popped a chip in her mouth. "You need me to give you the Heimlich maneuver? I just re-certified last week. I'm sure I can save you."

"*Sally...*"

"What?"

Ellie wanted to bang her head against the wall.

After getting home from her parents', and experiencing at least twenty-five meltdowns, she told everything to her best friend. And after some laughs at Ellie's expense, Sally drove over to her house, agreed to stay the night and help get her ready for today.

No matter how much Sally had tried to convince her, Ellie still didn't understand why she was about to go on a date with *Spencer Hurley*. Her student's father.

"Should I do this, Sal? I shouldn't be doing this. I mean I don't think I should be doing this. There are like a gazillion reasons plus ten why this is a horrible idea."

Sally pulled her hand out of the bag before dusting off the crumbs on her pants. Which Roxy eagerly helped with. "Okay, I guess we need to do this *again*. For what I think is like the thousandth time since last night. I won't even talk about the phone call or the freak-outs before you called me. By the way, I'm still pissed I wasn't the first call as you walked out of the park." She narrowed her eyes at Ellie. "I'll remember that."

Ellie threw her hands in the air. "Focus woman. I'm about to walk the plank."

"Are you already doing role play?" Her eyebrows shot up. "I would've thought you'd pick principal-teacher rather than pirate."

Ellie dry heaved. "Why would you say that? Bob's our principal."

Sally shrugged. "I wasn't talking about him. I'm talking about McHotPants and his punishment. You've been a very naughty teacher."

Ellie looked around the room in awe. "How does your brain come up with this stuff?"

"Books. Speaking of, did you read the new one by Quinn Sparks? Apparently, she got all the juicy bits from her fireman husband." She fanned herself. "Let me tell you—"

"Sally, focus! Please."

"You're no fun. Fine, let's try a different approach this time. How long has it been since you've dusted off those cobwebs between your thighs?"

"Sally!"

"What?" Her brows snapped together. "It's a legitimate question."

Ellie's jaw firmed as her teeth gritted. She could feel her migraine coming back.

"Down tiger. Listen, you can't deny you both have insane chemistry. Shit, I get second-degree burns just from your stories. Okay, you've had some, how should I put it, not the best encounters, but you aren't about to walk down the aisle to this guy. Why can't you roll around in bed a few times and call it quits? Nothing wrong with getting your girly bits serviced. Think of it like a car. We all need routine service." Sally winked at her. "Plus, angry sex is the best sex. Think about all that rage you can use to your advantage."

That's basically what my mom said. Oh my God, is Sally in on this with her? Wait a second....

"Did you just compare my vagina to a car?"

"Yeah, and I also said the person driving said car is an angry ball of rage when she comes in contact with Spencer's motorcycle. You'd think he cut you off in traffic or something, sheesh."

"How are you my best friend?"

"'Cause I'm awesome." Sally wiggled her brows before stuffing a chip into her mouth.

"I don't even know where to start with your ridiculous words and your analogies. I'll give you this one, though. We somehow do have a weird chemistry, and that kiss—"

"You bitch! You never mentioned *anything* about a kiss.

You're only now telling me there were lips locked! I should murder you where you stand."

Ellie at least had the decency to look sheepish. "I guess I kinda left that detail out. All twenty times I told you the story."

"You think? If we weren't getting you ready for your date, I'd punch your lights out."

Ignoring her, Ellie continued. "I'm not one to just, as you put it, roll around for a few good bump and grinds then quit. You know this about me. Also, how about we not forget the elephant in the room—"

"Do not call Roxy an elephant." Sally covered the dog's ears.

"For freak's sake, you two are incorrigible." Ellie rolled her eyes. "I'm talking about Belle. I can't sleep with her *dad* then end it. I still have to see her, and unless they move again, which I doubt, I'll be her teacher for at least two more years. That will be two years of parent-teacher meetings. I mean I can handle them if he's lousy in bed, but what if he's mind-blowing? He's probably mind-blowing. That kiss alone almost killed me. Sally, I'd never be able to sit there in front of him knowing what those fingers could do…"

"Ahh, so you've noticed those beauties too. There is something about his arms, hands, and fingers that just…."

"Sally. Pay attention." And don't talk about his hands. Who knew Ellie had a thing for hands?

"I'm trying. This is your fault. You brought it up."

"Sally…"

"Don't Sally me. You're both adults. You can handle adult things. Besides…" Sally stood. "I know you. If you don't take this chance, you'll regret it for the rest of your life. And then I'll have to hear about it from now until the retirement home we end up in. I don't know about you, but I don't want to hear about the one that got away for the next fifty years 'cause you never jumped the bones of Mr. McHotPants."

Dang, she did have a point.

"What's the worst that could happen?"

"I somehow betray Belle and I won't be able to help her." The reality of that happening had bile rise in her throat. She would never let that happen. Or what if she ended up falling for Spencer and he turned out to be as big of a jerk as she thought. What if he found out about her own learning disabilities and used that against her somehow?

"You aren't looking at this the right way. What if this could be the thing that helps Belle even more?" Sally asked before sneaking a chip to Roxy.

"Huh?"

"I think all you really need to do is fuck his brains out once maybe twice then forget the whole thing happened."

"Sally..." she warned.

Ignoring Ellie, she continued. "Hear me out. What if you being around Belle actually helps her? It's like you can be a built-in tutor. I can picture it now." Sally looked away in a dreamy state. "You wake up next to McHotPants after five earth-shattering orgasms 'cause you and I both know that man will satisfy you, *many times*. It's the next morning, you feel like you can't walk, but your stomach growls. You figure it's time to get out of bed, and once you do, you try to pull that whole walk of shame bullshit. Anyway, you walk out of McHotPants' bedroom and bam, Belle is there. She's got two books in her hands and sad eyes. She needs help and who's better to help her than you?"

Ellie looked at Sally horrified. "Do you hear yourself?

There are so many things wrong with that statement I don't even know where to begin."

"How about the five orgasms?"

"Sally, I swear to all things sweet and delicious, you're out of your fucking mind."

"You love it. Okay fine, maybe having some bow-chicka-wow-wow and then walking out of the bedroom with his kid being there isn't the best scenario, but you're missing the point. You're thinking too much into this, Ellie. Sure, you've had some problems with the dude, but why are you complicating it? Get your jollies rocked then deal with the outcome later."

Ellie stared at her. *Deal with the outcome later? What if that outcome could end her career? Or, hurt Annabelle?*

"Then you can tell me how big his dick is."

"Sally!"

Her shoulders went up. "If you don't tell me, are we even best friends?"

"Oh my God, you need to get laid or admitted into a mental hospital."

"Duhh, I've been saying that forever now. About the being laid part not the other. When you see someone show an ounce of interest my way let me know. Mommas got some cobwebs to dust off too. In the meantime, though, let me live through you and McHotPants. Do it for me, not you. Okay?"

"I question our friendship."

"I'll question it if you don't go out with this guy, screw his brains out and then tell me every detail."

Before Ellie could say anything, the doorbell rang causing Roxy to bark and dart toward the noise.

"Showtime." Sally turned and headed to the front door.

"Belle, you've gotta wait. You can't barge into someone's house."

"But Dad, it's not just someone, it's Ms. Ryan and Roxy in there." Belle danced in excitement. "I can hear Roxy barking."

Just as Spencer was about to tell her to calm down the front door swung open, almost knocking him back.

Then before he knew it a black and white ball rushed past him and headed right for his daughter. His first instinct was to protect his girl, but he soon realized the dog was licking Belle's face trying to get into her lap.

"Roxy! I missed you!"

"Mr. McHotPants, it's nice to see you again." That had Spencer's eyes darting away from his daughter to the front door.

What did she call me?

"Ms. Sally!" Belle shouted.

"Inside voice, kid. Damn, I think you blew out my eardrum." He placed his finger in his ear, wiggling it.

"But we're outside. Dad, that's my art teacher."

Spencer smiled at his daughter's enthusiasm. He had to admit, he was a little confused, though. "Yes, kiddo. I met her when I picked you up after your test a few weeks ago, remember?" Spencer held out his hand to Sally. "Nice to meet you again, and what did you call me?"

"McHotPants."

"Okay..." His brow arched.

"I missed you too, Roxy. Thank you for my kisses. Guess what? We get to play all day today."

"Hopefully, your dad and Ellie will too." Sally winked at Spencer as a wicked smile appeared on her face.

This just got interesting.

Ellie came flying around the corner shaking her fist in the air. "Sally!"

Holy shit, she was beautiful.

No matter how hard Spencer tried, he couldn't get over how breathtaking Ellie Ryan was. And right now, was no exception.

Fuck him, her dress.

Was he drooling, because he felt like he was drooling?

That deep green dress molded to her curves, begging for him to touch them.

Close your damn mouth, dumbass.

Man, he thought she was beautiful yesterday, but today...whoa. He bit back a groan as he forced himself to look away.

"I swear to all things, Sally, you don't think before you speak." Ellie stomped to the door. "There's a child here."

"All I said was play. I didn't say—"

"That's it. You've lost all your house privileges, give me back my key." Ellie held out her hand as her other snapped to her popped out hip.

Why was her stance sexy as fuck? Spencer took a deep breath as all the blood in his head migrated south.

Fuck, he wanted her.

"Over my dead body." Sally mimicked Ellie perfectly.

"You wanna go, sister?"

"Remember what I said about all that pent-up aggression?" Sally squared her shoulders. "It doesn't have to be used only during *playtime*. I've got enough to take you to the ground and keep you there. Trust me. Cobwebs and all."

What the hell was going on? Spencer looked between Ellie and Sally.

Just as he was about to step in, they laughed. And as

they laughed harder, Ellie held her stomach trying to breathe.

Whoa.

Hearing her laugh like that was like music to his ears. This was one of those deep, can't breathe, about to pass out genuine belly laughs. Spencer wanted to hear it again and again. But more importantly, he wanted to be the one to cause it.

"Love you, El."

"Love you too, Sal."

And just like that, it was all over.

Ellie turned her attention to Belle who was happily playing with Roxy on the ground. "Hey princess, I see you've got someone who likes you."

"I love Roxy so much," Belle said as she scratched Roxy on the belly.

"She loves you too, sweetie."

After getting a grin from Belle, Ellie *finally* turned her attention to him. Spencer watched as her eyes rounded before her mouth formed a tiny 'o'. "Wow."

"I can say the same about you." He smirked.

"Ouch!"

Spencer's eyes snapped to Sally who was now rubbing her arm.

"That heat, Ellie. Dang. I'm pretty sure I just got a second-degree burn. Now, I'm gonna have to go to a walk-in."

Ellie punched her in the arm. "One more word and you're giving me back your key. I mean it this time."

"You'll have to pry it from my cold dead hands first." Sally rubbed where Ellie had punched her.

"That could be arranged."

Wow, these women were something else.

Sally chuckled, before grabbing Ellie by the shoulders and pushing her out of the house and right into Spencer's arms.

"Geez, Sally, are you trying to kill me? Or him?" Ellie pointed at Spencer before pulling out of his embrace much to his disapproval.

"Nope, just moving things along." Sally laughed with a mischievous grin. "I'll lock up the house." She then reached for a bag just inside the door. "Here." She shoved it into Ellie's chest, turning once more to grab a leash that had been hanging by the door. She then proceeded to hand it to Belle.

"You kids go have fun and El if you don't call me by tomorrow morning, I will come over here and dig your grave myself." She winked.

"Sally..." Ellie growled.

"Ms. Sally," Belle grabbed her attention. "Why don't you come with me? We can paint with Roxy and you can meet my grandpa." Belle pointed over her shoulder.

Everyone turned.

Spencer groaned the moment he saw his dad leaning against the car. *I thought I told him to wait.*

Why in the hell had Spencer agreed to drive him, Belle, along with Roxy to Ellie's parents' house? This was his own fault.

"Whoa. Shiver me timbers." Sally turned to Ellie. "See, I can do the pirate thing too. Now, I see where McHotPants gets it from. Far too old for me, but damn. Momma can appreciate."

"Belle!" Spencer shouted, trying to stop whatever the hell was about to come from Sally's mouth next. "You don't know what Ms. Sally is up to and you can't invite someone else over to Mr. and Mrs. Ryan's house. That's not polite."

"Sure, she can." Sally looked at him like he lost his mind. "I've got nothing but time today and I'm sure I can be of service." Her brows wiggled as a scary smile appeared on her face.

Sally then turned to Ellie who was glaring daggers in her direction. "I can grill *Grandpa* about McHotPants. Have no fear, best friend of mine, I'll report back."

"Don't you dare."

"Yo, gramps!" Sally screamed. "I'm Sally Johnson, Belle's art teacher, and this chick right here's best friend. Sweet Miss Annabelle asked me to come play with you and Roxy at mom 'n' dad Ryan's house. I've got tons of stories about Ellie I'm willing to share as long as someone feeds me. You down?"

Randal pushed himself from the car with the Hurley's signature smirk on his face. "Hell yeah, I'm down."

Belle jumped to her feet, Roxy barking along next to her. "Yay!"

"*Dad,*" Spencer warned.

"Come along, Gramps," Sally laughed as she quickly did a side step into the house before stomping out, closing and locking the door behind her. "We'll take my car." She winked at Spencer. "Gives these two lovebirds a few extra minutes alone."

"Sally..."

"Don't you worry your little head there, El," Sally gleamed. "I won't tell them the story about you ripping your pants at summer camp and then trying to fasten the life vest around your waist only to fall into the lake."

Ellie gave her a dirty look.

"I'll leave that story to Papa Ryan."

"I'm telling Dad you called him papa again," Ellie growled.

"He loves it. I'm like the daughter they never had."

Ellie rolled her eyes. "Yeah, you would have sent him to an early grave."

"We almost did a few times, didn't we?" She winked. "Might as well tell them those stories too." With that, Sally shooed Roxy and Belle toward her car in the driveway which Randal eagerly jogged over to.

"I like you," Randal said, opening the car door.

"Do you like me enough to have another son hidden away somewhere?"

"No can do, sweet thing. If only I were thirty years younger."

Sally shrugged. "Age is but a number."

"Sally!!" Ellie screamed.

Sally held up her hands. "I kid. I kid."

Before either Spencer or Ellie knew it, Sally was gone. She'd peeled out of the driveway, his dad, his kid, and Roxy all going along with her.

Holy shit.

"What just happened?" Spencer stared at the space where the car once was. "I honestly have no idea, but I never do when it comes to her."

"My kid didn't even say goodbye. I don't think I'm ready to handle that yet." He turned back to Ellie.

"That's Sally for you. She could charm the pants off anyone." A look of horror flashed across her face.

Would Sally try to charm the pants off his dad? Oh, shit.

"It'll be fine." Ellie shook her head checking to make sure the front door was locked.

Spencer looked back to the empty street. "Should I worry about her driving? She does have my kid in her car."

"No, Sally would jump into a burning building if it

meant saving a kitten let alone a child, or apparently your dad. They're safe. I promise."

"Okay, then." Spencer had waited long enough. He cupped Ellie's cheeks in his hands. "Before we get this party started, I have to do this."

"Do what?"

"This." He brought his lips down to hers.

CHAPTER EIGHTEEN

"This is really nice," Ellie remarked as she picked up a strawberry from the plate and popped it into her mouth. Even though she had reservations about this whole thing, she had to admit, so far everything had been pretty damn close to perfect.

Spencer's smile morphed into a wide ear-to-ear grin. "I'm glad you think so. We're still pretty new here, and I don't know any good restaurants." He shrugged. "I figured a picnic in the park would be nice."

"It's lovely." She picked up a banana from the basket. "I've never had a picnic before."

As Ellie watched Spencer's face brighten, she had to smile. It was hard not to.

She didn't get it though. How could he be so sweet and yet, at the same time, been a complete asshole to her?

Okay, in his defense since the coffee shop, he hadn't been an asshole.

Maybe she should give him a chance, if nothing else, the sex would be great right?

And, it *had* been a while.

While Ellie contemplated the sex, her mind drifted back to how he'd acted *after* the coffee shop. Like right now, he'd made this whole picnic for her. If *this* was the Spencer she first met, there wouldn't have been an issue.

Well, maybe a little. Ellie still had trouble understanding why he was attracted to her. She got why she was attracted to him, but the other way around...

"I'm glad you like it. It's been a while since I've done something like this," he said, popping a pretzel into his mouth.

Ellie cocked her head at him. "Eat?"

Spencer's face lit as a chuckle escaped his mouth. "No. This." He waved his hand over the food.

"Again, I say *eat?*"

When he looked at her, his whole face broke into a huge smile. "Dating."

Dating.

The word made her throat dry. Hell, Ellie couldn't remember the last time she went on a date... She resisted the urge to look at her lap. Cobwebs were an understatement.

"After Belle's mother, I didn't want to try."

That made Ellie sit up straighter, as she gave him her full attention.

"Actually, if I'm being honest here, I didn't think I ever would again."

Ellie's face pulled together as Spencer sat crossing his legs. "For the longest time she'd tainted my view of all women," he began. "I can't believe I'm going to say this but you should know."

Ellie watched as pain flashed through his eyes, which then turned to anger.

"I was stupid, and I have no excuse for myself. I met a pretty girl at a bar one night and before I knew it, we were back at my place. Don't ask me how we got there, because I have no idea. That was my first mistake of many. I was so beyond wasted I did the one thing you *never* forget with a one-night stand..." he sighed. "The next morning, she left. I thought that was the end of it."

Ellie placed her hands in her lap. "But it wasn't."

"Not by a long shot. At first, I had a hard time believing her. But I went to the doctor's appointment. I saw Annabelle on the screen when she was nothing but a small peanut." A sweet smile broke out on his face with the memory.

"I knew at that moment that baby was mine. I didn't have to question it, because I felt it. Even after all the stories of her mother sleeping around, I knew. I knew with everything inside me. That's when it all started." Spencer picked up a blade of grass and picked it apart as he spoke. "I tried. I swear I tried when it came to Belle's mother. I mean how could I not? She was going to be the mother of my child. We had to work it out, you know?" He shook his head as he pulled at the grass. "I can't count the number of times she threatened to abort our daughter if I didn't give her money, buy her things, you name it. She used our child as a payday loan, Ellie. I'd like to say that was the worst, but it wasn't."

Ellie's lips thinned.

"Once Belle was born, it got really bad. If it wasn't her coming home at three in the morning drugged up, it was her stealing money, my car, pawning my stuff. Then she left. Just up and left. I moved us in with my dad and for the first time since Belle was born, I had help. I could breathe again. My dad helped me raise her."

"Your dad is a wonderful man. A little out there but wonderful."

"And Sally isn't?" The corner of his mouth turned up.

"You got me there."

He went back to playing with the blade of grass. "A few years went by and boom. She was on our doorstep one night, begging for another chance, saying how she couldn't live knowing her child was out there and she wasn't a part of her life. What was I to do? I wanted my girl to grow up with a mom. I should've known better, though. It was fine for a few months, then it all started again, but this time it was worse. My dad hated her. He wouldn't let her into his house, and how could I blame him? I was so blindsided by the fact Annabelle could have a mom I looked past all the garbage. I blame myself every day for not putting my foot down and kicking her out sooner."

"You can't blame yourself for how someone else acts."

Spencer looked at her with a plea in his eyes. "You'll agree, just wait. As Belle got older, Dad and I noticed she was a little behind. Not a lot, but enough for us to notice. Her first teacher mentioned she saw some signs of a possible learning disability. She was still pretty young, but there were a few tests to get Belle an early diagnosis. And then each year she'd be retested. She was diagnosed with dyslexia and learning disabilities. At first, I was angry, not at Belle, but in general. I didn't know what to do to help her. I went to Belle's mother and let her know." He let out a deep growl. "She shrugged it off and asked for money in the same breath. Hell, if I was thinking clearly, I would have thrown her out of our life then, but no, I was an idiot. Fast forward and you come to the last time we ever saw her. She came to the house begging for who knows what. When I told her no, she got pissed. However, this time instead of directing her anger at me, she looked over my shoulder and stared into the eyes of the daughter we shared and said, she was stupid and a waste of space to her face. The next day, I filed for full custody and after a lengthy battle, we won. We haven't seen or heard from her since." He threw the blade of grass. "That doesn't stop the scars she left, though. I didn't even know Belle remembered the words, but to this day she's never forgotten them."

"I hate her." Pure loathing ran through Ellie. "I mean I *really* hate her," she growled as her fists clenched the banana making it ooze out of her fingers. "You give me her name right now. I'll find her and I will beat the shit out of her." Ellie saw red. "I'll get Sally to drive me, so I'll have a clean getaway. Come to think of it, though, she'd probably also want to beat her ass. And then once I tell Dad, who would tell Bob, they'd want a piece of her too."

"Ellie..."

"I wonder how many people we can fit in dad's truck? We'd have to take the truck since it has room to hold the body in the back before we dispose of it."

Spencer laughed causing Ellie to dart her head toward him.

"This is why I'm glad I'm trying again. I've never met anyone like you."

"Huh?" Ellie asked as she looked at her hand to see the decimated banana. *Did I do that?*

Spencer gently took her hand discarding the fruit before wiping it away. "The love you've shown for Annabelle is undeniable. I'm pretty sure you'd die for her."

"In a heartbeat. I'd die for any of my students."

Ellie watched as he cleaned off the last pieces of banana on her hand. "I believe it."

"I understand where Belle is coming from, that's why." She pulled back her arm as he watched her.

Spencer's face twisted in confusion. "I don't understand."

159

How could he?

Ellie's heart went to Belle. To know her mother said those things to her face...Yeah, Ellie knew exactly how that felt. How those words could leave scars so deep, they'd never heal.

"Explain, please?"

How could she, though? How could she open up that part of her again? Yeah, Spencer had told her all about Annabelle's mother, and yeah, her heart hurt from it. But...

She looked around at everything he'd done. He was a good man. Ellie knew that. Look at how he was with Belle in the park yesterday, or how he'd fight tooth and nail for his daughter...

Ellie chewed the inside of her cheek deciding what she was going to do.

Maybe, just maybe it was time for her to let go of how he treated her, and let him in. She couldn't deny there was something between them. Ellie looked into his eyes and saw the concern. But something stopped her. "Tell me why you were such a jerk to me when we first met?"

"*What?*" Spencer yelled in shock. "Hold on, sure I know calling Talley wasn't my best move but I've never once been a jerk to you."

It was Ellie's turn to raise her brows. "The first time we met you pretty much stomped in my classroom accusing me of being a horrible teacher. Then you talked to me like I was beneath you."

Spencer's mouth hung open. "I never did that."

"Yes, you did."

"Wait, is that why you said the bottom of the shoe thing?"

Ellie stared at him.

"Holy fuck, are you for real right now?"

"Do not use that tone of voice with me, mister." See, this is what she was talking about. She couldn't even ask him a question without him getting defensive.

"Here you go again, getting pissed at me and I don't get what I'm doing to piss you off." He looked at the sky before he said his next words. "I'd be a lying fool if I didn't say it also turned me on."

Excuse me...

"There's that fire in your eyes again," he growled, looking back at her. "I don't know why, but every time I see it, my dick jumps."

"Whaaaat?"

This had taken a strange turn and she didn't quite know what to do. Ellie looked around the park.

"What are you doing?"

"I'm trying to figure out where we went from you being a jerk, to talking about how I make your dick hard."

Sally was going to love this.

"I'm just being honest. I thought that's what this whole thing was about. Do you think I willingly tell everyone how Annabelle's mother nearly bankrupted me and scarred my little girl for life?" He ran his hands through his hair as he cleared his throat.

Spencer was right. He didn't have to tell her anything about his past and yet he did. And no matter how much Ellie hated it, he would never truly understand why she'd gotten so upset without telling him. Where would you even start, though? She took a deep breath. "You aren't the first one."

"The first one what?"

Her throat tightened as the memories came back. "Look at me the way you did, and assume I'm a not good enough."

"I-I didn't."

161

"You did," Ellie stated with fact. "That's why I understand where Belle's coming from. My whole life people have looked at me the exact way you did, and more than once. Not unlike Annabelle, when I was a kid, my parents noticed something was off with me." She pulled her legs to her chest. "I remember getting so mad. I'd see the kids around me in class reading or doing word searches and I couldn't. I couldn't figure any of it out. I faked what I could, and Sally," The tears swelled in her eyes. "She'd always let me copy her work when I couldn't do it. Word searches were the worst. How could you find a word in a jumble of letters when that's all you saw to begin with? I hated it. I hated every second of it. It took me going a few years in school before a teacher suggested I be tested for learning disabilities."

"Ellie..."

"It helped a lot. I was placed in classes where I got one on one attention. My parents worked with me every day. So, did Bob..." She turned to him. "Principal Talley. He's been my dad's best friend for years and kinda a dad to me too. I got the help I needed, but that didn't stop the bullying from kids *and* adults." Ellie looked away as she said her next words. "I understand why those words scarred Belle's heart because they were said to me. The doctor that was doing one of my re-evaluations, he just... I don't know if he was having a bad day, he hated I was overweight, which he made sure I knew, or if he truly wanted to crush the soul of an impressionable child? His words of being no smarter than a box of rocks on the side of the road, and telling me I might as well give up, rooted deep inside of me for years. I hated everything about me. I believed his words. I let him tell me my disabilities shaped me and I was nothing."

"Baby..."

The pity in Spencer's voice hardened Ellie as she looked at him. "No. Don't. It might have taken a while but I'm thankful for him. Without his words, I would've never fought as hard as I did to get to where I am now. Because of him, I get to fight every day for my students who are just like *me*. I get to be their living proof that a learning disability no matter how severe it is, does not define you. Because of *him*, I worked my ass off to be the top special education teacher I could be, along with getting my certification to administer the test. I am better because of him. I get to help children who are exactly like me."

"To use your same words. I hate him." Anger flared through Spencer's eyes. She couldn't help the chuckle that escaped her. He looked like he was ready to murder.

"*That's* why I can't stand it when anyone looks at me like I'm less. Like I'm beneath them for any reason. I let those feelings consume me for far too long and I refuse to let them ever again."

Spencer grabbed her hand bringing it to his lap. "I'm so sorry I made you feel like you weren't good enough, Ellie. I don't have the words to truly explain how sorry I am."

"Why did you get upset that day? Why did you come into my classroom like you'd already placed me in the not good enough box?"

"Belle's old school. We had problems. Her teachers... they were horrible. One morning, I was headed to school for a conference and I overheard them making fun of her openly in the hall. When I asked Belle about it that night, she confessed how her teachers and all the kids picked on her. As her dad, I felt like I'd failed. I put her into that school trusting they would help my baby. Instead, they were just as bad as her mother. And when I saw you... I just. I lost it. Then with you being late I I..."

Spencer shook his head in frustration. "It's no excuse. I should've handled it better. No one should make anyone feel like they aren't valued." He squeezed her hand. "I'm so grateful for everything you do for my girl. From the bottom of my heart, Ellie, I am so unbelievably sorry for ever making you feel the way I did."

Ellie watched him, as she heard the sincerity in his words and his actions. But more importantly, she felt them in her heart.

She didn't know what to say. And even as her mind still told her to guard herself, her heart said to let him in.

Give him a chance. Don't let those words of your past rule over you anymore. Don't let that one asshole change what you've pushed so hard to become. Give it a chance, Ellie. You already know in your heart you should. What are you waiting for?

Ellie looked him in the eyes before she leaned over and kissed him lightly on the lips. "I forgive you."

Ellie would've sworn she handed him the winning lotto ticket, with the way Spencer's face brightened before he pulled her in for another kiss.

"Fuck yes."

"If we're going to explore whatever this is between us," she said with a laugh at his childlike amusement, "we're gonna have to figure out the whole school thing. Talley might freak out."

"We'll deal with that when the time comes, let's just enjoy right now."

She could do that.

Ellie sat back and watched him from the corner of her eye. She felt like a teenager again. One thing she knew for sure, she liked Spencer. And maybe now, she'd finally pull up her big girl panties and allow herself to enjoy it.

"Before I forget." Spencer pulled out a brown paper bag from the basket. "Since we've had this heart-to-heart, I think we both deserve something. Don't cha think?" He smirked at her.

"Is that what I think it is?"

"Depends. If it's what you think it is, do I get a kiss?"

"I'll give you my damn dog if that's what you want."

Spencer laughed. "A kiss will do, but don't give Belle that option. She'll take the dog in a heartbeat." With a bigger smile on his face than before, he pulled out two croissants.

"I'm in love."

Spencer coughed almost dropping the pastries.

"I'm talking about the flaky goodness. I love *them*, geez." Ellie held out her hand. "Gimmie, gimme, gimme."

Spencer handed her one of the croissants. "Here. Remember I'm the one who gave it to you."

Ellie took a large bite closing her eyes as a small moan escaped her lips.

"If you make that sound each time, I'll make sure you have croissants every day for the rest of my goddamn life." He moaned, closing his eyes.

Ellie laughed as she ripped off another piece and tossed it into her mouth. It was like everything was easy between them now. Like it was always meant to be. She winked at him. "You can't deny they aren't damn good."

"You're right. I can't deny it." He popped some in his mouth.

They both sat in silence for a few minutes watching the leaves sway in the wind. Spencer was the first to break their silence. "I don't know about you, but I feel like we just skipped ahead three years in our relationship," he laughed as he finished the last piece of his food.

Humm. Ellie looked back at her lap. *Nope, still got them cobwebs.* "Oddly enough I feel kind of the same way. Wow, three years and I still haven't gotten laid." She turned to him with a smirk. "Sally is going to eat you alive when I tell her you haven't put out in three years."

Spencer's eyes darkened as they filled with lust. "I'd rather eat you."

Spoke too soon.

Ellie coughed a few times as the piece of croissant went down the wrong pipe.

"You're freaking adorable when you're uncomfortable. I love it." He sat back on his elbows. "I never thought I'd feel this."

"Indigestion? Because that's what I'm feeling right now. It happens a lot when I panic."

He laughed. "No, it's just with Belle's mother." He stopped looking at her, his eyes shining. "I'm really glad that I met you."

Ellie's stupid heart did a weird thing.

"If I give you another croissant will you stay this way forever?"

She was a goner. "I can't make any promises, but those pieces of heaven can get you a lot of things."

"You're making me hard again thinking about what I can barter for them."

Ellie swallowed. Why'd she say that out loud? Oh man, was this the heat Sally was talking about? Now, she got it.

As Ellie opened her mouth, her phone buzzed. Figuring it was better to avoid the situation and stop the conversation she grabbed it. When she opened the message, she saw a photo from Sally.

"You've got to be kidding me." She let out a groan.

"What is it?"

Ellie shook her head as she looked at a picture of Roxy covered in head to toe blue paint, with a message saying: *Oops and I expect a call tomorrow morning if you aren't doing McHotPants. I'm headed home. Love you. Call me or I kill you. Kisses.*

Shoving the phone in Spencer's face Ellie fell back onto the blanket. "Kill me."

Spencer burst out into a hearty laugh. "We better head to your parents' before it's too late. Maybe we'll get there before they glue sequins on Roxy?"

"She'd probably like it." Ellie snorted as she rolled onto her side before standing. "The she-devil that she is would demand I put them on her all the time. Thank everything all my mom has is non-toxic washable paint at her house. It's gonna be a bitch to get Roxy clean."

Spencer jumped to his feet. "We'll make my dad bathe her. It's probably his fault."

"I'm blaming Sally. This has her name all over it. Damn, this is gonna suck. Roxy *hates* water."

Spencer folded the blanket putting it on top of the picnic basket as Ellie rolled her eyes. "And of course, Sally left before she would have to clean up the mess."

"Why does that not surprise me?"

"That's 'cause you've met Sally," Ellie groaned. "Let's go check out the damage."

"Not before we do this." Spencer pulled her into his arms and kissed her, taking full possession of her mouth.

CHAPTER NINETEEN

SPENCER LOOKED at a smiling Ellie as she laughed at his father's joke for the tenth time.

There was something about all of this, that felt right. And, as he sat there at the dining room table surrounded by Ellie, her parents, his dad, and Belle, he never wanted to forget this feeling.

As Ellie sat across from him, next to Belle, at his daughter's insistence, he felt a deeper pull to her. Watching her and Belle, he understood Ellie more. He also admired her for how far she'd come.

Ellie would be a perfect role model for his daughter.

Something inside his heart swelled.

Spencer's eyes glanced around the room before they found their way back to Ellie, as she happily munched on her meal. Holy shit, Spencer was still taken aback by her beauty. But it wasn't just that, it was her as a whole. Every part about Ellie Ryan was the whole package. The package *he* wanted.

Then his eyes caught a splatter of blue paint behind Ellie's head on the wall, causing him to chuckle.

When they arrived back at the house it was pretty chaotic if you asked him. Roxy had gotten loose from the bathroom and had been running around spraying water, soap, and blue paint all over the place.

It was hilarious to see Ellie arguing with her dog, trying to convince her she'd never see another piece of chicken for the rest of her natural-born life if she didn't march her ass right back into the tub.

Sure as shit, that dog took one look at Ellie, called her bluff, and then made a run for the back door. Spencer thought he cracked a rib laughing as hard as he did at the scene.

Everyone had run after the dog, as Roxy continued spraying paint and soap everywhere. Then, Shannon, the angel that she was, walked out of the kitchen with a piece of chicken.

Roxy came to a screeching halt before sending a glare toward Ellie. The dog then high-tailed it to the bathroom, jumped into the tub like a perfect lady and barked signaling she was ready for her chicken.

That had Ellie calling Sally on the phone promising her a slow painful death the next time she saw her.

All in all, it had been perfect and he loved every second of it. From running around after Roxy to Ellie screaming death threats. Even to Belle dancing around laughing as Ellie stopped running after Roxy and ran after Belle instead, with a smile on her face screaming how she was going to get her.

Like he said, this was right.

All of it.

And, right now, as Ellie sat next to his daughter, she purposely made sure Belle was a part of the conversation. She'd ask her opinion, agree or disagree with her. Hell, they both tried to hide their peas under the same napkin when they thought no one was looking.

They were *all* looking.

Spencer's heart beat faster as he focused on Ellie's face. This is exactly where he wanted to be.

"Son, if you keep looking at her like that, she's gonna call the police. You're sittin' on the border of creeper city there, population you."

Spencer shot his head to his father who had their Hurley signature smirk on his face. "Dad."

"Don't you dad me." Randal pointed his fork at him.

"Fine, *Randal*."

"Boy, I think you forgot who you're talkin' to. Might I remind you I can bury you six feet underground in a second flat."

"I only *let* you believe that. Makes you feel like you've still got it, but we all know I'd win." Spencer smiled at his dad as he sent a wink to Belle.

"Don't you use my grandbaby against me. I'll tell everyone here the story of how you stole my car when you were fifteen, hit a tree, and were so scared you thought you'd died you peed your pants."

"*Dad!!*"

"Don't worry, Spencer," Dean chimed in with a mischievous smile on his face. "Randal here already entertained us with that one. I must say, I thought my little girl was bad sneaking out to Sally's and stealing skin movies from the back of the video rental store but—"

"Dad!" Ellie's face heated. "If you say one more word, I'll never bring Roxy here again."

"I don't know why you always get embarrassed, dear. Being curious about bodies is a good thing. We didn't punish you or Sally, did we?" Shannon reminisced as she tossed a pea into her mouth. "Why do you think we kept taking you back to the video store?"

"Mom!"

Shannon shrugged before turning to Spencer. "If the videos are any indication of her curiosity, you're in for a treat."

Spencer choked on his water as he tried to breathe. *Holy shit.*

"That's it. We're done. You'll never see Roxy or me again." Ellie dropped her head in her hands but Spencer could see the blush on her cheeks. Was it possible to like this woman even more? Apparently, it was.

He filed the new information in the back of his mind for later. They were definitely going to talk about those movies.

Randal with a lopsided grin turned to him. "You picked good, son."

"What's a skin movie?" Belle asked before hiding another pea under her plate.

"Ahhhh." Ellie flipped her body toward Belle in a panic. "It's a movie about monsters that take people's skin and then eat them!"

"They eat something alright," Shannon mumbled.

"*Mother...*"

"A monster movie! I love monster movies!" Belle's face glowed. "Do you still have any? Maybe we can watch one."

Spencer knew he should jump in and handle the situation, but how could he when it was a perfect opportunity? "Yeah, Ellie, do you still have any of those movies?"

The instant snap of her head to him had Spencer biting his tongue. When Ellie narrowed her eyes, giving him that fire he fucking loved, he couldn't help it. He winked.

Ellie turned back to Belle after shooting him another death glare. "Sorry, Belle, they are a bit too scary for you."

"I can handle anything! That's what you say in class. We can handle anything as long as we put our mind to it and try hard."

Ellie's mouth open and closed like a fish out of water.

"Never thought your own words would be used against ya, now did you?" Randal snickered as he took a bite of his dinner roll.

"Hush your face, old man."

"Old man?" His hand went to his chest. "I thought you liked me?"

The whole table laughed as Ellie scrambled to change the subject. "Roxy took that garden gnome from the backyard thinking it was a toy. She only made it a few feet before it fell and shattered!"

"Are you talking about Gnome Man? I thought someone stole him from the yard." Her mother's face scrunched. "You said you saw someone steal him."

"You lied?" Belle's eyes widened as she looked at Ellie.

"No. I mean yes. I mean well..." she sighed. "Maybe."

"Don't be too hard on her, Bella. Your dad lies all the time."

"Dad!"

"Grandpa, no he doesn't. Do you dad?" She turned to him.

Spencer never had to pull off a straight face like he did now. Holy shit, this had been the most entertaining meal of his life. "Never, kiddo."

Belle quickly turned to Randal. "Grandpa, it's not right to lie. We're Mr. and Mrs. Ryan's guests. We need to be respectful while we're in their home."

Everyone turned to Belle in shock.

Holy fuck, where did my kid learn to talk like that?

"Wow, well mannered, and smart." Shannon beamed from her spot next to Dean.

"That's my girl." Randal's chest puffed out.

"Then behave yourself, Grandpa."

"Damn, first schooled by Ms. Sally and now by my own grandbaby, what's today come to?" Randal sat back in his chair tossing his napkin on the plate.

"That's what you get for making a scene, Grandpa. You brought this on yourself."

"Right through the heart, kid, damn."

"And you shouldn't lie either." Belle moved her attention to Ellie. "But since you have Roxy, I'll let it slide."

As Spencer watched the scene play out in front of him, he almost pulled a muscle in his stomach as he fought to stop his laughter.

Holy fucking shit this was perfect. Every last second of it.

"I really like Ms. Sally," Belle continued like she hadn't just put half of the room in timeout. "She has lots of fun stories about you."

"Ugh."

"She told us about the time you were in a talent show and when you both got on stage you forgot your lines and started singing show tunes at the top of your lungs." She giggled. "You got all the words wrong so the only thing Ms. Sally could do was be your backup dancer and let you go."

Dean chuckled. "I'd forgotten about that until Sally brought it up. Come to think of it, I think I still have the tape."

"Don't you even dare, Dad," Ellie growled as she glared at him.

"That's okay, Ms. Sally said she has lots of pictures of the two of you."

Ellie pushed her plate out of the way before she banged her head on the table.

"You know, Ms. Ryan, you're kind of dramatic." Belle cocked her head.

"We hid our peas together. I thought we had a bond?"

"It's not a secret now since you just told everyone." Belle grabbed the napkin tossing it to the side showcasing their pile of discarded peas.

"God, I love this kid!" Dean hollered, as he smacked his hand on the table in a fit of laughter. "Wait until Bob hears about this."

"Thank you." Belle smiled sweetly at him. "I really like Ms. Ryan, she's my favorite. She's the best teacher I've ever had. Thanks for being her dad."

"No problem, kid."

Ellie stopped banging her head and looked at Belle. "How about when we aren't in the classroom you can call me Ellie or Ms. Ellie like you call Ms. Johnson, Ms. Sally."

"Okay." Belle's whole face beamed.

"Come on, kids, let's finish up dinner so you can play with Roxy a little more before you guys head home." Dean pushed away from the table.

"But I don't want to go home. I like it here!"

"You'll be back," Shannon remarked with a smile.

"With Roxy?"

"Of course."

"I'm right here you know," Ellie snapped. "Roxy is my dog after all."

"True, but how can you deny that sweet face?" Her mom nodded her head toward Belle who was now leaning down with her head snuggled next to Roxy.

"You've got me there."

"The kid's good," Spencer interjected. "Trust me, she knows how to get her way."

"I learned from the best."

Spencer righted his shoulders.

"She's talking about me, boy. Calm yourself," Randal corrected him.

"Dad..."

"Again, stop dadding me."

"Fine. *Randal,* knock it off, or I'm sending you back on the first plane I can."

"I'd like to see you try." His dad stood taking the discarded dishes toward the kitchen.

Ellie watched as Belle jumped out of her seat grabbing her plate along with Ellie's. "I'll take this. Come on Roxy you can help me bring them to the kitchen."

Obviously, Roxy was all over the word kitchen and followed the girl with a wag of her tail.

Once everyone was out of the room but her and Spencer, Ellie spun to him. "I should kill you. How could you leave me floundering like that?"

Spencer sat back in his seat with his fist on the table as he watched her. "It looked like you were handling it just fine."

Ellie glared at him which was returned by his smirk as amusement danced in his eyes. "Stop looking at me like that."

"Like what?" His eyes scanned her again.

She pointed at his face. "That."

"It's my face. I can't help it." Spencer smirked before leaning in closer. "So, about those movies?"

Damn her parents.

"I want to hear all about them."

You know what, screw it. So, what if she dabbled in adult movies? Clearly, he liked it if the look he's giving me is any indication. Go for broke here, El. Channel your inner Sally.

"Maybe I'll show you one day." With that, she got up and left the room and headed down the hall leaving Spencer with his eyes about to pop out of his head.

CHAPTER TWENTY

AFTER WATCHING Ellie escape down the hall, Spencer lost it. Shit, Ellie got him going like never before. After being with her all day, the stories and now after her parting words.

He groaned deep in his throat.

Thank fuck everyone was out of the room.

His eyes darted back down the hall. The way she swung her hips as she walked away...

Fuck!

Spencer wanted her.

No, he *needed* her.

Even just a small taste of her lips again. His body heated at the thought. To feel those curves under his hands....

If he had to wait another five minutes, he'd be a dead man.

Taking a quick look around he saw Shannon and Dean talking in the kitchen and Belle playing with Roxy and his dad on the floor.

He looked down the hall. He couldn't wait.

Spencer pushed back from the table, making sure to check over his shoulder one more time.

He was in the clear.

Spencer took off toward the direction Ellie went. As he came to a closed door, he heard the sound of running water.

Bingo.

He only had to wait thirty seconds before the door opened to reveal a startled Ellie. That look on her face only served to ignite him further.

He had to taste her.

As he grabbed onto her hips, his lips found hers as Spencer pushed them back into the bathroom.

Her taste, her scent, the little moans that escaped her. He couldn't get enough. Their kiss was hungry. Desperate. But he wanted more.

Pulling back from her lips, he started peppering kisses along Ellie's jawline. As he felt her hand push against this chest, he pulled back panting as he looked at her.

"What are you doing?" she whisper-shouted.

"I just–" He gave up talking as he brought his lips back to hers once more.

"Spencer..."

"I had to taste you. I couldn't wait another second."

"This is my *parents'* house. Belle, your dad."

He kissed along her neck, making Ellie throw her head back giving him better access. "Shh, it's just a taste. We'll be quiet." The fact that a few rooms over was full of people only urged him on more.

Spencer's right hand skimmed down her body. When he reached her hips, he squeezed.

Fuck she felt good. Molding to his grip like she'd always meant to be his.

The little gasp that came from her lips went straight to

his dick. His hand moved lower, just skirting under her dress. He was so close to finally touching her. Seeing her, tasting her.

It consumed him.

The heat that poured off them was fire inducing. Now he finally understood what Sally had been talking about. With each touch of Ellie's creamy skin, his fingers burnt.

He needed more. Fuck, he needed all of her.

As Spencer reached the hem of her dress, he was struck dumb the moment Ellie pushed his fingers away.

"You take too long."

Before he could argue, Ellie shocked the shit out of him pulling up the bottom of her dress to her waist exposing her luscious thighs, and sexy as fuck black lace panties.

"Fuck me," he groaned as he stared at the apex of her legs.

Holy shit his dick had never been harder in his life. Seeing Ellie with her legs bare and her pussy only covered by a thin piece of lace was his undoing.

Not to mention her take-charge attitude.

Holy. Fucking. Shit.

"Yes ma'am." As he held her eyes, his fingers skimmed her exposed thigh. "Understand, Ellie Ryan. I won't be fucking you right now."

"Why the hell not?" With a growl, she pushed away his hands again before lowering her dress. "Bastard."

"Stop." He grabbed the material yanking it up. "*Never,* I mean *never* hide from me."

Ellie looked at him, her eyes wide, her mouth slightly open. *That's right baby, I'm in charge here.*

His fingers brushed over the lace covering her lush mound. "What I was saying before you sent fire my way again..." His eyes darkened. "I won't fuck you this time. Oh no, my sweet Ellie. That's gonna wait until you're in *my* bed. Sprawled out naked where I can finally let my eyes get their fill of you. 'Cause when I fuck you, it will be... All. Night. Long."

He kissed her shocked mouth with a hunger he didn't know he'd possessed inside of him. But then again, this was Ellie, nothing should surprise him anymore. He pulled his lips back, breathing hard. "Right now, we've only got a few minutes before someone comes knocking." Spencer slid his fingers up and down the lace, causing her to shiver in his arms.

"Oh, oh, um oh, well okay, then well...what are you going to do?" she breathlessly asked as his fingers inched their way to the side of her panties.

Before she could get out another word, he stared deep into her lust-filled eyes. "Mine now." His fingers gripped the crotch of the lace and pulled.

Hard.

The rip echoed throughout the bathroom causing his heart to race, as the material easily fell from her body.

He brought his prize to her face, letting them dangle in front of her eyes. As they rounded in shock, he couldn't help the wicked smile that appeared on his lips.

"Why the hell did you do that?" At his smile, her eyes turned to fire as she reached for his new treasure.

He easily kept them out of her reach. "Shhh. Time for talking is over." With zero effort Spencer hoisted Ellie onto the sink spreading her legs as he lowered himself to his knees.

"Wow, you didn't even groan."

Spencer looked up at her, his brow cocked. "Did you just insult me?"

"No."

"I think you did." He bit the inside of her right thigh causing Ellie to yelp. "Don't insult me, Ellie." Ignoring her protest, he finally feasted his eyes on her core. "Holy shit, I knew you'd be perfect." The image staring back at him had his mouth watering. She was lush, ripe, and had the smallest dusting of hair.

Holy shit, he was about to lose it.

Spencer felt the tip of his dick dripping, soiling his boxer briefs. If he wasn't careful, he'd come before he even touched her.

"Spencer..."

"Quiet, didn't I say the time for talking was over?" He leaned in. "It's time for me to claim my prize."

"I am not some object to claim, there buddy."

"You talk too much." He bit the inside of her thigh again, this time closer to her core causing Ellie to let out a small gasp as he licked the spot he'd bitten. "That's right baby, feel me."

"Holy moly."

Slowly, Spencer brought his lips closer to her center biting and nipping along the way. The feel of her skin against his lips was more than he could handle.

He'd fantasized about this for weeks now.

"Crap on a fucking cracker," Ellie moaned as his hot breath reached her center.

Her words had him smirking. *Just you wait.*

Spencer looked at her from between her legs and waited until her eyes found his. Once they did, he *finally* brought his mouth to her core.

When her eyes closed, he had to do the same. Spencer knew she would taste like heaven he just didn't know how good that would be. She was tangy and sweet all at the same time.

Fuck him.

He'd never get enough.

"Please," she begged.

Hearing her plea sent shockwaves directly to his dick. *Anything you want, baby.* He circled her nub with his tongue before pulling it into his mouth, sucking.

"Oh, fuck me."

"Soon." Spencer grabbed her hips pulling her center closer to his mouth. He wanted more.

"Holy crap. Holy crap." Ellie rocked her hips into his mouth begging for more.

If she wanted more, he'd gladly give it to her.

Quickly his fingers found her center.

Fuck him, she was soaking.

He trailed his fingers down her slit, coating them with her essence before entering her. As he felt her walls clench around his fingers, he could only imagine what they would feel like around his cock.

"More," she moaned. "Give me more."

"Gladly." Spencer pumped his fingers inside her as her walls tightened.

Fuck him, his dick wasn't even inside her and yet it was seconds from bursting. If he wasn't careful, he'd make a fool out of himself.

That's when Ellie moaned out his name. "Spencer, that's it. That's it. Oh, I'm there. Effe me, I'm coming!" Her words came out in a hushed shout as her legs clamped around his head pulling him into her shaking body.

However, at the exact same moment, a loud cracking noise echoed through the bathroom.

Before they knew it, Ellie was thrown into the air landing directly on top of him as the sink broke from the wall and crashed to the floor.

Within seconds the whole room was soaked, including them.

"Ahhhhhh!" Ellie jumped from his lap, and somehow in the process ended up punching him in the gut knocking the wind out of him.

"What do we do? What do we do?" Ellie raced to the sink using her hands to shield away the water as she tried to make it stop.

All Spencer could do was lay on his back coughing as he did his best to inhale without dying.

"Make it stop! Where the hell is all this water coming from? Stop demon water, stop!!" Ellie shouted as the water mocked her attempt by spraying her directly in the face.

To make matters worse, that was also the exact moment the bathroom door flew open.

"What the hell is goin' on in here?" Randal barged through the door ready to fight off any intruder that dared to enter his new friend's home.

Spencer finally being able to take a breath turned to see not only his dad, but Ellie's dad also standing there.

Both of their eyes were seconds from exploding out of their head as they surveyed the room.

Then to Spencer's absolute fucking horror, Ellie's mother was right behind them shoving his daughter away with Roxy.

Fuck me.

His daughter.

Spencer's eyes shot back to Ellie. Thank God, her dress had fallen back into place.

"Boy, haven't I told you in the past you gotta be careful about these things? Look at what happened to you last time. I swear I thought I raised you smarter than this." His dad stepped into the bathroom pushing a screaming

Ellie still trying to block the water with her hands out of the way, before he reached the valve and shut everything off.

"All righty then." Dean winked at him. "I'm gonna get these two demolition contractors clothes to change into." Dean laughed as he walked the opposite way out of the bathroom.

"Son, hanky panky is fun and all, but not when it breaks a sink in the process."

"There was no hanky panky!" Ellie screamed at the top of her lungs.

"Dear," Shannon appeared from around the corner with a pile of towels. Spencer had never been so relieved that Belle was not there. "We were all young once, Ellie. I mean your father and I never broke a sink, but we did break a few bed frames."

"Shoot me now!!"

"Don't be such a prude, young lady. You are after all the ones who just broke our decorative sink. Unless he didn't finish you off. You should be flying high right now." Shannon tossed Spencer one of the towels.

"Holy fuck, somebody get a shovel from the garage and hit me over the head with it."

He couldn't help it. Spencer shifted his body as he burst into laughter while Ellie rambled on about plotting her death.

Damn, not once had he ever been caught, but this was... shit, this was something else entirely.

Not only was he caught red-handed with Ellie. But they somehow broke the sink and now the room was covered in water.

No one ever said he did things subtly.

His eyes went back to Shannon as she scrutinized him.

Oh, hell no. He knew what that look was. Especially coming from her. Time to defend his honor.

He jumped to his feet. "Mrs. Ryan, I can assure you Ellie was extremely satisfied."

"Spencer!" Ellie snapped toward him.

"What? I can't have her thinking I'd be lousy for her daughter." He turned back to Shannon and his dad. "Mistakes were made."

"I'd say so. Breaking the sink is a big mistake, son."

Spencer shrugged with his signature smirk on his face. "But what a story."

"You will not tell a single soul this." Ellie grabbed another towel from her mother. "I will murder every single one of you, if so much as a peep gets out."

Shannon handed Spencer another towel. "Please, dear, it's Shannon, never Mrs. Ryan to you." She smiled at him, which he gladly returned.

"You'll have to ask her about it Monday at school, Bob." Dean snorted walking through the hall. "Yeah, if you don't mind heading over to the home improvement store that would be great. Yeah sure, sure. Text me a picture of the sink. Yeah. Okay. See you soon, Bob." Dean walked into the bathroom with two pairs of sweats in his hand.

"Did you just tell Bob?" Ellie squeaked.

"How else did you expect me to get him over here to replace the sink? He wanted to know details."

"And you told him!"

Dean shrugged as the corner of his mouth rose. "I told him what I know."

Ellie groaned. "I take it back, don't get the shovel, just lay me out in front of the car and run me over, please."

"You're being a bit dramatic, dear."

Ellie shot a glare toward her mother and then snapped it

toward him. "Hey, what's that look for?" Spencer held up his hands in surrender.

"This is all your fault. All of it."

"How?"

Ellie let out another growl directed at him.

"Please, if you plan on having makeup sex do it in a bed this time. Your father and I don't want to buy stock in house appliances."

"Someone hit me with a car, run me over, stop, then back up, and run me over again. Please, I'm begging you."

"I'll pay for the damages," Spencer announced.

"For running over my daughter?" Dean cocked his brow.

"No." He laughed at Ellie's groan. "No one's running Ellie over."

"Says who? I'll do it myself," she huffed.

"I'm talking about the sink." Spencer darted his eyes to Ellie giving her a glare.

"Don't you dare look at me like that, mister. I'm still blaming all of this on you."

Shannon handed him another towel. "No, that's fine, dear. Consider this a freebie."

"Is no one listening to me over here?" Ellie yelled, stomping her foot.

"Yes, dear, we're all listening to you beg someone to run you over. Wait a second, why don't you ask Spencer?" Shannon winked at him. "After all, in French, orgasm is called *La Petite Mort*, meaning the little death."

"Oh my God, I fucking can't."

Randal barked out a deep belly laugh. "I like her, son. I like her a lot."

"Me too, Dad."

"Here." Dean handed him clothes. "Change and then we'll meet in the living room."

Ellie grabbed a pair of sweats from her dad with a huff. "If you think I'm leaving this room again, you're mistaken. This is where I live now."

"That's fine, El. Bob will be here in about an hour. I'm sure he'd like to ask you a few questions." He turned to Spencer. "You too for that matter. Bob's another father to her."

"I'm out." Ellie pulled the pants on under her dress before putting the top on letting her wet clothes soak through. "Peace out, losers." Ellie raced out of the room, leaving a water puddle wherever she stepped.

Spencer's hand went to his stomach as he laughed harder.

"She is an odd one, but we love her," Shannon said as she followed her daughter out of the room using the last towel to clean up the water Ellie was leaving behind.

"You did good, son." Randal nodded at him before doing the same laugh as Dean while they both walked away.

"Holy shit." The smile on Spencer's face said it all.

Quickly he changed into the dry clothes.

One thing he knew for sure, he was in for a wild ride when it came to Ellie. And he liked it.

Once he made his way into the living room, he saw Ellie pacing the floor as their parents talked like he and Ellie hadn't just destroyed the bathroom.

"Pace on the towel I put down, dear, you're getting everything wet."

Spencer's lips pulled back into a wicked smile as he heard Ellie ask for the shovel again.

Before he could make it over to her, though, the back

door swung open. Belle and Roxy came running through the house. "What happened?"

"Nothing you need to concern yourself with, Bella," Randal said, still laughing. "Your dad accidentally fell into the sink causing it to break and spray water everywhere."

Belle looked at all of them before the Hurley smirk appeared on her face. "Sure..." She turned to Ellie. "I wonder what Travis will say about this on Monday."

"You better not." Ellie sent her an evil look. When she saw Belle's face morphing into an ear-to-ear grin, her mouth dropped. "I'm gonna get you." They both laughed as Ellie chased Belle around the room.

"The towel! Don't make me run after you cleaning up puddles, Ellie!" Shannon grabbed the towel from the floor before chasing after Ellie and his daughter.

"See, this is what I'm talking about. I can't be missing things like this." Randal laughed before waving his hand around the room.

"We don't get these moments a lot. We need to enjoy them when we do," Dean agreed. "I think you're making the right decision."

"I know so. It'll be better this way."

"What choice?" Spencer asked looking at his dad.

Randal ignored him as he turned to Shannon who'd given up chasing after a soaking wet Ellie. "You said there was a house for sale a few blocks over?"

"Yes, the Henderson's recently moved out of state to be closer to their grandkids."

"Then that settles it."

Spencer's brows darted to the ceiling. "You're moving here?"

Belle skidded to a halt in front of them. "Are you?!" She jumped up and down waiting for his answer.

"Darn tootin' I am. I can't believe I hadn't done it sooner. What's keeping me back home anyway? You're here, your dad's here. Your grandma passed away a long time ago before you even got to meet her. Why shouldn't I be where my family is?"

"Dad?"

"Plus, I want to be close to my future daughter-in-law." He winked at Ellie who completely paled at his words. "I gotta get all her secrets and get on her good side."

Spencer's eyes darted from his father to Ellie. And as he stood there a loss for words, the more and more Spencer liked the idea.

He turned back to his dad. "Welcome home."

CHAPTER TWENTY-ONE

THREE DAYS! That's right. It had been three days! Ellie stormed into the teacher's lounge on Wednesday morning, ready to break something.

Three. Fucking. Days.

To say Ellie had been pissed, would be an understatement.

After leaving her parents' house on Sunday, Spencer drove her home. Might she add in the same car as a chatty grandfather, a barking dog, and a giggling little girl.

Her anger slashed through her again.

No, that wasn't what annoyed her. Nope, not even in the least. Nor was it when Spencer walked her to the front door, did a quick check to make sure no one was in there - which was sweet. He gave her a toe-curling kiss, smacked her on the ass, and pushed her and her dog inside the door.

That was the last she'd heard from Spencer freaking Hurley.

Bastard.

Ellie didn't know what she was expecting, but it sure as

hell wasn't radio silence after you know, going to chow-town on her lady bits.

As Ellie walked past the table in the lounge, her foot accidentally hit a chair. "Get out of my freaking way you jerk." She glared at the chair like it was now her mortal enemy.

This was all Spencer's fault.

If that stupid picnic hadn't been perfect, and Ellie deciding Spencer was worth the chance she would have gone the rest of her life hating him and no one would be the wiser.

Least of all her va-jay-jay. That stupid thing got a little action and now she was a freaking hussy trying to get her to travel to bang town, even if that meant jumping Spencer's bones showing up at his front door.

Yep, her lady bits had lost its ever-loving mind.

Only *half* the cobwebs were cleared... Stupid asshole.

Her mind drifted back to the bathroom. She groaned.

She was never going to live any of that down. Between Bob, her parents, and how could she forget Sally.

Freaking Sally...

Ellie wanted to punch something. Anything. Maybe the stupid chair.

Then, of course, there was Monday morning. At first, she didn't know how to handle seeing Belle. This was definitely new territory for Ellie. You know having the father of one of your students make a meal of your downstairs and all that.

Thankfully though, it did seem Belle believed the sink had broken on accident. Okay, so she might have suspected something but in Ellie's mind Belle had no idea and that's how it was going to stay.

None of that really mattered, though, because Belle was

a freaking star. She had no idea why she ever doubted the girl.

As Ellie had waited nervously in the classroom Monday morning, which might she add, she was thirty minutes early for the first time in her life.

Belle walked in with her shoulders back and that Hurley smirk on her face. She looked Ellie right in the eyes before sending her a wink. Belle then promptly turned to Travis and started talking about Jimmy and his dog.

Ellie's jaw hit the floor.

Nothing. Not even a single word was uttered about the weekend. Damn, she knew she liked Belle for a reason.

Not once had Belle mentioned her father the past two days, which Ellie was thankful for, or at least she thought she was.

Three days later and she wasn't sure if Spencer was dead or alive. Which made her even angrier because if he was dead, she wanted to be the one to do it.

Maybe he changed his mind. Maybe it was all a one and done thing, or you know the fact that they broke a sink, sprayed water all over the place, her mother and father and hell even his dad made a game out of it. Maybe once he got back home, he'd decided she was too much trouble and said forget about her.

And then there was Bob.

Freaking Bob.... She was still mortified at what he'd done once he'd shown up.

He'd stormed in with his tools in hand, went straight up to Spencer, crossed his arms over his chest, and demanded to know what his intentions were with Ellie.

Fuck her, right?

No wonder Spencer gave up.

She let out another growl.

"I don't think the chair's gonna fight you back," Sally said, sipping her tea from the other side of the table.

How had I missed her when I walked in? Ellie threw her head back. "Is it too early to ask you to shove your head in a car door and close it?"

Sally looked at her watch. "Yeah. You can't make those requests for at least another hour."

Ellie stormed over to the coffee pot after sending Sally a death glare. However, the moment Ellie saw the pot empty she snapped. "That's it. I'm going to fucking murder him." She gritted her teeth as she spun on her heel.

"Not today, killer." Bob blocked her exit with his arm.

As Ellie tried to sidestep him, her fists clenched as he easily blocked her attempt each time. "Oh, come on," she shouted when his arm blocked her again. "Just let me do it once. That's all I'm asking. Then he'll stop being an inconsiderate asshole."

Bob's brows shot to the ceiling as he looked down at Ellie.

"What? Stop looking at me like that, you dick."

Sally put her mug down. "Whoa."

Bob pointed at Ellie as he looked at Sally. "Why's she so angry this morning?"

Sally shrugged. "Hell, if I know? She walked in here, tried to pick a fight with that chair, went to the coffee pot, threatened death, and then you walked in."

Ellie growled louder. "I'm right here! Do not talk about me like I'm not in the freaking room. I'm so tired of everyone doing that. I matter, you know? I'm. Right. Fucking. Here."

Bob looked at her like she had ten heads.

"Shove off. How long have you known me? I'll answer, my whole freaking life. Give me a break today, okay?"

Bob stopped blocking the door before looking at Sally. "You know what? This sounds like your territory. I'm not getting involved." Deciding it was best to leave, he grabbed the coffee pot from Ellie's hand before going back to the door. "I'll go deal with this, and you," he pointed to Sally, "deal with her."

Sally saluted him. "Aye, aye, Captain."

Ellie's eyes thinned at both of them. "I am not something to be dealt with. How many times do I have to tell people that? And if you keep talking about me like I am not here, I'll stab both of you with a pen." Her hands shot to her hips as she narrowed her eyes on them further.

Right as Bob was about to step out of the lounge, he stared at Ellie ignoring her rant. "If this is about *him*, I'll deal with him too." With that, he left the lounge taking the coffee pot with him.

Before Ellie could open her mouth, Sally tapped the back of the seat next to her. "Come sit. Tell momma all about it."

"Uhh."

"Don't uhh me, sister." Sally pulled out the chair. "Sit your ass down. We've got two minutes before either of us needs to be in class. Momma doesn't have all day."

Ellie sent her an evil look before giving in and walking to the chair. "I can't deal with all this without caffeine and Talley's stupid face just took the coffee pot. How am I going to function without my liquid gold?" Ellie threw herself into the chair letting her arms flail around her.

"Here have some of my tea."

"It's not the same," she whined.

"Sure, it is. If you put the amount of sugar and creamer you do in your coffee in the tea you won't even know the difference. Now drink it and shut your pie hole so we can figure this shit out. The moment you walk into your classroom like…" She pointed at Ellie, waving her finger around. "That, you'll be eaten alive. Don't make me remind you of Travis."

Ellie banged her head on the table keeping it down. "Why am I the way I am?"

"It's what makes you perfect." Sally grabbed the back of Ellie's hair pulling her head up. "Tell Aunt Sally all the bits that's got your brain all flustered. Then we can go back to talking about how big Mr. McHotPants' dick is."

"Shoot me now."

"Whoa, Ms. Ryan are we really watching a movie today?" Travis asked almost fearful as he walked into the classroom and saw the projector on.

"Yes."

"Are you okay?"

Travis might have been a pain in her ass most of the time, but he was sweet. A little annoying, okay a lot annoying but still sweet. "I'm good, Travis. I just figured we could all use a break before we start work on the book report." Collective groans rang throughout the room. "Hey, none of that. We can start the book report now if you want instead?"

"No!"

"That's what I thought." Ellie walked to the front of the room.

"Ms. Ryan," Belle's voice startled her. "Are you sure you're okay? You look weird."

Ellie turned to Belle with a forced smile on her face.

"I'm good, sweet pea. Don't you worry your little head about it."

In the end, what Ellie felt didn't matter. Well it did, but there was something about Belle that pulled to her. And each day she got to be with Belle, she felt it more and more.

No matter what happened between Spencer and her, Ellie would make it a point to help Belle anyway she could, just as if she was her own child.

"Yeah, you do look weird. Ms. Ryan, did you accidentally show your other class your underwear?" Travis shouted still concerned but now had a mischievous grin on his face.

Ellie rolled her eyes. "No one has seen my underwear." *Except Spencer who'd stolen my destroyed pair...*

Travis watched her suspiciously. "We're still your favorites, right?"

"We're watching a movie, aren't we?"

He studied her as his lips pursed. "It depends. What's the movie about?"

Ellie took a deep breath. *Universe, if you love me at all, give me a fucking break today.* "It's a nature documentary about slugs."

"What?" Travis jerked back with a gasp. "Guys, she hates us. We've been demoted to the bottom."

"Tea is *not* the same as coffee," Ellie grumbled into the cup Sally had given her. "I'm usually better equipped for this."

"Slugs are awesome!" Belle's toothy smile brightened the room, making Ellie chuckle for the first time in days.

"Girls aren't supposed to like slugs." Travis cocked his brow at Belle.

"Boys shouldn't be so narrow-minded they have to put girls in a box," she shot back.

Oh, hell yes, get 'em, Belle. Sexism can suck a dick.

"I'm gonna tell Jimmy you like slugs."

"I'll tell him myself at lunch. He'll think it's cool."

Travis looked at her before a smile appeared on her face. "You're probably right."

Belle sat back in her seat proud of herself. *I'm proud of you too, girl.*

Ignoring their commotion, Ellie walked to her computer to start the movie. "It's actually a nature documentary about the rainforest."

"Why the rainforest?"

"Rain is calming," she answered before bringing up the main menu. "Don't fall asleep. That's all I ask."

"You got it!"

"I'll make you take notes if you do."

"We won't!" rang out in unison.

As the movie started, everyone settled while Ellie sat at her desk. The conversation she had with Sally played through her head.

Maybe Sally was right?

Why was Ellie waiting for Spencer to contact her? And as Belle so gracefully reminded her, that was stupid and sexist. She was a strong independent woman. She could reach out to him.

Ellie pulled out her phone and brought up Spencer's number. *Okay, El, don't screw this up. You're not going to screw this up. This is gonna be easy. All you're doing is checking in, it's not like you're asking the guy to marry you. It's okay, just take a deep breath and ....* Oh, for fuck's sake. What the hell was her problem now?

Screw it. She typed out her message and hit send before she could chicken out.

Hi.

Not even ten seconds went by before she received a text from Spencer.

Took you long enough! Damn, I was worried you were going to make me suffer another day. It's been three days, woman. Are you kidding me?

Hold up. What? Ellie read the message again before sending back her reply.

Huh?

She didn't have to wait long.

I was beginning to wonder if I needed to bribe you with croissants for a week, so you'd talk to me again. You've been killing me here. Do you know how hard it's been to not pack up Belle and drive to your house?

Ellie's eyes almost popped out of her head.

Wait. You were waiting for me to contact you?

She sent her question as her heart raced. *He was waiting for* her? No way.

Yeah! At the risk of sounding like a loser, I've been checking my phone every five minutes. Like I said, it took you long enough.

Ellie sat back and try as she might, she couldn't keep the

smile off her face, or her stomach doing a weird flip thing. Oh man, she was going to have to tell Sally she was right. *Great. That will go right to her head.*

Ellie's phone buzzed making her look at it.

Have dinner with me Friday night?

She cursed her body as her stupid va-jay-jay jumped at the thought.

Ellie, just so you're aware the moment I saw your text, my dick got hard. You know, honesty and all that.

Her face heated as her eyes darted to the kids in her room. Oh crap, she needed to end this conversation. This was *not* the time or place.

Fuck, I'm tempted to say screw it and tell you to have dinner with me tonight but I know I've got to get this new website done for my client by Friday morning, and if you're here, I won't think of anything else besides you being naked. And I already think about that enough as it is.

Whoa. Definitely not the time. She clenched her thighs together.

Dad's back home. Dropped him off Sunday night. He's already packing to move here. So, you won't have to worry about whatever he'll come up with out of his mouth. It will just be me and Annabelle. Say yes.

Ellie bit her lip as her face broke into a smile. Why not? Life was short.

Okay.

Her phone buzzed right away.

Fuck yes.

She rolled her eyes at his reply.

You're a piece of work, Spencer Hurley.

The corner of Ellie's mouth turned up as she sent her message. But, she liked it.

Bring Roxy. Belle would love that.

As she was typing her reply another text came in.

And some extra clothes...

She had to swallow her laugh.

Better yet, never mind. I'd rather see you in mine in the morning.

Ellie gulped as she did her best to hide the fact her body shivered at his words.

That's mighty presumptuous, Mr. Hurley.

She received his reply instantly.

You are owed that punishment for making me wait... And I'm sure as fuck looking forward to it.

CHAPTER TWENTY-TWO

THE NIGHT COULD NOT HAVE GONE BETTER if you asked
Spencer. It felt like it'd taken eighteen years to get here, but
it happened.

Ellie was in his living room.

Roxy and Belle were on the floor wrestling and he was
sitting next to the girl he couldn't wait to get naked.

He looked over at the clock. Damn, it still wasn't Belle's
bedtime.

Spencer closed his eyes as he tried to calm his body
before he looked at the clock again. *Hurry the fuck up!*

Giving up, his eyes moved to his daughter playing on
the floor. She'd been a freaking champ about all this. On
Wednesday night, after Ellie agreed to come over, he had a
sit down with her.

He'd explained, at least the best he could, what was
going on between him and Ellie. Belle at first asked some
questions about what it meant, but soon, shrugged it off and
realized she'd get to see Roxy a lot more.

Spencer had explained to Belle why she couldn't talk
about it at school. Talley might have been aware of them,

but he got the sinking feeling he was turning a blind eye. He needed Belle to fully understand, Ellie could lose her job if somehow people found out. Other than, Sally.

After what felt like pulling teeth, Belle informed him she got it and he needed to lighten up. She wasn't a child, which surprised him. He'd rolled his eyes at her as she continued on and on about Ellie and Roxy and all the fun they'd have.

Spencer had no idea why he'd been worried. Clearly, his girl was a hell of a lot smarter than he knew.

He looked around his living room again. Ellie being there with him and Belle fit. Yep. He liked this.

Spencer sat back on the couch, as he watched Ellie pick up another slice of pizza.

From the corner of his eye, he saw Roxy's ears perk up. *Here it comes.* He laughed as Roxy left Belle and ran over to Ellie.

"Don't even think about it, chica. I saw Belle give you her crust. Ain't gonna happen. This is mine. Momma doesn't share."

"Would you share with me?" Belle asked.

Ellie nodded. "With you, yes. With her, hell no." She turned back to Roxy. "You've already had dinner." To make a show of it, Ellie turned her pizza around and bit the crust.

Roxy's eyes widened in betrayal before she barked.

"Do not yell at me, young lady."

Roxy barked again before falling onto her back, her tongue flopping out of the side of her mouth.

Oh man, Roxy was gonna get it.

Trying to save her, Spencer tapped the seat on the couch between him and Ellie. "Come on, Rox, leave your mom alone. Don't forget you got the end of my crust too."

The dog turned to him and huffed like she was pissed he'd told on her.

"Roxy." Spencer stared her down, a sharp edge in his tone when he called her name.

Slowly, the dog climbed onto the couch and glared at him. She would have been more intimidating if she didn't let out a small burp. Then she kissed him.

"How in the heck did you get her to do that?" Ellie asked, flabbergasted. "She never listens to me."

Spencer scratched Roxy's chest. "I have a way with women. What can I say?"

Roxy promptly burped in his face again.

"Gross, Roxy, you don't do that in someone's face." Belle laughed as she jumped to her knees. "Hasn't anyone taught you manners?" She looked at Ellie.

"Hey, I try my best. She doesn't listen to anyone."

"She listens to me and Dad." Belle looked back at the dog. "Roxy, come."

She did.

"Sit."

Roxy sat.

"Rollover." And wouldn't you know it, the damn dog did that as well.

Ellie's eyes rounded. "But you don't have any food!" Ellie snapped her attention to Roxy glaring at her. "I don't know whether I should be pissed or impressed."

Roxy barked once more before crawling over to Ellie's feet. She then looked up at the pizza in her hand.

"For Pete's sake."

Spencer laughed. Yep. There was no place he'd rather be than right here. Maybe the bedroom, but this was good enough for now.

"Ellie," Belle got their attention. "Dad said we're having a sleepover tonight. Do you want to sleep in my room?"

Spencer jerked as Ellie choked on her food. He smacked her back as he tried to help her breathe. Once she was no longer on the verge of dying, Ellie shot him a death glare.

He turned to Belle. "We've got grown-up things to talk about tonight while you're in bed. Besides would you rather have Roxy as your bedmate or Ellie? You only get one."

The fact Belle thought about it before turning to Ellie with an apologetic look had him holding in his amusement.

"Sorry, Ellie. I pick Roxy."

"Wow, that hurts." Ellie placed her hand over her heart. "I'm pretty sure I'll never recover from this. My favorite girl picked my dog over me."

Belle's whole face beamed. "I'm your favorite?"

"Of course, you are. You had doubts?" Ellie held her finger over her mouth as her face softened. "Shhh, don't tell the others."

"Did you hear that, Roxy. She said I'm her favorite!"

Roxy turned to Ellie giving her the side-eye. "Geez Rox, you're my favorite dog, she's my favorite girl, you good with that?" Roxy barked once before she turned to Belle to lick her face.

"No respect." Ellie popped the last bit of the crust in her mouth. "I'm glad I didn't share with you now."

Something inside Spencer threatened to break as he listened to Ellie's laugh. That's it. Night's over. He turned off the TV. "Time for bed, Annabelle."

"But Dad, it's Friday. Can't I stay up with you guys? Grandpa would let me stay up," she whined.

"Don't bring him into this." Spencer stood grabbing the empty pizza box.

"But it's true."

"I thought you'd want to show Roxy your room and where she's sleeping?" *That's how you win against your daughter.* He hid his smile as he brought the box to the kitchen.

"I want to show you both." Belle grabbed Ellie's hand. "You can tuck me in. Dad doesn't do it every night anymore, but he does sometimes. You can do it tonight."

"Hey." Spencer walked back into the room. "I only stopped 'cause you told me to. You said you were too old to be tucked in."

"Not by Ellie. She can read me a story."

"Ouch." He looked at her like he'd been shot. "I read to you every night you let me. Did you forget?"

An evil smirk appeared on her face. "Ellie's better." Belle took off running dragging a laughing Ellie behind her while Roxy eagerly followed along.

It took forty minutes to get Belle and Roxy settled into her room. Ellie had to admit she loved it. She loved every minute of it.

Crawling into Belle's bed as she read to her, after she'd shown Ellie her room, felt like a dream come true. It only took about ten minutes before Belle had fallen asleep on Ellie's arm, while Roxy was passed out at the end of the bed, on her back, snoring.

However, when Spencer tried to move Annabelle off Ellie's arm so she could get out, she had to stop him. Just a little while longer with Belle in her arms was all she wanted.

Spencer understood the plea in her eyes before leaning against the wall watching them.

Ellie didn't care, though. As Belle slept soundly in her arms, she tucked a piece of stray hair behind her ear.

She loved this little girl.

Ellie's throat tightened. How could you love someone as much as Ellie loved Belle when you'd only met them a month before? More importantly, how could Belle's mother give this up? How could she have walked away from this?

From Annabelle?

If Belle was her child, no one would've been able to pull her away.

The moment Belle snuggled deeper into Ellie's side, she was done. Annabelle Hurley owned her heart.

After a few more minutes of watching her sleep, Spencer gently tapped Ellie's arm, nodding to her, it was time. Ellie didn't want to let her go, but she knew she had to.

Sooner or later the gallon of water she'd had with dinner would rear its ugly head.

Carefully, Spencer lifted Belle's arm giving Ellie the room she needed to move. Once she was gone, Belle curled onto her side as Spencer kissed her forehead goodnight.

Ellie watched transfixed as he tucked Belle into bed before giving Roxy a quick pat on the head.

He then grabbed Ellie's arm pulling her out of the room, quietly shutting the door behind them.

Spencer placed his finger over his mouth telling her to still be quiet as he dragged them to the living room.

Joke's on him, Ellie couldn't talk even if she tried.

Once they were back in the living room, Spencer yanked Ellie into the seat next to him. "I haven't had someone put Belle to bed with me since we moved out of my dad's."

Ellie nodded as her eyes moved to the hallway leading to Belle's room. "Annabelle is an extraordinary girl. You're lucky to have her."

"She's lucky to have you." Spencer tugged Ellie into his lap. "I will never forget what you just did for her."

"I loved her." Tears threatened to fall from her eyes. "That's what I did."

Something flashed in Spencer's eyes but Ellie didn't have the time to figure it out. Before she knew it, he kissed her.

"Wait. Wait." She pushed his chest. "We have to stop."

"I can't." His voice was raw with emotion.

"We have to, what if Belle hears? What if we wake her?" She pushed against him again but failed when he wrapped her legs around his waist.

"Belle is out like a light. She won't wake up for another seven hours, but you're right." He picked Ellie up, tossing her higher on his waist.

"Put me down, you fool. You're gonna kill yourself. Then I'm gonna have to explain to Belle how you died trying to hoist me in the air." She clung to him hoping not to fall.

"Bedroom," was all he said as he took a step toward the opposite end of the house. Once Spencer reached his room, he tossed her onto the bed as he kicked his door shut.

"Don't toss me around like a rag doll, Mr. Hurley." Ellie scrambled on the bed trying to sit up. When she pushed her hair out of her face, she looked at him. Her heart slammed against her chest as Spencer stared at her like he was ready to pounce. His eyes held a hunger Ellie had never seen before. "Spencer..."

He took two steps toward her, as she fought the urge to

move back. The room heated around them as he took another step.

"I want you."

She wanted him too. More than she'd ever wanted another person.

"No, I *need* you." He placed his left knee on the bed as he advanced toward her ready to strike and fuck if that didn't make her hotter.

Spencer grabbed her ankles, yanking them toward him. "Ahhh!"

"I think you're wearing too many clothes, Ms. Ryan." His hands went to her shirt before ripping the material over her head causing her to sit up.

"Spencer!" She wasn't ready for that. Holy shit she was not ready for that at all. Her hands subconsciously went over her middle.

"What're you doing?" he growled.

"Don't growl at me."

Spencer's hands pushed her shoulders making her fall back onto the bed. "Why are you hiding?" He tried removing her hands from her stomach but she held on tighter. "Didn't I tell you in the bathroom never hide from me?"

"That was different." *Oh God, make it stop.*

"Ellie..." he warned.

"Stop, okay." She shook her head. "I get it, you want me, but give me a second to wrap my head around that. I'm not saying no. I just need a minute."

He crawled onto the bed, his right knee going in between her legs as he kissed the top of her breast. He then moved his lips up to her neck. "What's wrong?" He nipped her collarbone.

"I can't think when you're doing that."

"That's the point. You're overthinking." He did it again causing Ellie to tilt her neck giving him better access.

"I can't help it. Have you seen you?" She waved her hand in the air at him.

"I'm not looking at me, Ellie. I'm looking at *you.*"

That's what bothered her. "You're like this perfect dreamy piece of cake with extra frosting. Add in sprinkles, nuts, chocolate sauce, and like a million sparklers. That's what you are. Then there is me, I'm that small pathetic cupcake in the back that's overcooked, with crusty bits and frosting that's two years expired. I'm just chilling in the back of the display case, hoping no one sees me and realizes how pathetic I am compared to the masterpiece that is the sparkler cake."

A wolfish grin appeared on his face. "Good thing I like cupcakes."

He grabbed both her hands forcing her to pull away from her body. "Ellie, I'm gonna let you in on a little secret." His eyes darkened as he looked down on her. "I love *your* cupcake."

Her breath hitched.

"I've been dreaming about this body for so long, I'm about to come in my pants and I haven't even seen your tits yet." That made her feel good.

He sat back pulling his shirt over his head. *Oh, my freaking God.* Her eyes widened. "You have yum-yum lines!"

He arched his brow.

Ignoring him, Ellie quickly got to her knees before reaching out to his hips. "These! I've always wanted to be with someone who has them!"

Spencer laughed before unbuckling his belt making his pants fall farther down his hips.

"Look how far they go!"

"If I'd known the sight of my body would distract you from thinking, I would've gotten naked in the living room."

"No more talking, more stripping." Her eyes danced as she reached for the button of his jeans.

"I agree." Before Ellie knew it, her bra was flung across the room, quickly followed by her pants.

"I was talking about you, *not* me!" she groaned, trying to reach for his jeans again.

"Not yet, let me get a look at you. I've been thinking about your tits since the coffee shop." He moaned. "Fuck me. They're better than I ever imagined." His hand caressed her breast making Ellie forget about trying to get him naked.

"Shit, I'll never forget what these look like." His fingers pinched her nipple. "I wonder how they taste." Spencer lowered his head as he brought the peek into his mouth.

Oh shit.

Ellie's whole body heated as Spencer's hand moved down her body, finding the edge of her panties.

"Better than I imagined." His fingers slipped inside the elastic, causing her body to heat even further.

"Please," she begged as his fingers found her core. "More. Please, Spencer."

He worked her body like it was his job, and he'd been doing it his whole life. She'd never felt anything like this before, and as his fingers pushed inside her, she exploded.

Holy fuck!!

As soon as Ellie began coming down from her high, Spencer was off the bed. He tossed her panties from her body before pushing down his jeans.

Ellie blinked a few times, once his boxer briefs followed suit. *Ho-ly shit! Sally was never going to believe this.*

"If you keep looking at it like that, I'm gonna come before I get inside you."

That was hot.

Really fucking hot.

Something came over Ellie as her heart pounded against her chest. "Prove it."

Spencer was back on the bed between her legs before Ellie had time to think. "You little shit."

"What? You know mom's gonna demand to know if you've satisfied me. Not my fault. I can't lie to her." She laughed as he pushed her legs apart. "Oh, Ellie. You have no idea what you just did."

"I hope it's less talking and more fucking."

"You're gonna regret that." Spencer grabbed the condom from the bedside table, before he quickly sheathed himself.

Damn, that was fast. He was back at her core before she blinked.

"Eyes on me."

Where else could she look? Everything about him captivated her. Especially his dick. *Hol-ly mol-ey.*

Spencer slowly entered her, gritting his teeth. "God damn, you're so tight. How am I gonna prove my manliness when you're gripping the life out of me?"

"Move," she begged. "Freaking put those yum-yum lines to good use and move."

She didn't have to tell him twice. Instantly, Spencer started moving as Ellie's body clenched.

"Ellie," he growled as his movements increased. Spencer's hand reached between them seeking out her clit. When he reached it, he rubbed vigorously sending her over the edge once more.

"Spencer!"

His thrusts became more erratic as he pounded into her. He grabbed onto Ellie's hips as he pulled her body into his, stilling as he emptied himself.

It took a few minutes before either of them could move. Spencer collapsed on top of her, doing his best not to crush her body as they both fought to breathe.

"Holy crap," she said, trying to pull in air. "I'm gonna feel that tomorrow."

"Good." Spencer kissed the side of her neck. "Ellie?"

"Yeah?" She kept her eyes closed as she answered him.

"Best damn cupcake I've ever had."

Her whole body shook as she laughed. After a few seconds, a yawn escaped her lips. Wow, she was tired.

"No yawning."

She barely opened one eye to him. "Why not, I'm tired?"

"Not tonight, baby." His hand slowly trailed down her stomach. "The night's still young."

"Psssh, sleep. I want sleep."

Ellie felt the bed bounce as he chuckled. "Oh, Ellie, my Ellie. What am I going to do with you?"

"Let me sleep." She yawned again.

Spencer's hands found her hips. "Not gonna happen, baby. I still owe you that punishment."

Her eyes shot open.

CHAPTER TWENTY-THREE

ELLIE ROLLED to her side as her body ached in places it hadn't ached in years. *Whoa boy, momma needs a stretch.* Slowly she sat up in the bed, wiping away the sleep from her eyes. *Did Roxy sleep on me again? She knows that kills my body in the morning.*

Morning...Shit. It's morning.

Panic rocked through her.

I'm late! Crap, I'm late for class!! Damn fucking alarm clocks! Ellie grabbed the blankets ready to toss them across the room and hurry her ass to school— *Wait. It's Saturday, not Friday. Stupid body you would pick the weekend to finally wake me up on time.*

Ellie tossed the blankets, and when she looked down, she froze.

I'm naked. Like naked, naked. What the hel—

That's when her brain finally kicked in.

Hoolliiee Crrraapppp!

Spencer Hurley had done things to her body she'd didn't even know existed. As the memories rushed back in, her face heated. Sally was gonna be in for the ride of her life when Ellie told her.

Five times.

Holy guacamole.

Ellie had gotten off five times last night. *Five times.* That was unheard of for her.

No wonder she was sore. As she stretched her arms over her head she looked to her side and saw a sleeping Spencer. Damn, he was adorable.

He was out cold. She couldn't blame him though, they'd both put in quite a workout.

Too bad her dang body's internal clock decided it was *finally* time to work.

Ellie looked back at a peaceful Spencer. Might as well let him get more sleep. Trying not to wake him, she placed her left foot on the floor. As her right foot followed, her stomach growled.

Maybe they have cinnamon rolls in the fridge? Ellie could go for a cinnamon roll right about now. Actually, make that a cupcake.

She blushed. *Bad, Ellie. Give your body a dang chance to recover.*

As quietly as she could, Ellie got out of bed, her eyes scanning the room as she looked for her clothes.

Top: check.

Bra: double check.

Pants: nothing.

Where the hell did he throw my pants? Ellie looked around the room again, only coming up with a pair of Spencer's sweatpants on his dresser.

Good enough.

There was no way in hell Ellie was going to walk out there without pants on. She shuddered at the thought.

She tiptoed over to his dresser and grabbed them, pulling them on over her legs. She didn't miss the love bites on her thighs, though.

Belle was wrong, her dad *did* bite.

Ellie's face broke into a sheepish grin as she carefully opened the bedroom door.

Fuck me! Her hand flew to her mouth holding in her scream as she fell back. Holy shit, the Hurleys were going to send her to an early grave.

As Ellie tried to stop her heart from exploding in her chest, she looked at the massive smile of one Annabelle Hurley, staring back at her holding a book in each hand.

Sally's words came rushing back to Ellie as she realized this was *exactly* what Sally had said. Down to the five orgasms and all.

Crap on a cracker. Sally was going to lose her mind.

Checking to see if they woke Spencer, Ellie turned her head back into the room only to see him still passed out. Maybe she should close the door? Her luck Annabelle would run in and jump on the bed and discover her dad butt ass naked.

No kid wants to see that.

Ellie took a small step out of the room, before closing the door behind her. When she turned back to Belle, the girl's eyes scanned up and down her body.

Oh crap, oh crap, oh crap. She was wearing Spencer's sweatpants.

Ellie's throat closed as she blurted out the first thing that came to her mind. "I spilled water on my pants and your dad gave me his!" she whisper-shouted causing Belle to raise her brow. "Then I got really tired and your dad felt bad about me sleeping on the couch, so he told me to take his room."

215

Both of Belle's eyebrows shot up.

"Nothing happened. I slept on the floor."

Belle continued to stare at her.

"I tripped and sprained my ankle and your dad took care of me. That's why I was in there." *What did I just say? Shut up, Ellie. Shut up!*

Ellie's body had gotten a mind of its own since she took a step away from the door and faked a limp. *What is wrong with you?*

Belle cocked her head. "I saw you walk out of the room fine."

"I was testing the weight on my ankle." *Stop talking!* "I'm much better than I was last night." *In more ways than one. Oh, for fuck's sake shut up brain!*

"Okay..." Belle gave her a strange look before holding up the book. "Can you help me with my report?"

Whoa. Sally called it so freaking hard.

What do I do? Ellie's eyes darted around the hall. That's when she noticed Roxy on her back with her feet in the air as happy as could be.

"I fed her this morning," Belle announced. "She seemed like she *really* wanted to eat."

"She always does." Ellie took a step down the hall wanting to get away from Spencer's room.

"Your ankle seems better."

Ellie snapped her head toward a smirking Belle.

When Ellie took another step her body limped, giving its best performance. *Would you freaking stop already?*

To make matters worse, Roxy after hearing their voices jumped to her feet and barked. She ran to Ellie giving her a kiss. "Shhhh. Not everyone is up yet, Rox."

Then to no one's surprise, Roxy nudged Ellie's legs pushing her down the hall toward the kitchen. Once they were there, Roxy grabbed the dog bowl Ellie had brought and tossed it at her feet. "Ouch, you jerk."

Belle's laugh echoed through the room as Roxy picked up the bowl and did it again, only this time it hit Ellie in the leg.

"Roxy!" Belle laughed as she did it again.

"It's only funny when it doesn't hit you." Ellie glared at her dog as she rubbed her shin. "All these bruises are from her." *Well, at least the ones on the bottom half of my legs.*

"Huh," Belle smirked. "I thought you ran into the desk at school? I've seen you do it. *A lot.*"

"Fine. They're from that too. But mostly her." Ellie walked toward the counter as Roxy picked up the bowl and tossed it at Ellie's feet once more. "Come on, Rox. We're guests here. We're not gonna do the second or third breakfast thing today."

At her words, Roxy looked her square in the eyes before picking up the bowl and tossing it toward Belle.

"Oh, no you don't, miss thing. You do not trade me in for Belle thinking she'll feed you." Ellie put her hands on her hips daring Roxy to do it again.

Roxy being who she was, fell onto her back kicking her feet in the air making adorable noises as her tongue flopped out.

"That's the cutest thing I've ever seen!" Belle cried, running to scratch Roxy on the belly.

"Don't fall for it, Annabelle. She's trying to fool you."

"It's working. Do you want a treat, Roxy? Ellie has them next to the food. You want me to get you one, girl?"

"Stand strong, Belle. Don't give in to her demands. You'll become putty in her paws. I'm serious."

"I can't help it." Belle looked at Ellie from the floor. "Look how cute she is."

Ellie crossed her arms as she watched Roxy kick her feet in the air, pretending to run. And try as she might, Ellie couldn't fight it either. "Damn. Fine. Okay, second breakfast it is, but hear me now she-devil. You will *not* get a second dinner tonight you hear me? And I swear if Dr. Richman yells at me again about your weight you're explaining yourself to him. Not me." Ellie grabbed the dog food she'd brought and tossed a few nuggets in the bowl.

Roxy barked as she bounced to her feet causing Belle to laugh harder.

"Here you ungrateful furball." Before Ellie could place the bowl on the ground Roxy was there gobbling it up.

No respect whatsoever.

Ellie's eyes moved to the clock on the stove. *Might as well get some food myself.* She opened the fridge looking for cinnamon rolls. *Damn. None.* Giving up, she turned to Belle. "What do you want for breakfast?"

"Chocolate!"

"You and me both." Ellie grabbed the milk from the fridge. "Please tell me you have good cereal? Like the ones with marshmallows in them."

Belle darted to the pantry grabbing the box out. "We do!"

"Thank the Universe." After grabbing them each a bowl for breakfast, they talked and ate for a few minutes. Once they finished, Belle placed both bowls in the sink.

"Come on, kid." Ellie pointed to the books on the counter. "Let's head to the table and work on your report."

"Okay!"

It only took around ten minutes before Ellie and Belle were in a groove as they worked on Belle's report. With Ellie's help during class, Belle had picked an easy to read book that had werewolves -*go figure*- and a village that needed to be rescued by the main character. It was a little advanced for Belle's reading level, but Ellie knew she could do it. And she proved it. When Belle came across a word she had trouble with, she sounded it out loud exactly how Ellie had taught her.

Watching Belle improve as she worked had Ellie's heart bursting. These were the moments she lived for as a teacher.

After Belle finished her page of the story, she turned to Ellie. "I like this. I don't even mind reading out loud."

A ridiculously wide smile spread on Ellie's face. "That's great, sugar plum. See reading out loud isn't all that bad."

Belle bit her bottom lip. "I guess. At least when I'm with you it's not."

Ellie cocked her head as she watched Belle close off. "You know, something just occurred to me. The other kids know 'cause I've worked with them for years. Annabelle, I'm just like you." Ellie pushed the book away focusing on Belle.

"You are?"

"Yeah." Ellie nodded. "I grew up going to all the same classes you do. I was diagnosed with reading, writing, and math learning disabilities when I was in the first grade. Dyslexia when I got to the third."

"That's me!"

"I know, honey." Ellie smiled sweetly at her. "Look at where I am now. I can read, write... math is still a little iffy." She shrugged. "But, I pushed. I worked my butt off and I now get to teach little girls and boys who are just like me, to show them they can do anything they want to do. Their disabilities won't stop them, they didn't for me."

Belle's eyes widened. "You really are just like *me*."

"I am. Learning something a different way doesn't make

you any less than students who learn a more traditional way. If you want my opinion, having this type of disability makes you more resilient. People like us have brains that are wired to figure things out in a way others' don't."

Belle's face scrunched. "It makes me different."

"No, it makes you, you. I know adults that would kill to be able to think outside the box as easily as we do. Because of how your brain works, you're able to problem solve on the fly. You can't tell me you don't do that. I've seen it. When you come across something you don't understand, you pull it apart and piece it back together in a way that makes sense to you."

"Sometimes I need help to figure stuff out. What if I can't read a word, or spell something no matter how hard I try?"

"You'll find a way." Ellie grabbed Spencer's phone that was sitting on the table. "These babies here are what I like to call pocket helpers. I don't rely on them, but when I come across words I can't spell, or a word I've never heard before, I look it up. There are resources everywhere. Phones, computers, teachers, your dad, Grandpa." She pointed to herself. "Me."

Belle's brows pulled together.

"Not knowing something off the top of your head is okay," Ellie continued. "People have to look things up all the time. I do it at least ten times a day, if not more."

Belle's eyes moved to the phone before she looked back at Ellie. "Would you show me how to look up something when I get stuck?"

"Of course, sweetie. Life's about finding what works for you and what works for you might not work for others."

Belle sat in her seat looking at the book. "My learning disabilities don't make me dumb?"

Ellie pulled Belle into her arms. "Don't ever think that, Annabelle. Just because you learn a little differently does not make you dumb." Her heart broke. How could she explain to Belle being different was okay? Especially, when it was something Ellie struggled with a lot when she was growing up?

"Do you think I'm dumb?"

"No." Belle shook her head. "You're the smartest person I know other than Dad and Grandpa."

"But I have the same disabilities as you."

Annabelle pulled out of Ellie's arms as she worried her bottom lip. "I hate that it's hard for me when it's easy for the other kids."

Ellie had felt the same way when she was younger. "That's something you'll have to learn to deal with, Annabelle. What if it was the other way around, what if it came easy to you, and it was hard for everyone else? How would that make you feel?"

"Normal."

Ellie's heart shattered at the word.

No. Belle didn't get it. At least not yet. Ellie needed to try a different approach. She waved her hand in the air as she shook her head. "Who wants to be normal? Normal is boring. Being different is where it's at."

The corner of Belle's mouth turned up. "Roxy's different."

"Don't remind me," Ellie chuckled before looking back to Belle seriously. "Different comes in many shapes, sizes, forms, abilities, you name it. Being different is what makes us all unique. I'd take being unique any day of the week than being *normal*."

"Does that include Roxy?"

"If we have to include her, sure." She smirked. "Roxy's

differences make her fun. Weren't you the one busting a gut 'cause she kept throwing the bowl at my legs?"

"It was funny." She nodded.

"Even though I want to strangle her sometimes, Roxy's food-driven personality makes her different. That's what makes her uniquely perfect in her own way."

Roxy barked from her spot on the floor next to them.

"I think she agrees." Belle gave Roxy a quick pat on the head before returning to her seat.

"Listen, Annabelle, you are a golden child. Never, and I mean *never,* let someone else make you think that you're not. You're special in every way possible. Anyone would be lucky to have you in their life."

"Not my mom."

The air was sucked out of the room.

"She didn't think I was special. At least not the way you do."

Ellie sat there dumbfounded as she searched for the right words. Words that didn't involve calling Belle's mother a fucking cunt. "Annabelle, that *woman* and I'm being very nice to call her that, was not your mom. Just because she gave birth to you does *not* make her a mom. A mom is someone who loves their child unconditionally, they sit by their bed when their baby is sick. They hold your hand when you're scared. They laugh and cry with you."

Recognition dawned in Belle's eyes as she looked at Ellie. "They read you stories at night?"

"Yes." Ellie's heart tightened. "They read you stories at night. And help you when you need it. Mom is something earned, Belle. Moms don't get that title just because they gave birth to a child." Ellie could see the wheels turning in Belle's head as she thought. She just wished she could make her understand how special she was.

"Can we read some more?" Belle picked up the discarded book. "I want to find out if Jasmin and the were-wolves can fight off the evil queen and save the village." She quickly found the page they'd stopped on. "Jasmin is a hero."

"So are you, Belle."

Belle beamed as she picked up the book and started reading out loud again. Once Belle finished reading the page, she pushed the book back toward Ellie. "I really do wish I had you all day."

"You say that a lot." As Ellie watched Belle something changed inside of her.

"It's true. Reading out loud with you is easy. I don't have to worry about what you're gonna say or laugh at me."

"I would never laugh at you."

"I know, that's why I like reading with you." Belle pointed to the girl in the book. "Do you think if the evil queen picked on Jasmin or her werewolf friends she would do something about it?"

Ellie sat back in the chair cocking her head. "She is. That's why she's fighting for her village. The evil queen picked on everyone and Jasmin had enough of it."

"How come there are people in the world like the evil queen? The ones that pick on others and make them feel like they aren't good enough?"

"I don't have an answer for you, sweetie. Sometimes people are jerks. No one really knows why they act the way they do."

"The evil queen is an adult, though. I thought adults weren't mean on purpose?"

Ellie wished she had an answer. Sometimes adults were worse than kids when it came to hurting others. The evaluation Ellie had all those years ago popped into her head.

"They shouldn't be," she finally said. "Adults should know better."

"What if they don't?"

"They deserve a kick in the head then."

A giggle escaped Belle. "I'd like to see that."

"You and me both. I've got a list a mile long of people that need a good kick in the head. Mr. Douglass is at the top."

Belle laughed harder. "If you kick him, can you record it?"

"I'll see what I can do." Ellie tapped the book. "We've got a few more chapters to read."

Belle nodded as she pulled the book to her lap as she began to read out loud. As Ellie listened to her, she couldn't stop her mind from wandering.

I thought adults weren't mean on purpose?

For some reason, that set alarm bells off in Ellie's head. *I don't have to worry about what you're gonna say or laugh at me.*

Adult... Like a lightbulb going off, Ellie's heart sank. *Annabelle didn't mean Grady, did she?*

There was no way... but then, that would explain why every time she asked about Grady's class Belle would shut down.

Ellie hadn't worked with her directly before. This was Grady's first year at the school. But Ellie couldn't see another teacher picking on a student. Okay, well, actually from what Spencer and Talley said, that was exactly what happened at Belle's old school.

That couldn't happen again.

No, there was no way. Besides, everyone that Ellie worked with knew her stance on treating someone differently and if they did anything to her kids they'd have to deal with *her*. And that was something no one wanted to deal with.

Not when it came to Ellie defending her kids.

She needed to get to the bottom of this.

Ellie wracked her brain trying to figure out what to do. She couldn't ask Belle directly about it. What if she was wrong? What if she was right? Belle had already gone through so much. And then there was Spencer.

No, she had to know for sure before she brought it up, and the only way to do that was to talk to Grady on Monday.

"Your turn," Belle announced, snapping Ellie from her thoughts.

Doing her best to push everything away, she took the book.

As she looked at Belle's smiling face, there was one thing Ellie knew for sure. If she found out Judy Grady had done *anything* to Belle...she was a dead woman.

CHAPTER TWENTY-FOUR

DAMN.

Spencer couldn't remember the last time he'd slept this well. As he stretched his body, he smiled. Ellie was a hell-cat in bed. They probably could've gone another round or two, but even he was running on empty by three in the morning. No wonder he slept like a baby.

Last night had been incredible, every moment of it. From the second Ellie walked into his house, everything fell into place.

But what really got him? When Ellie tucked Annabelle in bed for the night. If he hadn't known before, there was no doubt in his mind then. Ellie loved his daughter like she was her own.

Spencer would never get the image out of his mind when Ellie begged to hold Belle a little longer after she fell asleep.

As he watched them from the door, he knew that was the moment he fell in love with Ellie.

It's funny, Spencer had spent years avoiding women at all costs. He never wanted to put Annabelle in harm's way again, and yet here he was. The woman he was in love with was also in love with his daughter.

Damn.

It might have been fast, but if he'd ask his dad, he'd gladly point out, things that were meant to be, didn't follow the rules of time.

If you know you know. And Spencer knew one hundred percent, he was in love with Ellie Ryan, and if the way she looked at him was any indication, Ellie was in love with him too. She just hadn't realized it yet.

As Spencer's eyes adjusted to the light, he glanced at the clock on his bedside table.

Fuck! It was ten o'clock. Annabelle had been up for hours.

Shit.

He reached for Ellie on the other side of his bed. They needed to get up. When his hand hit cold sheets, panic raced through him.

Of course, she wasn't there. It was ten o' fucking clock.

Spencer jumped from the bed and found discarded pajama bottoms before pulling them on. He swore to everything, if she left without saying goodbye, the punishment she got last night was nothing compared to what it would be.

When he grabbed the handle of his door, he heard the distinct sound of paws walking on the hardwood.

Roxy.

Good. That meant Ellie hadn't left. He'd be lying if he said he wasn't a tad disappointed. Blindfolding and tying her to the bed last night had been fun. He could only imagine what other punishments he could come up with. Then again, knowing Ellie he was sure he'd get the chance.

Spencer opened his door to find Roxy standing there, wagging her tail as she held her food bowl in her mouth.

"Hey, Roxy girl."

She wagged her tail harder causing her whole body to wiggle. "You hungry, Roxy Foxy? Your momma didn't feed you?"

Roxy tossed her food bowl directly onto his foot.

"Damn, Rox, that hurt." Spencer grabbed her bowl as Roxy nudged the back of his leg. "Okay, okay, you want food. I get you loud and clear."

Roxy nudged him harder forcing him to walk toward the kitchen. "Shit. Is this what Ellie deals with every morning? No wonder she's always late."

Spencer's face lit into a ridiculously huge smile as he turned the corner into the kitchen. There in front of him, were *his* girls reading at the table.

He leaned against the doorframe, crossing his arms over his chest as he watched them. The love he felt before only grew stronger.

"Ellie, can you help me with this word, what's it mean?"

Spencer watched as Ellie took the book from his daughter. "Sure, let me see." After looking it over she placed it in between them. "Sometimes we can use the words around this one as context clues."

"Context clues. You talked about that in class. You said they're like clues to help us figure out the word we don't know."

"Yep, you smart girl. See, what do you need me for?"

"You're right. I don't."

"Ouch." Ellie jerked back. "The pain. I think you shot me."

"I'm kidding." Belle gave her the Hurley smirk. "Maybe."

228

"After all we've been through this morning, I thought we were friends."

"We are. Can we get back to the word?"

"My poor heart." Ellie shook her head. "Yeah. Let's start the sentence over and find the clues. 'As Jasmin walked into her village, she was *parched,* she felt like she hadn't *drank* anything in days.' What do you think the clues tell us about 'parched'?"

Belle thought for a second before saying, "Thirsty? She wants water."

"Yeppers." Ellie nodded. "See, I knew you could do it." Ellie gave her a high-five.

That's when Roxy decided she'd waited long enough. She tossed the bowl into the kitchen with a loud bark.

"You are *not* getting a third breakfast you overeating pain in my butt!" Ellie pushed back from the table. The moment she turned around and saw Spencer leaning against the wall, she screamed throwing her hand over her chest. "Don't do that! How many times do I have to tell you Hurleys to stop sneaking up on me!"

Spencer pushed himself off the wall with a laugh. "Maybe you should be more observant."

"Says the man who slept till ten," she mocked. "Maybe you should pay for my adult diapers. One of these days, I'm gonna pee myself 'cause of the two of you."

"I think I can add that to my budget."

She shot him a glare.

As he took another step closer to them, something flashed in Ellie's eyes. It was gone before he could figure it out, though. Just as he was about to ask, she picked up a pencil and tossed it directly at him.

"What was that for?"

"Payback."

"You'll need to throw harder next time." Spencer pointed to the pencil lying on the floor a foot in front of him.

Ellie huffed as Belle giggled. "Whatever."

"Mornin', Dad."

"Morning, kiddo." Spencer kissed Belle on the top of her head. "Did you have breakfast?"

"Yep." She popped the 'p'. "Ellie let me have the good cereal."

"Did she now?" He looked at Ellie who shrugged. "Thank you for feeding her."

"You're welco—" Spencer grabbed her arm pulling her to his body.

"Hey Neanderthal! I am not a rag doll." When she narrowed her eyes at him, he kissed her trying not to overdo it since Belle was there. "Morning, cupcake."

At his word, her cheeks flushed causing him to wink at her.

"I should throw the book at you this time."

"You might have better aim."

Ellie tossed her hands in the air giving up. "You two are gonna be the death of me."

"Can Roxy chew on the pencil?" Belle asked, making Ellie dart her head to her dog.

"Leave it."

Roxy dropped the pencil before she barked at Ellie. "I mean it, Roxy, don't even think about it."

Roxy jumped into a play stance, barking once more before she picked up the pencil and made a run for it.

"Roxy-Ann!" Ellie charged after her. "Get back here. There's lead in that, you moron!"

"I'll help!" Belle leaped from her seat and ran after Ellie who was running after Roxy.

As Spencer stood in his kitchen watching his woman

and his daughter run around the room after a dog, the corner of his mouth turned up into that signature Hurley smirk.

Yep. He knew with everything inside of him. One day, he was going to marry Ellie Ryan.

CHAPTER TWENTY-FIVE

ELLIE HAD to admit the weekend with Spencer and Belle had rocked. Like really rocked. Saturday, they ended up at the park, and Sunday, they watched cartoons in a blanket fort they'd made in the living room.

Of course, Saturday night Spencer had upped his game, making Ellie lose her freaking mind in the bedroom. Who knew sex could be so mind-blowing? If they kept this up, she was positive they'd win some weird kinky world record. Her va-jay-jay sure wanted to give him the award.

That poor girl needed some recovery time.

Even with the weekend being phenomenal, Ellie never got that sinking feeling in the pit of her stomach to go away. The more she thought about it, the more she believed she knew the answer.

As that feeling ate her alive, she had to talk to someone about it. That's probably the reason Sally was marching along right next to Ellie as they headed to the Teacher's Lounge.

Sunday night, after leaving Spencer's, much to Belle's and his protests, she spilled her guts to Sally.

Ellie had to stop her from finding Grady's address and paying her a visit that night. She couldn't blame Sally's knee-jerk reaction to hunt her down, though. Ellie was right there with her. But she knew by the off chance she was wrong... Yeah, she didn't want to deal with Bob and his bitching about paperwork.

Besides, being on school grounds would save them both. Ellie couldn't murder Grady if there were witnesses.

So, Monday morning it was.

As they walked through the halls, the feeling in her stomach worsened. How could anyone pick on a child? Let alone Annabelle. She was the sweetest, kindest, most funny girl Ellie knew. Spencer had done an incredible job in raising her.

Her mind drifted to Spencer. The love he had for Annabelle was unmatched. He would do anything for her, and he had. Heck, he'd picked them up and moved just so Annabelle would have a chance at a better life.

Her heart tightened.

Spencer was the perfect father.

No, Spencer was the perfect guy. Forget about the mind-blowing sex, there was so much more to him. He was loving, caring, funny, the list went on and on. And when it came to Ellie, they might have had a rough start, but he'd well made up for it.

Spencer was everything Ellie could've ever wanted in a guy. And how things stood now, she couldn't see her life without him. Without Annabelle, without his insane dad—

Ellie stopped dead in her tracks causing Sally to collide into her back.

"Dang, warn a person."

Ignoring Sally's annoyance, Ellie turned and stared at

her, her eyes on the verge of popping out of her skull. "I'm in love with him."

"Yeah," Sally gave her the duh look.

"I love him. Holy crap, I love him." The color drained from her face. "I love Belle too." She really did, and the more Ellie thought about it, the more she felt it in her heart. She was madly in love with Spencer Hurley and his daughter.

Whoa. She needed to sit down.

"Are you only now just figuring this out?" Sally rolled her eyes. "I could've told you that a week ago. You really need to get with it, sister."

"Sally, I'm not joking."

"Neither am I. You've loved Annabelle since she walked into your classroom. Spencer not long after that."

Annabelle.

The reason why Ellie was at school forty-five minutes early.

Ellie saw red as anger, like she'd never felt before, ran through her. If Grady so much as looked at Belle wrong, she's a dead woman.

No one and Ellie meant no one, messed with her girl.

"There's the demon that comes out when someone screws with your kids." Sally looked in her eyes. "Let's go, boss. We've got garbage to take out."

Ellie took off to the lounge, Sally right behind her. If Grady wasn't there, Ellie didn't care. She would find her. She'd hunt her down, no matter how long it took.

Thankfully, as they opened the door to the lounge, they were greeted with Judy Grady sitting at the table drinking her coffee.

"*Grady,*" Ellie growled her name getting her attention.

Judy put down her mug arching a perfectly sculpted eyebrow at Ellie. "Yes?"

"Don't play dumb with me. I know *exactly* what you've done." Ellie's fists clenched at her sides as Judy rolled her eyes.

"I can't play dumb with someone who *is* dumb. They won't get it."

The fuck did she say? "Excuse me?"

"You just proved my point. Hurry up, I don't have all day for you to figure out your big words to talk to me. What do you want?"

"Can I hit her? I really want to hit her." Sally took a step closer to Judy, but Ellie held her back. "Come on. Let me do it."

Ellie let go of Sally's arm keeping her focus on her target. "I came in here ready to give you the benefit of the doubt. But you, Mrs. I don't know who the fuck you think you are, just told me all I needed to know."

Judy Grady then did the one thing that always made Ellie snap. Grady looked at Ellie like she was beneath her.

"Oh, now you've done it," Sally chimed in.

"Don't you dare look at me like that." Ellie gritted her teeth. "Wait, is that how you've looked at Belle?"

"Belle?" Grady said almost dismissively. "Are you talking about the new girl who's taking after your footsteps? Poor girl never had a chance."

"What's that supposed to mean?"

"Exactly how it sounds. Really, I'm not sure how you made it through school let alone got your teaching certifications. Do you need me to spell it out for you? And here I thought you at least had two brain cells. I guess I was wrong."

Ignoring her jab at Ellie, she stared down at her. "I believe you just insinuated there was something wrong with Belle?" Ellie's nostrils flared as she slammed her fist onto the table, making Grady jump. "Listen here, you little bitch. You can say whatever the fuck you want about me, I don't give a rat's ass. You're not the first to try to degrade me 'cause you think you're better than me. Newsflash. You aren't original here, *sweetie*. I've heard it all before, my weight, my disabilities, you name it. That's not where you fucked up. The second you went after *my* child you signed your death wish."

"Please, do you hear yourself right now? You're even more pathetic than I thought."

"She's digging that hole deeper, isn't she?" Sally remarked.

"Pathetic? You wanna know what's pathetic? A grown-ass woman picking on a little girl. How do you sleep at night?"

"Soundly," she replied. "It's not my fault some people are put on this earth only to hinder others. Before Belle came into my class, the cumulative average was a B plus. Now it's a C minus. All because of *her*. Uhh, having her read out loud is a joke. The girl stumbles over her own name. We all can't be intelligent." She looked Ellie up and down. "But those that are, shouldn't be punished because some of the stupid ones want to pretend they can make it."

"Did you fucking call her stupid?" Ellie's rage boiled over while Grady shrugged.

"I know sure as hell you aren't talking about Annabelle Hurley. That girl is the smartest, bravest, most beautiful inside and out angel, I've ever met. You're lucky to have even been in the same room with her. How the hell do you call yourself a teacher? You're a bully, and do you know what I do with bullies?" A chilling smile appeared on Ellie's face. "I fucking destroy them."

Grady waved her off. "Go on back to your little class full of imbeciles. That means stupid if that was too big of a word for you."

That's it. This woman was fucking dead.

Before Ellie knew it, she lunged through the air ready to take her down.

"Ellie, no!"

Someone grabbed Ellie around the waist holding her back. "Let me go! I will fucking destroy this piece of shit."

"That's enough!" Talley came into the room. "Mrs. Grady, you better have a good explanation for this."

"She tried to attack me. Did you see that?!"

"We've been standing here since Ms. Sally threatened to hit you."

"Then why aren't you calling the police, she tried to attack me."

"Fuck yeah, I did. And as soon as I'm free, I *am* going to attack you." Ellie tried again but she couldn't break the hold. *Wait. We've who is we?*

Ellie turned and let out a scream finding Spencer Hurley's face only inches from her own. Ellie darted her head around the room, and sure enough, she spotted Annabelle standing there with her mouth hanging open holding a familiar little brown pastry bag from the coffee shop.

Oh, no!

"That's our cue." Sally took two giant steps toward Belle. "You and I are gonna take those little goodies and eat them in the art room." She then pushed a shocked little girl out of the room, but not before turning back to Grady one last time, sliding her finger across her throat.

"Mrs. Grady," Bob Talley began once they were gone. "You better have a damn good explanation as to why I shouldn't fire your ass right now. "

"Fire me? For what? I did nothing wrong."

"Telling my kid she's stupid. Making her read out loud, even when you know it made her uncomfortable?" Spencer spat as he glared at her, his eyes hard. "Don't even get me started on what you said to Ellie. She can take care of herself, though. But my kid... how fucking dare you? I should let Ellie go."

"Mr. Hurley, let me handle this." Bob held up his hand before turning back to the vile human. "Judy, you need to come with me. We'll wait in my office for the superintendent to arrive."

"She tried to attack me!"

"And you're extremely lucky Mr. Hurley was there to stop her."

"This is ridiculous."

"Now Mrs. Grady, or I'll be forced to call the resource officer and have him escort you."

"This is fucking bullshit. I'm filing charges," Grady yelled as she stomped out of the lounge.

Before Bob followed, he turned to them. "I will try my best to help you, Ellie, but I don't know if I can."

"I'd do it again." Ellie finally yanked herself out of Spencer's arms. "In a heartbeat. She went after *my* girl, Bob. If I lose my job over this, I can still sleep at night."

"I couldn't." Bob shook his head, the anger still radiating off him. "You have to promise me right now, this will not happen again. It's the only way I might be able to save you."

"I can't make you that promise and you know it. If one of my students needs me, I'm there."

"Ellie, I'm serious." He stared down at her but Ellie stared back, her eyes just as hard. "So am I."

"Jesus, Ellie." Bob's hand went to his hair in frustration. "I'm gonna see what I can do. In the meantime, for the love of all things, don't fight anyone else. Fuck, do you know how much paperwork this is gonna cause me?" He shook his head as he left the room.

That's when Ellie finally turned to look at Spencer.

CHAPTER TWENTY-SIX

SPENCER HAD PLANNED it out with Belle the night before. They'd get up early, head to Ellie's favorite coffee shop, grab her most beloved pastry and surprise her at school.

It might have been a little selfish on his part, but he wanted to see her again. After Ellie had left the night before, his house felt cold.

Belle felt it too.

What Spencer hadn't expected, was running into Bob Talley when they walked into the school. After he'd gotten the 'I'm watching you stare, and if you do anything to Ellie, you'll be a dead man,' look, he got the nod of approval from him. Then, with a quick, "I saw her walk toward the Teacher's Lounge, follow me," they were off.

When they made it to the door, it was something out of a movie. Ellie and Sally were arguing with someone Spencer hadn't met yet, all the while the woman dismissively brushed the girls off.

The moment Spencer was about to say something signaling they were there, he understood what was going on.

All three of them, Spencer, Bob, and Belle somehow froze in place as the scene played out in front of them.

As the words registered in his head, the blood drained from Spencer's face.

It happened again.

He failed his daughter all over.

It took everything inside of Spencer not to fucking snap, and just as he was about to, he stopped. He realized exactly what Ellie was doing.

She was standing up for his little girl.

Not only that, but she was about to fight for her.

Literally.

It all happened so fast, one moment Spencer was holding Ellie back, the next Bob was standing in front of them saying he didn't know if he could help Ellie.

Then Bob left leaving them alone.

When Ellie finally turned to him, the worry in her eyes, the pain, the love...

Spencer grabbed her face and kissed her.

He kissed her, hoping she would understand the words he was trying so desperately to convey.

This woman.

He *loved* this woman.

Spencer pulled back from her lips still keeping Ellie's face cupped in his hands. "I love you."

Her eyes widened as they held unshed tears.

"Shhh." He brought her back into his arms cradling her head in his neck. "Don't cry, baby."

Ellie's body shook as he held her tighter. "My baby," Ellie cried. "She went after my baby right under my nose. How could I've let that happen? How could I've been so blind?"

Spencer understood what she felt. He was fighting the

same feeling. It's what he felt the first time it happened at Belle's old school and now... well now, he felt it just as much.

He pulled her head back, wiping away her tears with his thumbs. "You did more for Annabelle than I did the first time it happened. You fought for her. Thank you."

"I love her."

He stared into her eyes. "We *both* love you too." As he watched her recognize his words, Spencer knew she understood. And the love he saw pouring back at him was enough to make his heart tighten.

"I love you, Spencer. I love you and Belle so much. I don't know how, or when it happened but I do."

He smiled at her before kissing her lips.

It took a few minutes until Ellie calmed down from the confrontation. Then out of nowhere, she jumped back from his arms. "Belle!" Her eyes widened in horror. "We have to get to Belle. She saw everything! I have to make sure she's okay!"

Before Spencer could stop her, Ellie took off out of the room, leaving him to chase her.

Ellie ran to the art room, almost colliding with the wall when she tried to stop. "Belle! I'm so sorry. I am so freaking sorry."

Belle, who'd been sitting at one of the tables happily munching on one of the croissants, looked up at them. "Why?"

"What do you mean why? You were there, you saw everything that happened," Ellie rushed out.

Belle turned to Spencer, quirking a brow his way. "She serious, Dad?"

He shrugged, he knew his kid, she might've been

shocked at first, but she knew the bigger picture here. "I think so."

Ellie snapped her head to him. "She's in shock." She looked around the room. "What do you do for shock, the Heimlich maneuver? Throw cold water on her? What damn it? Tell me what to do!" Ellie ran to the sink looking for a cup.

"Ms. Sally?" Belle's head turned to the woman sitting next to her, who was also eating one of the pastries.

"Let her go, kid. She has to have this freak out before her brain will work again."

They all turned to Ellie who'd given up finding a cup and tried holding the water in her hands. "I'm coming, baby. I'll save you!" The second she took a step toward them, she slipped.

Spencer was there in a heartbeat before she ended up on the floor. "Chill, babe. You need to calm down."

Ellie shot him an evil look. "Do not tell me to be calm! Our baby is over there about to have a meltdown. I'm trying to save her."

"*You're* having the meltdown. Belle is fine."

"I am not." She stomped her foot on the ground. "I am having a cool-up—" She stopped when he raised his brow at her, giving her the Hurley smirk.

"Shit." Ellie's body relaxed.

"Now she's good," Sally chimed in, popping a corner of the croissant into her mouth.

"Does she go through these a lot?" Belle asked.

"Sometimes. Although, your dad seemed to snap her out of it faster than I ever have." Sally winked at him. "Thanks for that."

"Anytime." He placed his hand on the small of Ellie's back pushing her toward the table.

"Why aren't you freaking out?" Ellie stared at his girl, who continued to snack on her food.

"Why would I freak out? You stood up for me," she explained. "You were like the werewolves protecting Jasmin. You called the evil queen out for who she was. A mean old bitch."

"Belle!" Spencer darted his eyes to his girl. "We don't use that language."

Belle rolled her eyes at him. "Bitch is a female dog. But, if you use the context clues, you can infer adults also use it to call out when someone is a jerk."

"Infer?" His brows shot up. "Where did you learn that word?"

"Grandpa." Belle moved her attention to Ellie. "Did I use it wrong? I think I used infer right. If one of you would give me your phone I'll check."

I'll be damned. The smile Spencer had on his face grew.

"She's a smart one." Sally tossed the last piece of the croissant in her mouth.

"The smartest." Ellie lowered to her knees, next to Annabelle's chair. "I am so sorry you had to deal with Mrs. Grady. If I'd known, I promise you'd have never been put in that situation in the first place. Will you forgive me?"

Belle jumped out of her seat and into Ellie's arms.

"I love you, Annabelle. So much."

"I love you too, Ellie."

Spencer watched as Ellie hugged his daughter before her eyes moved to the brown bag on the table. "You brought me croissants?"

"We did." Belle pulled out of her embrace. "Dad and I wanted to surprise you and ask if you and Roxy would have dinner with us tonight?"

"I'll have dinner with you every night." Her eyes

gleamed. "I'd do anything if someone brings me these delicious goodies." Ellie stood grabbing the brown bag.

"Uhh." A sheepish look appeared on Belle's face. "Ms. Sally and I might have eaten them all."

Ellie jerked back. "How could you?"

"They're good." The little girl shrugged before pointing at Sally. "She ate the last one, though. I said we should save it for you."

"Annabelle, I thought we were friends?" Sally had the gall to look upset.

"We are. But I'm not gonna take the blame. Did you see what she did to Mrs. Grady?"

"Touché, kid." Sally threw her head back as she barked out a laugh.

"You ate my croissant." Ellie glared at Sally. "You bitch."

Belle turned back to Spencer. "See, I used that word right too."

CHAPTER TWENTY-SEVEN

It'd been two months since the fallout with Judy Grady. Ellie had ended up on disciplinary action for two weeks, which Ellie couldn't complain about. All things considered, a small suspension was nothing compared to what could've happened.

Grady was escorted out of the building with the superintendent, and as far as Ellie knew, she'd lost her teaching certification.

Good. She deserved all she'd gotten and more.

It hadn't helped Grady had called the police, though. Thankfully, Officer Jones, and Detective Bower, told Ellie she'd be fine. She never actually touched Grady. And, it was her word against Ellie's.

Thank all the things, Ellie had everyone on her side.

She had to admit, Jones was a tad intimidating though, and then of course, Sally had offered for him to arrest her, with a wink.

Sally... Man, Ellie didn't know what to do with her. Maybe Officer Jones arresting her would be good for her.

Then again...

Nah, Ellie pushed those thoughts away. Trying to figure out Sally was a headache. Besides, she had other things to focus on.

Like the fact last weekend, Ellie had moved in with Spencer and Annabelle. It had been easy; Ellie and Roxy had pretty much been living there anyway.

Roxy barked from the backseat of the car, scaring Ellie out of her thoughts. "Give me a heart attack why don't you?"

"She knows where we're going."

"Did you tell her?" Ellie gave her the eye. "Belle, I swear if you told her, you're not picking the movie tonight."

A giggle escaped Belle as she shook her head. "I didn't, but Dad did."

She'd kill him.

"Great. Now I won't be able to get her out of the car." Ellie groaned as she pulled into Richman Veterinarian Hospital. *Freaking great.* And all she wanted was for today to go smoothly. She could already hear the accusation in Doctor Richman's voice about overfeeding Roxy.

After Ellie parked, she tried to pull her dog out of the car. "Come on you, big lug. You did this to yourself."

The dog barked, giving her the eye. "Don't you look at me like that. You knew this day was coming. Now get your butt out of the car."

Roxy huffed, narrowing her eyes at her.

"Come on, girl," Belle said, patting Roxy on the head. "If you go inside, I'll give you a treat when we get home."

"Belle!"

The girl looked up at her with that damn smirk. "It worked didn't it?"

Ellie's arm was almost yanked out of its socket when Roxy dragged her toward the door.

"For the love of all things..." Ignoring her ridiculous dog, and the laughing girl by her side, Ellie walked through the front door.

"Morning, I'm Ellie Ryan, here with Roxy." She smiled at the woman behind the counter. Ellie had been here enough times to know she was Holly Richman, Doctor Richman's wife.

"Hi, Ellie." She smiled at her. "It's nice to see you again. Let's get a weight on Ms. Roxy pants." Holly stood, grabbing a clipboard before walking around the counter to the scale.

"Do we have to?" Ellie groaned.

"Trust me, I hate this part, too." Holly sympathetically looked at her then to Roxy. "The scale is the devil."

"Preach it." Ellie followed Holly over to the device. "Up you go, you glutton." She tried pulling Roxy onto the scale but the dog was having none of it. "You made this mess yourself, now you gotta face the moment of truth. On the thing, Rox, or no more treats for you."

Roxy quickly jumped onto the scale and wagged her tail as she expertly waited for a treat.

"You're ridiculous." Ellie narrowed her eyes at the dog.

"Got it," Holly remarked. As she wrote down Roxy's weight, she walked back to the counter.

"Look out!" Ellie yelled as Holly tripped over the dog bowl full of water that had been on the floor. The clipboard in Holly's hand went flying through the air as she screamed and fell to the ground.

Not even a full second later the door to the backroom flung open as a panicked Doctor Richman ran in. "What happened?"

"Nothing," Holly grumbled as she laid on the floor in the puddle of water. "Absolutely nothing."

Doctor Richman walked over to his wife and in one fluid move picked her up and placed her back on her feet. "You only work at the front desk maybe twice a week, and yet, you somehow manage to hurt yourself each time."

"I'm not hurt," she said, checking the palms of her hands.

"I don't know what I'm going to do with you."

"Beats me." Holly brushed off her shirt before retrieving the clipboard she'd tossed.

"Mom, what'd you do this time?" A boy came walking out of the same door Doctor Richman had come from, with a dog hot on his tail.

"Why do you have to assume I did something? I don't appreciate the accusation from my son or husband." Holly glared at them.

The boy ignored her, looking back at the doctor. "Do we gotta take her to the hospital again, Dad?"

"Not this time." Doctor Richman shook his head as a smile appeared on his face. "But it's only eleven, the day's still young."

As Holly opened her mouth to say something, Annabelle pushed past Ellie. "Jimmy!" She saw the Corgi at his feet. "Is that Lord Waffles? Do I finally get to meet him?"

Jimmy's whole face lit when he saw her. "Hi, Annabelle, yep this is Waffles! Come meet his holiness."

Belle took two giant steps toward the dog before she dropped to her knees. "Hi, Waffles. I'm Jimmy's friend from school."

As Ellie watched them, the Corgi turned to her and glared. "What's that look for?"

The Corgi looked at her again, his eyes narrowing further.

"Ignore him," Holly said as she handed her husband the clipboard. "He's angry I put him on a diet this morning. Any adult that goes near him he has a grievance with."

Doctor Richman looked down at the chart. "Looks like Waffles isn't the only one about to be on a diet."

When Roxy whined from beside Ellie's leg, she looked down at her dog. "Told you."

"Mom, Dad, this is Annabelle, she's the girl I told you about from school," Jimmy said, scratching the still glaring Corgi on the head.

"It's nice to meet you, Annabelle, I'm Ben, Jimmy's dad, and that's Holly, his mom."

"I know," Belle replied. "Jimmy talks about you guys all the time."

"Does he now?" Ben asked, looking at his son.

"Well, it's mostly about Waffles and the rest of his animals."

"Figures." Holly rolled her eyes at Jimmy.

Belle stood holding out her hand to each of them. "You can call me Belle. It's nice to meet both of you." She then pointed to Ellie. "Jimmy, Mr. and Mrs. Richman, this is my mom, Ellie."

Ellie's heart stopped.

"She's not my real mom but she told me a mom is a title you have to earn and just 'cause someone gives birth does not make them a mom. But to me," Belle looked at her with love in her eyes, "she's the best mom in the world."

The words caught in Ellie's throat as tears formed in her eyes.

"I get that," Jimmy stated. "I'm adopted. But they're still my mom and dad."

"You're adopted?" Belle darted her attention to the boy. "I didn't know that."

"It doesn't matter if I'm adopted." He shrugged looking at his parents. "Ben and Holly are my mom and dad, just like Helen is my sister, even though we aren't related by blood."

That's when Belle turned to Ellie studying her for a moment before turning back to Jimmy.

Before anyone could say anything, Ben pointed to Roxy. "Come on, Roxy. It's time." He looked down at his Corgi. "You too, Waffles. You can keep Roxy company when she gets her shots."

At the word shots, Roxy yipped before she dodged under Waffles' belly, trying to hide.

"You do know we can see you, right?" Ellie looked at her dog, her brow arched. "Hiding under a dog that's only four inches off the ground isn't your best move."

Waffles snapped his head back to Ellie sending her another evil look. "My bad. Four and a *half* inches."

Waffles huffed as he nodded his head once before gracefully walking over Roxy's body and into the back.

Jimmy laughed before grabbing Annabelle's hand. "I'll show you where we keep the animals. We've got a snake right now."

"No way! That's awesome." Belle let Jimmy pull her through the door, but not before she turned back to Ellie. "Love you, Mom."

Her heart clenched. "Love you too, baby."

Ben smiled at her before taking a step toward the way Belle and Jimmy had escaped to. He turned back to his wife. "Don't touch anything while you're still wet, Holly." He glared at her. "I mean it, Grace. You'll end up electrocuting yourself."

"Stop calling me Grace. I hate that."

"Never." He winked before leaving the room with Roxy following.

"I love him, but one of these days I'm going to strangle him." Holly turned to a closet that was next to the counter. She then pulled out a clean pair of scrubs with dogs on them.

But Ellie couldn't focus on her, though. No, her attention was on the door. The same door Belle had walked through.

Mom... She called me mom.

Ellie's face broke into a huge grin as she followed everyone and pushed through the backdoor in search of her baby.

CHAPTER TWENTY-EIGHT

Spencer looked around his living room and hoped everything would go according to plan.

But knowing Ellie, who knew what could happen? He chuckled.

He'd spent the better part of two months figuring everything out. And now, now it was time. He couldn't wait another day.

They had already built a wonderful life together and now he wanted to make it official.

Spencer looked at the clock on the wall. Ellie would be home any minute from her last tutoring session of the night.

He then looked to his dad, who was giving Roxy another cup full of dog food. "Alright everyone, places."

Ellie pulled into their driveway and grabbed her bag from the passenger side of her car. Tonight, her session went later than normal but that was okay. She'd stay all night to help one of her kids if she had to.

That's who she was, and who she'd always be. There was no use in denying it.

As she walked to the front door something felt off, though. She didn't hear Roxy barking or Belle laughing.

Her brows pulled together. And why were the lights off? Did they go somewhere?

Oh crap, was tonight the night they had plans to eat at Randal's new house? *Shit. Dang it. Why do I always do this?*

Ellie swung open the door. "I'm late. I'm freaking late again. Why can't I get my shit together to save my life?" She threw her bag down in the dark entrance ready to make a run to the bedroom and change.

"Ellie, you're not late," Spencer groaned.

She let out a scream when she heard Spencer's impatient voice through the dark. "Don't scare me like that! How many times do I have to tell you? I think I *did* pee this time. And why the hell are the lights off if you're here?"

"Can you be quiet for a second?" he grumbled.

"Where are you? I'm gonna smack you."

"Ellie, turn on the freaking light. I swear."

"If you talk to me in that tone of voice one more time, I'll—" She froze the moment she turned on the light.

There in the middle of the living room stood Spencer holding a single red rose. Annabelle right in front of him, holding one of her own.

"What's going on?"

Belle handed her the flower. "This is for you."

"Uhh, thank you." She took it not really sure what was going on.

"Oh, and this." Belle opened the palm of her hand showing Ellie a tiny silver ring. "Dad and I wanted to know if you'd marry us?"

Ellie's heart stopped.

"That was supposed to be my line, kid. Way to steal my thunder." Spencer shoved the rose in Ellie's hand before dropping to one knee, sending a glare toward his daughter.

"Oops." She giggled.

Spencer turned back to Ellie, who wasn't sure if she was breathing or not.

"She's right. Ellie Ryan, every day with you is better than the last. I love you more than I thought was possible. I need to spend the rest of my life with you. Growing, learning, and loving. You're everything I could've ever wanted for me and Annabelle." He tried clearing his throat as his emotions were raw. "I want you to be the one to teach Belle all the drive and determination you have inside of you. To prove to her and me, nothing can ever stop us if we put our minds to it. Ellie, I wanna be able to wake up every morning next to you as my wife—"

"Except when you spend the night with me in a blanket fort," Belle interrupted.

"My bad. Minus those nights." Spencer chuckled at Belle before turning back to Ellie. "Would you do me the honor of becoming my wife?"

"And my mom!" Belle ran to the document on the coffee table before tossing it in Ellie's hands.

Still in shock, Ellie's eyes glanced at the top of the paper. *Application for Adoption.*

Her mouth dropped as tears clouded her vision.

"Will you adopt me? I know you're already my mom, but we can make it official."

Before Belle was even finished saying the words, Ellie was nodding.

Ellie then turned to Spencer. "Yes! Yes, to both of you!"

Spencer jumped off his knee and placed the ring on Ellie's finger, followed by Belle placing her small ring there as well. He then brought them both into his arms. "Love you, both, so much."

"Yippie! I didn't know how much longer I could keep quiet." Shannon ran out of the kitchen, Dean and Randal, right behind her.

"Congrats, son. Took you long enough. If Ellie were my girl, I would've put a ring on her finger on day one."

"Dad..." Spencer warned.

"Boy, don't dad me."

"*Randal.*" Spencer smirked at his dad, causing him to shoot him a glare.

"Bob is gonna be pissed he missed this." Dean walked to Ellie pulling her in his arms. "Congrats, El. You get to be the one to tell Bob he wasn't invited."

"Leave her alone, Dean. Let her have this moment."

Ellie looked around the room. "Why are all of you here?"

"You think we'd miss my boy asking the woman he loves to marry him?" Randal scoffed, shaking his head. "Ellie, I thought you were better than that?"

What? She looked around the room again, only to find Roxy in the corner eating a *way* too large bowl of dog food.

What the hell? "Why does Roxy have that much food?"

"How else do you think we kept her quiet?" Spencer winked.

Ellie darted her attention to Belle. "You were at the vet. You heard what Dr. Richman said!"

Belle shrugged. "You gotta do what you gotta do sometimes."

Ellie's mouth fell open as Belle winked at her.

"Close your mouth, dear, remember what I told you."

"*Mom!*"

Shannon waved her off, before patting Belle on the back. "Grab your bag and Roxy's treats."

Belle ran out of the room before coming back with a bag in one hand and Roxy's container of treats in the other. "Come on, Roxy, we've got places to be, grandma and grandpas to terrorize."

Randal turned to Dean with a smirk. "Feels good to be called grandpa doesn't it?"

"Sure does." Dean looked to Annabelle, before smiling to his daughter.

"Just wait until the terrorizing starts."

Belle tapped her foot on the floor. "We're waiting."

"It's already begun." Shannon turned back to her and Spencer. "You two lovebirds have fun. We're keeping Belle all weekend."

"Grandpa, me, and Roxy are gonna spend the weekend with Grandma and Papa Ryan. We're gonna camp out in their backyard."

"I didn't agree to that. What are you tryin' to do, kill my back?"

Belle looked at Randal, giving him puppy dog eyes. When Roxy flung herself onto her back kicking her feet in the air, Randal gave up. "Fine. You two are a pair let me tell you."

"Come on, Gramps. Time to go. We've got to stop at the store for marshmallows."

As everyone laughed at Belle, they all made their way to the door, but not before Belle turned back to her and Spencer. "Try not to sprain your ankle this time, Mom."

When Ellie's eyes narrowed at the traitor, Belle laughed while running out the door.

"What was she talking about?" Spencer arched his brow looking at Ellie.

"Nothing!"

"That's not what Belle told us." Shannon winked at both of them before she pushed the men out of the house, closing the door behind her. "Bye! See you Sunday night."

"What just happened here?"

"Your guess is as good as mine. But I think Belle just wrapped not only my dad but your parents around her finger."

Ellie's smile spread from ear-to-ear as she looked at him, shaking her head. "How the hell am I going to survive the rest of my life with you two?"

"Hell, if I know. Can you imagine what she'll be like when she's a teenager?"

"No!" Ellie jerked back. "She's not allowed to grow up. She stays right where she's at!"

A deep chuckle escaped his lips. "She's gonna grow up, Ellie. We can't stop that. Believe me, I've tried."

"Take it back."

Spencer moved closer bringing Ellie into his arms, kissing her lips. "Don't worry baby, we'll have more."

"More what?"

"Kids. I want as many as you'll allow me."

Kids.

Her and Spencer's kids.

A beautiful smile appeared on Ellie's face as the thought of little Spencer and Ellie's running around.

She liked that. She liked that a lot.

Spencer kissed her again, distracting her from the fantasy. When she looked into his eyes, the love she saw pouring out of him had her heart skip.

"I never thought this was in the cards for me, Ellie Ryan. I never knew I'd be able to love someone as much as I love you."

Ellie's expression softened as she looked into the eyes of the man she loved with everything in her. The man that accepted her exactly the way she was. "Well Spencer Hurley, there's one thing I've learned throughout my life. We all have learning curves to go through. Some are like Annabelle and me, figuring out how to cope with our disabilities. Some are like yours, learning how to trust and love again."

The Hurley smirk appeared on his face. "I love learning. And I really love learning *your* curves." His eyes heated as his hand went to Ellie's hips. "And I'm about to re-learn them. Let's get to making Belle some brothers and sisters. Time's a wastin'."

Before Ellie could reply, Spencer tossed her over his shoulder and ran toward their bedroom ready to start doing just that.

Thank you for reading Learning Curves, I hope you enjoyed it. If reading about Lord Waffles, the judgmental Corgi piqued your curiosity, check out Holly and Ben's story, Stumbling Into Him. There is a sneak peek of chapter one on the next page followed by my Fun Facts for Learning Curves.

STUMBLING INTO HIM SNEAK PEEK

CHAPTER ONE

"Watch out!"

Holly Flanagan heard a commotion coming from the other side of the park. Ignoring the shouting, she bent over focusing on picking up her Corgi, Waffles, most recent deposit. With Holly's track record, though, she should have known anyone yelling "watch out," "take cover," or "that's about to fall" was directed at her. Even after years of being the spokesperson for "unlucky," "klutzy," and "clumsy" she still disregarded the shouting as she carried on with her dog parent duties.

Before she could register what happened, she was knocked onto her back with a pain radiating from her mouth and nose.

"Well, at least the sky is pretty today," Holly mumbled as she tried to get her bearings. She reached for her mouth as she felt the pain start to spread.

"Ma'am, are you okay?"

Holly closed her eyes pondering that exact question. Was she okay? She'd just been hit with something in her mouth. She was pretty sure some part of her face, she didn't know which part, but she was sure something was bleeding. Waffles started barking uncontrollably, and her head hurt. So, was she okay?

Holly sighed. Yeah, she was fine. This was just another day for her, and so far, if being hit by an unknown projectile to the face was the worst thing that happened to her, she'd considered it a good day.

Opening her eyes, she gasped. Above her, only a mere few inches from her face was by far, the most handsome man she had ever laid eyes on. He had dark brown hair and deep blue eyes that were richer than the ocean. His jaw was chiseled, with a light dusting of scruff, in the alpha male, I'm in charge here kind of way.

Wonderful. Okay, let's add embarrassing yourself in front of a Greek God to your lists of attributes for the day. Hey, it can only get better from here, right?

She realized she was staring at him for what could have been considered too long. She quickly jerked her head forward trying to right herself. Unfortunately for her, she slammed her head right into the Greek God's forehead.

Freaking wonderful.

Not only was her mouth hurting, her head now pounded.

Absolutely freaking wonderful!

"Shit," she heard the Greek God say through the wave of pain coursing through her body. Taking the chance, she opened her eyes once more only to see her Adonis holding his own head. And, to make matters worse, Waffles started barking at her, then looked at his recent deposit still on the ground, and then back at her.

"For the love of all things. I was trying to pick it up," she mumbled taking her hand away from her mouth to deal with his majesty, Lord Waffles. However, the second her hand came into view she saw the blood and screamed.

"Oh shit. Lady, you're bleeding," the Adonis said before reaching his hand out to grasp her mouth.

"What happened?" she asked as panic started to course through her. Did she break her nose? Was she unconscious? Was she dying?

The Adonis removed the hand that covered her mouth and tilted her chin back. He then gently held onto her jaw and slightly opened her mouth. "I was tossing the Frisbee with Ripley, and somehow it veered off course. I tried to warn you to watch out."

Typical. She groaned. *Hot guy throws Frisbee. Said Frisbee hits me in the face. Hot guy then insinuates it's my fault for not getting out of the way fast enough. I mean, I know I'm generally invisible to men like him, but, damn. You'd think these extra wide hips would make me more visible. Instead, invisible me is at fault for being in the firing line of a dang Frisbee.* She glared at the Frisbee sitting next to her. Ignoring the object, she moved her attention back to the Adonis.

Holly tried to speak, but he was still holding onto her jaw. "I can't tell if it's a busted lip or worse," he said as he examined her.

Holly ripped her face from his hand. She'd be able to tell if it was just a busted lip. She'd had enough of them from falling down, objects to the face, and even falling up the stairs. She reached into her pocket and pulled out the napkin she had stuffed in there from her soft pretzel. She blew off some stray salt and started feverishly wiping at her mouth.

"Let me see," he demanded, before taking one of the

napkins from her hand. He started dabbing at her lips as well.

Well, Holly. This is the most action you've had in months. And, if some hot guy who typically wouldn't have paid any attention to someone like you, is all over you, you might as well enjoy it while it lasts.

She turned her head to face him fully. Waffles, who was now crawling into her lap demanding attention, started to kiss the underside of her jaw.

Why thank you, Waffles, for bringing the attention of my double chin to the Adonis.

"Thanks buddy for trying to help me clean up your mom," the Adonis remarked before quickly abandoning his job of cleaning off the blood to pat Waffles on the head.

"He's not trying to help you," she remarked. "He's trying to remind me I still need to pick up his poop and then give him his treat."

"Shouldn't your mom be the one getting the treat if *she's* the one picking up your shit?" he asked the dog.

Waffles, ever the one to argue, looked at the man whom now was sporting a mischievous grin, with the most judgmental side-eye he could muster. She had to give it to her dog, though, no one came between him and his treats.

The Adonis once again pat Waffles on the head before moving back to Holly's mouth dismissing the pups glare. "I think it's just a busted lip, but, your front tooth..." he coughed while he looked away.

"My front tooth?" Holly quickly ran her tongue along her front teeth. Sure enough, she felt a jagged piece. "Oh, crap." She rapidly pulled her phone from her pocket and launched the front-facing camera.

As soon as she saw her appearance, she jerked back.

You've had better days, Holly. Ignoring her outward appearance, she hastily opened her mouth.

"Oh no."

Staring back at her was a chipped front tooth along with a busted lip. *Wonderful. Thank you so much, Universe. Thank you, so very much.* She didn't know whether she wanted to laugh or cry. *Unlucky, clumsy, klutzy, Holly, strikes again,* she thought.

As her eyes flooded with tears, a sudden cold nose hit her arm distracting her. She looked to her left and saw one of the most beautifully colored gray and black Australian Shepherds she'd ever seen. Thankfully, her love of animals overrode any sadness and pain she was feeling. "Aren't you a cutie?" she softly said.

"That's Ripley," the Greek God chuckled deeply. "I'd thought you'd be more concerned about your mouth than a dog."

Ignoring him, she reached out to pet Ripley. "You're so pretty." Ripley must have agreed because she barked.

"Ma'am, I'm not a human doctor, but I think we should pay more attention to your injuries instead of the dogs."

"Human doctor?" she mocked ignoring both of the pups, going back to her injuries. "As opposed to what, an alien doctor?"

"I haven't worked on any aliens that I know of, but I did neuter a cat named Alien once. Does that count?"

Holly's eyes widened. "Oh great, you've got a body of a Greek God, and now you're also a vet. Which means you love animals. Freakin' wonderful. You're like the most perfect guy, and here I am on the sidewalk with blood pouring out of me with a chipped tooth." She pushed Waffles off her lap and stood. "Please excuse me while I find a place to die of embarrassment."

A corner of his mouth lifted. "You're funny."

"And you're hot. So, we've now successfully established which groups we belong to." Annoyed at herself more than anything she angrily started to stomp away from the Greek God.

"Hey, wait up!"

She hastily turned around. When she saw Waffles sitting at the foot of the Adonis, her eye started to twitch. Of course, her dog would betray her. "Waffles, come." She pulled on the leash slightly, but Waffles wouldn't move. "Lord Waffles, get your butt over here."

The man cocked his brow. "Lord Waffles?"

"Yeah," she answered. "He thinks, he's a freakin' king. Hence the "lord" and I love waffles."

The Adonis threw his head back in laughter before he bent and started to pet her dog. To make matters worse, the betraying Corgi rolled over onto his back asking for belly rubs. *That's it. No more treats for you!* She glared at him.

"Who's a good boy?" the Adonis cooed. "You've got a weird name, but to each their own."

Holly's eye began to twitch more vigorously. She started trudging back towards her bastard of a dog and the Greek God when her foot hit an invisible rock causing her to trip. Within a split second, she ended up falling right into the arms of the bane of her existence at the moment.

"Whoa, are you okay?"

"I'm fine," she grumbled as she righted herself. *Go ahead and add this to the, "it can only happen to me" list.*

"I feel like you need to walk around with a warning or at least a crash helmet," he joked.

"Not the first time I've heard that," she replied. Quickly she bent down and retrieved Waffles. "Well, if you'll excuse me. Not only do I really need to find a secluded place to die of embarrassment, I also need to call my dentist, or go to the walk-in. Maybe both." She turned on her heel and started power walking down the sidewalk. As she passed the spot she'd tripped at; she examined the cement. Figures, there'd be absolutely nothing there. If there were a sporting category on tripping over invisible objects she'd win gold twice over.

"Hey," she heard from behind her. She kept walking, doing her best to hide her humiliation and ignore the Greek God.

Unfortunately, that was short lived. "Hey, I want to make sure you really are okay?" he asked when he caught up to her in two point three seconds. *Stupid short legs!*

"I'm fine," she said.

"Your lip's still bleeding pretty bad."

She glared at him. "Wonderful."

"Hey..." He reached for her arm stopping her escape.

"What?"

"Let me help you. My practice is only a block from here. I've got all the supplies to clean up your lip. I also can get a better look at your tooth."

"You're a vet." Her eyes started to twitch more.

"I am pretty sure if I can surgically remove nuts from an animal I can look at your busted lip." He shrugged.

She couldn't help but laugh. He did have a point.

Sighing she looked at her Adonis. "Thank you for the offer...." She trailed off.

"Ben. The names Ben Richman." He held out his hand for her to shake.

"Thanks for the offer Dr. Richman, but there is a walk-in clinic not far from where I live."

"Call me Ben. And, please let me do this. It will help me sleep at night knowing the woman I maimed with a

Frisbee is somewhat okay." She watched as his eyes widened pleading with her. Even Waffles who was still in her arms looked at her and whined. "Oh, for the love of... fine. Lead the way, Ben."

"Perfect." His mouth curved into a smile. "Follow me." He whistled loudly. Ripley was instantly by his side. Before they started their journey, he quickly bent down and fastened her leash.

Holly started following the Adonis, Ben.

She looked at Waffles who was enjoying being carried. "Guess you get an extra trip to the vet." She burst out laughing when Waffles closed his mouth and glared at her.

ALSO BY MOLLY O'HARE

Hollywood Hopeful Series

Hollywood Dreams

Risking It All (Danny and Lexi's Story) – *Coming soon*

Stumbling Through Life Series

Stumbling Into Him

Stumbling Into Forever

John & Emma's story – *Coming soon*

Teased Series

Teased by Fire

Lucas & Miranda's story – Coming soon

Standalone Novels

Nothing But a Dare

Learning Curves – *This book*

Stay up to date on New Releases

Sign up for my newsletter by clicking the link or going to my website: MollyOHareauthor.com I also have a Reader Group on Facebook. Come hang out with me: Molly's Marvelous Clan

ABOUT THE AUTHOR

Hey, thanks for coming to my about the author to check me out! Has anyone told you, you're beautiful and amazing lately? Just in case they haven't, I am!

So you want to know a little more about me? Well okay then. Much like any author out there, sleeping doesn't come easily to me. As it turns out, I've got horrible insomnia. Like, scary horrible. Anyway, when I was younger, to help myself fall asleep I'd tell myself stories. Each night I'd pick up where the story left off previously until it was complete. Then I started writing them down. A few months later, here I am, sharing my lack of sleep with all of you. Who said the stories in our heads can't be fun for others?

Fun Facts:

I had a teacher that was a lot like Ellie. I owe her the world.

I recently got a new Corgi and I named him Frank.

Figment is my favorite Disney Character.

My husband is now reading all of my books.

I paint when I need a break from the world.

Sometimes, I go on car rides, just to get lost in the world for a few hours.

Made in the USA
Las Vegas, NV
07 September 2021